Claire Fuller was born in Oxfordshire in 1967. She gained a degree in sculpture from Winchester School of Art, but went on to have a long career in marketing and didn't start writing until she was forty. Her first novel won the Desmond Elliott Prize. She has an MA in Creative and Critical Writing from the University of Winchester, and lives in Hampshire with her husband and two children.

SWIMMING LESSONS

Ingrid writes letters to her husband Gil about their life together. But instead of giving them to him, she hides each in the thousands of books Gil has collected. Despite their two daughters, despite their beautiful but dilapidated house by the sea, despite Gil's talent as a writer, their marriage has been troubled. When Ingrid has written her final letter, she disappears from a Dorset beach. Eleven years later, her adult daughter Flora comes home to look after her injured father. Secretly, Flora has never believed that her mother is dead, and she starts asking questions — without realizing that the answers she's looking for are hidden in the books that surround her.

CLAIRE FULLER

SWIMMING LESSONS

Complete and Unabridged

CHARNWOOD
Leicester

First published in Great Britain in 2017 by
Fig Tree
an imprint of Penguin Books
London

First Charnwood Edition
published 2018
by arrangement with
Penguin Random House UK
London

A catalogue record for this book is available
from the British Library.

ISBN 978–1–4448–3707–0

Published by
F. A. Thorpe (Publishing)
Anstey, Leicestershire

Set by Words & Graphics Ltd.
Anstey, Leicestershire
Printed and bound in Great Britain by
T. J. International Ltd., Padstow, Cornwall

This book is printed on acid-free paper

For Henry, Tim and India

Prologue

Gil Coleman looked down from the first-floor window of the bookshop and saw his dead wife standing on the pavement below. He had been amongst the shelves all afternoon, thumbing through the second-hand books from front to back, pausing at folded-over corners, or where the text had been underlined, flicking through the pages to persuade them to offer up what might be hiding between the leaves. The cup of tea that Viv had brought for him had cooled, forgotten on the window seat. At about three o'clock he had picked up *Who Was Changed and Who Was Dead*, a book he recognized and thought he might already own. It had fallen open, and there, tucked between the pages, he had been surprised to see a folded sheet of thin yellow paper with faint blue lines.

Trembling, Gil had sat down beside the cup and turned the book sideways so he could open the note without removing it. One of his rules was that the things he found must never be taken out from their original location. He lifted both the book and the piece of paper up to the rain-streaked window. It was another letter, handwritten in black ink, and when he squinted he could read the date — 2nd July 1992, 2.17 p.m. — and, under that, his own name. The text below was smaller, and the writer had paid no attention to the lines provided but had

1

allowed their words to slope downhill, as if they had written them at speed.

He patted the breast of his jacket, swapped the book to his other hand and dipped into the inside pockets, then tapped the sides of his trousers. No reading glasses. He moved the letter nearer and further away from his face to bring the writing into focus, and leaned closer to the window. The light was poor; the storm which had been forecast for Saturday had arrived a day early. When Gil had locked his car in the car park beside the Jurassic Crazy Golf playground, he saw that the wind had wrapped a plastic bag around one of the front claws of the Tyrannosaurus rex, so that the creature appeared to be about to step over the wire fence on its way to do some shopping. And as Gil had walked along the promenade to the bookshop, the wind had gouged troughs in the grey sea and flung the top edges of the waves towards the land, so that now, standing amongst the old books, he could taste salt on his lips.

A blast of rain rapped on the window, and that was when he turned to look out and down to the narrow street below.

On the pavement opposite, a woman in an oversized greatcoat stood gazing along the road. Only the tips of her fingers showed from the ends of the sleeves, while the bottom hem came almost to her ankles. The coat was a dirty olive colour from the rain — the cast of the sea after a shower — and it occurred to Gil that his daughter Flora would know the colour's proper name. The woman pushed a strand of wet hair

2

off her face with the back of her wrist and turned towards the bookshop. The gesture was so shockingly familiar that Gil stood up and was unaware of knocking over his cup of tea. The woman tilted her heart-shaped face to look up, as if she knew Gil was watching, and in that moment he understood the woman was his wife; older, but without doubt, he thought, her. The rain had flattened and darkened her hair, and the water dripped off her chin, but she stared at him in the same defiant way she had when he'd first met her. He would have known that expression and that woman anywhere.

Ingrid.

Gil slammed his palm against the window-pane, but the woman turned away and stared down the street again, towards the town, and, as if she had seen the person or car she was waiting for, strode off. He hit the window again, but the woman didn't stop. He pressed his cheek sideways against the cold glass and saw her for a moment more before she was gone from view. 'Ingrid!' he called pointlessly.

He snapped shut the book he was holding and, clasping it to his chest, hurried down the stairs, then to the front of the shop and through the door. From behind the till Viv called to him, but he kept going. Outside, the rain pasted his grey hair to his forehead and soaked through his jacket. The street was empty, but he marched along it, every two or three steps breaking into a trot, searing his lungs. By the time he reached the high street, Gil was puffing and struggling to catch his breath. He stood on the corner and looked up the hill. The pavement was empty. In the other direction, towards the sea, some tourists hurried, the squall bowling them closer to the water. He limped after them, scanning the people ahead for the large coat and glancing through the steamy windows of the cafe and the bakery. He weaved around a young woman with a buggy and, ignoring a stab of pain in his hip, crossed the road at the corner without checking for cars. He was on the promenade, eight feet or so above the beach. In the distance, a man walked at an angle against the gale while an ugly dog jumped and snapped at the wind — too fierce for May, more like an autumn storm. Gil slowed but continued to shuffle, head lowered, along the promenade until below him the sand ended and the breakwater boulders and the massive concrete blocks began, wet with leaping spray. The rain flew in his face and the wind buffeted him, pushing him into the metal railing at the edge of the walkway, tilting him over it as though he were being passed from hand to hand in a violent dance. Between the rocks, about a dozen paces further along and below him, Gil thought he saw a jut of olive and the whip of lifted hair.

'Ingrid!' he shouted, but the wind took his words and the woman, if that's what it was, didn't even turn her head. He continued along the promenade in her direction. Twice he stopped to lean out over the railing, but the angle and the height of the walkway, together with how she was hunkered down, meant he lost sight of her. When he judged that he must be above Ingrid, he tipped forward over the railing again, but couldn't now even see her coat. He put his head and torso in the wide gap between the top and bottom bars, and, with the book in one hand and the other on a vertical post, Gil inched his left leg over the lower railing, swivelling it awkwardly so his foot remained on the lip of the promenade, while he negotiated his right over the bottom rail. When he was on the other side he clung on to the wet post with his free hand and cantilevered his body out, but his left foot in its leather brogue slipped.

It seemed to Gil that he fell in slow motion into the void, so there was plenty of time to think about the fuss his eldest daughter, Nan, would make, and how worried Flora would be, and then he thought whether, if he survived this fall, he should ask his children to promise to make a pyre of his books when he did die, and what a sight that would be. The fire, a beacon announcing his death, might be visible as far as the Isle of Wight. And Gil considered that if today was the 2nd of May 2004, which he thought it probably was, it meant Ingrid had been gone for eleven years and ten months exactly, and he also thought how he should have made it clearer that he had loved her. All this went through his mind while he fell between the rocks, and then there was pain in his arm and bursts of light in his head, but before the blackness swallowed him up he saw the book open beside him, its spine cracked in two.

1

The ringing woke Flora from a deep sleep. Richard, lying next to her, had a pillow over his head, so she climbed across him and out into the cold and gloomy room. She stepped over the debris of clothes, empty bottles and dirty plates on the floor, picked up an old tablecloth which she kept on the sofa to hide the greasy stains left by the previous tenants, and wrapped it around her like a cloak. The ringing stopped. Flora sighed, and at the end of her out-breath the ringing started again. She listened and then rummaged through the clothes until she found her jeans with her mobile phone in the pocket. *Nan*, the display said. Richard rolled over in the bed with a groan and Flora went through to the bathroom.

'Nan?' she said, pulling the light cord and wincing at the glare.

'Hello? Flora?'

'Oh God, I'm so sorry,' Flora said. 'I should have called. Happy birthday for yesterday.'

'Thanks,' Nan said, 'but I'm not calling about that.' Her tone was urgent, worried, and a creature uncoiled itself inside Flora's stomach.

'What is it?' Flora's voice was a whisper. She sank on to the lino, slotting herself between the bath and the basin's pedestal. Close up, the abstract swirls and eddies embroidered on the tablecloth transformed themselves into silvery-blue fish swimming over her knees.

'What?' Nan said. 'I can't hear you properly. The reception's terrible. Flora? Hello?' Nan's voice was too loud. 'It's about Dad,' she shouted.

'Daddy?' Flora said, her mind already spinning towards all the possible scenarios.

'There's no need to worry immediately, but . . . '

'What?'

'He's had an accident.'

'An accident? What? When?'

'I can't hear you,' Nan said.

Flora stood up, stepped into the bath and opened the window on to the gap below ground level. It was dark outside, confusingly dark. A blast of wind blew in, and above her shapes of trees and shrubs thrashed back and forth. 'Is that better?'

'That's better,' Nan said, still shouting. 'Dad fell off the promenade in Hadleigh. Cuts and bruises, concussion maybe, a sprained wrist. Nothing serious . . . '

'Nothing serious — are you sure? Should I come now?'

' . . . or maybe he jumped,' Nan continued.

'Jumped?'

'No, don't come now.'

'Off the promenade?'

'Flora, do you have to repeat everything I say?'

'Well, tell me then!'

'Are you drunk?'

'Of course not,' Flora said, although she may still have been.

'Or stoned? Are you stoned?'

An unexpected laugh bubbled out of Flora.

8

'No one says stoned any more, Nan. It's high.'

'So you're high.'

'I was asleep,' Flora said. 'Tell me! What's happened?'

'Have you just got up? It's nine thirty in the evening, for goodness' sake.' Nan sounded outraged.

'In the evening?' Flora said. 'Isn't it morning?'

Nan tutted and Flora could imagine her sister shaking her head.

'I was up all last night,' Flora said. She had no intention of telling Nan that she and Richard had stayed in bed for the past two days. That twice Flora had pulled on jeans and a jumper and run to the shop on the Stockbridge Road to buy another couple of bottles of wine, a lump of plastic Cheddar, sliced white bread, baked beans and chocolate. Richard had offered to go, but Flora needed those ten minutes away from him. When she returned and let herself in through the basement door, she dropped the bags and her jeans, and climbed back under the covers.

'Doing what?' Nan said. 'Oh, Flora, you're not late with an essay, are you?'

'Are you in the hospital? Can I speak to him?'

'He's sleeping. Flora, there are a couple of other things.' Her sister sniffed and rustled as if wiping her nose, and then took a deep breath. 'He told me he saw Mum outside the bookshop in Hadleigh, wearing his old greatcoat, the one you used to dress up in, and that he followed her down to the breakwater boulders.'

Adrenalin rushed through Flora, like a wave

surging out from her centre to her limbs, the ends of her fingers, and up to her head. 'Mum? In Hadleigh?' The scent of coconut came to her, inextricably linked with the colour of golden honey, sweet and clean from amongst the thorns and dying flowers of gorse.

'He didn't though,' Nan said. 'He just thought he did. It's probably his age or the concussion.'

'Yes,' Flora whispered. The wind splattered rain at her, and she ducked back inside the bathroom, leaning towards the window to keep the phone signal strong.

'Flora, are you still there?' Nan said into her ear.

'Still here,' Flora said. 'I'm coming to the hospital. I'll pack a bag and get the next train.'

'No, don't do that. Dad's sleeping. I was hoping they might discharge him tonight, but it's too late for that now. It'll be tomorrow morning, after someone from the mental health team has seen him.'

'The mental health team? What's wrong with him?'

'Flora, calm down,' Nan said. 'They're just ruling things out. It's probably a urinary infection. Come over tomorrow. I'll meet you at home and we can talk.' The Swimming Pavilion: home. They both still called it that, although neither lived there now.

'I want to see him.'

'You will, in the morning. Make sure you check the bus timetable for the ferry. Don't get stuck like last time.'

Flora had forgotten her sister's irritating habit

10

of thinking of everything that anyone might require.

When they had said goodbye, Flora put her phone on the side of the sink and brushed her teeth. As she turned to go, she knocked her mobile and it fell into the toilet with a plop.

⋆ ⋆ ⋆

The light was on in the main room — kitchen, bedroom and sitting room — but Richard, who must have got up, was now back under the covers with his eyes closed. The dirty plates had gone from the floor and were stacked on the table, the remains of the food scraped into the bin. In her food cupboard Flora found a packet of curry-flavoured savoury rice and dropped her phone inside. She sat on the sofa, trying to imagine her father broken and bruised in a hospital bed, but she could only see him wiry and brown, striding beside her over the heath, or showing her another book he'd found. She thought about her mother walking around Hadleigh right now, or sitting in a shop or a pub or a cafe. It made her hands shake and the creature in her stomach flip over. And then she realized that her mother wouldn't be in any of those places; she would be waiting for them at home.

Flora watched Richard sleeping. There was no noise of wind or rain in the main room. The ceiling bulb shone full on his face and he looked different without his glasses, not just younger, but blanker, more unformed. She kneeled beside

11

the bed and scrabbled underneath it for her suitcase.

'Who was that?' Richard said, opening one eye.

'No one,' Flora said, tugging at what she hoped was a handle.

'Why are you wearing that? Isn't it a tablecloth? You must be bloody freezing. Come back to bed.' He lifted up the duvet to reveal his torso.

'Oh,' she said, 'I'd forgotten about that.'

'What?' Richard craned his neck forward to stare down at his own body. He clawed with his free hand on the shelf below the bedside table and brought up his glasses. When he put them on, he gasped in mock surprise. Between the brown hairs that covered his chest and flowed from his belly button was an anatomical drawing of his insides — ribs, sternum, clavicle and the start of his pelvis, the wrapped snake of his intestines — all in indelible black felt-tip. 'You have to come back to bed.' He leaned over to pull her towards him. 'I don't have any arms or legs yet. You need to finish your drawing or I can't go back to work.' He smiled.

'Did you know it's nine thirty?' Flora said, giving another yank on the suitcase handle and toppling backwards on to the carpet.

'Nine thirty? In the morning?' Richard dropped the duvet.

'No, in the bloody evening,' Flora said.

Richard reached out again for the shelf below the bedside table. This time he brought up his phone plugged into his charger, and Flora felt a flash of irritation not only that he had remembered to charge it but that he had been sensible enough to put it somewhere safe.

He gave a long whistle. 'Nine thirty. Maybe it's nine thirty tomorrow and we missed the whole of Saturday. Work is going to be really pissed off with me.'

Flora gave up on the suitcase, went to the drawer where she kept her underwear, and rooted through it.

'Is everything all right?' He sat up in bed to watch her.

'It was Nan,' Flora said. 'On the phone.'

'Your grandmother?'

'Nanette. My sister.'

'I didn't know you had a sister. Older or younger?'

'Five and a half years older,' Flora said. She dumped a handful of knickers and bras in the middle of the floor. She returned to the chest of drawers to go through her jeans and jumpers.

'What did she want?'

'I have to go home.'

'Right now? As in, this instant?'

'Yes, right now,' she said as she dropped another pile of clothes on the first and turned to him. 'As in, immediately. Daddy's been taken to hospital, and I need you to get up, so I can get my suitcase from under the bed.'

'Daddy?' Richard said.

'Yes. Gil, my father. Do you have to repeat everything I say?' Flora stood with her fists on her hips. Richard got out of the bed, found his pants and jeans, and pulled them on. He bent to

13

get her suitcase, and sat on the side of the bed, watching her pack. The case had belonged to her mother and was made of blue cardboard with rounded corners. Flora was facing away from him, but she could feel Richard's mind working.

'Hang on,' he said. 'Gil? Your father's called Gil? And isn't your surname Coleman?'

Flora sighed. She hadn't realized he knew her surname. It had taken a little less than two weeks for Richard to work it out. That wasn't bad; once, she had discovered that a boy had only slept with her after he had found out who her father was. She never returned his calls.

'*That* Gil Coleman?' Richard said. 'The Gil Coleman who wrote *A Man of Pleasure?*' She knew without turning around what the expression on his face would be, and that was why, she reminded herself, she must never sleep with a bookshop assistant again.

'That's the one,' Flora said, pressing sketchbooks and a box of charcoal on top of her clothes.

'My God. Gil Coleman is your father. I can't believe it. I thought he was dead. He hasn't written anything else since that book, has he?'

'I expect you think it's all a bit *I Capture the Castle.*' Flora tried to laugh it off. But looking at Richard from where she sat on top of the case, trying to lock it, she could see he had remembered that there was something else; another thing that was memorable about Gil Coleman apart from the book he had written. It was coming and it was best to get it over with, and then she could leave and not see Richard

14

again. The suitcase clicked shut.

'Wait,' he said, sitting up straight, with one hand on his forehead and the other in the air, as if she had been doing something to stop him thinking. 'Wait, I know this story.'

'It isn't a story, Richard. It's my family.'

'No, of course, sorry.' He was still trying to remember when she turned away from him and dropped the tablecloth around her feet. She opened the case again, took out a clean pair of knickers and pulled them on. She found her jeans, sniffed the crotch and stepped into them. She didn't look at Richard, because she couldn't bear to see the dawning of that little piece of knowledge.

Flora picked up a bra, tried to hook it together, missed the catches, tried again, and heard him say a short, embarrassed 'Oh'. When the bra caught, she squatted beside the bed and fought her way into a T-shirt that had been lying there. Richard leaned forward and gently took hold of her wrist. The black shoulder socket she had drawn on him flexed as his arm moved, and he said, 'I'm sorry. About your mother.'

'There's nothing to be sorry about,' Flora said brightly. 'She might not be dead.'

'But,' Richard said, 'I thought she — '

'The newspapers,' Flora spoke over him, 'got it wrong.'

' — drowned . . . a long time ago,' Richard finished.

'I . . . ' Flora started. 'She's lost, that's all.' The coconut smell and the golden honey colour came again, her mother turning in sunlight. 'We don't

15

know what happened. And it was eleven years ago. But now she's back. Daddy saw her in Hadleigh.' Flora couldn't hide her excitement.

'What?' Richard still had hold of her wrist.

'I can't go into it now. I just have to get home. He needs me.' She sat on the floor beside him. She knew she wouldn't see Richard again, because he would look at her differently now he had learned who she was. She hated it when her parents became the thing men found most interesting about her.

'Let me drive you.' His hand slipped from her wrist and now held her fingers. 'Is Hadleigh where your father lives?'

'Nearby. I'll get the last train, it's no problem. You probably need to get back too.' She was aware of the change in his posture at these words, a realization of what she might mean.

'When does it go?' Richard stood up, pressed his phone.

'About ten, I think.'

'That's in fifteen minutes. Flora, you won't make it. Take my car.'

16

2

Dear Gil,

It's four in the morning and I can't sleep. I found a pad of this yellow paper and I thought I'd write you a letter. A letter putting down all the things I haven't been able to say in person — the truth about our marriage from the beginning. I'm sure I'll write things you'll claim I imagined, dreamt, made up, but this is how I see it. This, here, is *my* truth.

If I asked, could you say when we first met?

I can tell you. It was the 6th of April 1976, although I'm being easy-going with the word 'met'. It was a Tuesday. Sunny and warm, with an excitement that spring had arrived and was going to stay. Louise and I had been sitting on the lawn outside the university library, ignoring the notices to keep off the grass, and talking about what we were going to do with the rest of our lives. Of course, neither of us knew what it would be, but we both agreed it would be different from our mothers' lives (keeping house, looking after children, not working), which we dismissed as parochial and pointless.

'I'm not worried about having money,' Louise said.

'Or things,' I said.

'God, no. Things — children, husbands,

houses, men — just tie you down. Stop you doing what you want to do. It's all about education now. That was the problem with our mothers — no education. No degree. What use were they to anyone?'

'No use at all,' I said. (We were so critical, so uncompromising.) I lay back on the grass. 'But I'd like to keep having sex. Now and again.'

'Of course. We can have as much as we want when we're away. No strings. No commitment. They have it, why shouldn't we?'

By 'they', Louise meant 'men'.

When we finished university, Louise and I were going to see what the world had to offer (places, people, and — inconsistently — men of course). We spent our evenings studying maps of South America, Australia, China, tracing routes, making plans and drinking cheap red wine.

That afternoon, Louise went to her history class and I went to fetch my bicycle from the racks. There, I found a note tucked between the brake cable and the handlebars of the man's bike I'd bought from a fellow student. The note, which was folded in four, said (I memorized it): 'Sir, in future, please be more careful when locking your bicycle. You appear to have attached yours to mine and now I have to walk home in the rain without an umbrella.'

The day was sunny, remember? The words had been written in pencil and in some places the point had gone through the paper as if the writer had rested it on a trousered knee. There wasn't a signature.

I glanced around, tucked the note into my

18

pocket, put a clip around one leg of my jeans and unlocked the bikes. I picked a daffodil from a nearby flowerbed, threaded it through the spokes of the bike next to mine and rode home. The next day another note had been tucked under the brake wires, although I'd propped my bike in a different spot. This one, in the same handwriting, made me laugh: 'You shouldn't pick the university's flowers,' it said. 'The bigwigs won't like it, and, no doubt, were the Dean to hear, you'd have to sit through one of his interminable speeches about university standards. I can assure you, it's not worth it, however beautiful the flower and welcome the gesture.'

After supper with Louise, I lay on my bed in the flat. I should've been working on an English paper, but started cutting up a yellow envelope which I'd lifted from the wastepaper basket. I shaped daffodil petals from it and glued them to a pencil, and when it was finished I laid the flower on my bedside table. It was the last thing I saw before I switched off the light. The next morning I tucked the home-made daffodil between the handlebars and the brake cable of the note-writer's bike. The bike was gone when I returned that afternoon, and the flower with it.

Then it was Easter, and I convinced my aunt on a crackling telephone line to Oslo that since my rent had been paid for the whole year, I may as well stay on in London. Every morning during the holidays, Louise and I cycled north through Regent's Park to the swimming ponds at Hampstead Heath, no matter the weather. We took hard-boiled eggs and Ritz crackers, towels and swimming costumes. Louise always wanted to go to the ladies-only pond and although it was further and I'd have been happy to take my chances in the mixed pond, I didn't argue because it was the water I went for: the chill of it as I lowered myself from the ladder, the verdigris hue of my legs as they kicked, the coot's-eye view of the pond as I swam, with the insects hovering and the sunbeams refracting and reflecting, or rain speckling the surface. I liked the slap of the water against the boards of the wooden jetty, the distant laughter and shouts of other swimmers, and how, if I ducked down, I could open my eyes into a secret underwater world of weeds, mud, bubbles and the quick flashes of other swimmers' limbs. I was disappointed that, unlike the men in their pond, in the ladies-only we were forbidden to swim naked.

When summer term started, so did the creative-writing module I'd signed up for, and in that first session we were still chattering at our desks when you came in. You put down your bag and leaned back on the lecturer's table at the front of the room and crossed your ankles until one by one we noticed you and stopped talking. You looked young for thirty-nine, and handsome. On the blackboard behind you was a pie chart showing the chemical composition of seawater.

The first thing you ever said to me was 'What's your name?' I remember thinking that your voice had been made for bed-time radio. The second thing you ever said to me was,

'Ingrid Torgensen, please would you lock the classroom door.'

I shuffled on my chair and glanced at my neighbour, who gave an embarrassed laugh.

'Well, come on. What's the worst that could happen?'

I hesitated another moment, then went to the door and put my hand on the locking catch. Behind me there was talk and laughter as you directed the class to push the tables and chairs to the side of the room. I looked over my shoulder and saw you unpacking your bag. You took out an object wrapped in tissue paper and unrolled it from its covering — an empty jam jar. It was 1976, remember, we were young and ready for something new, excited by possibility. You placed the jar on the carpet, then sat cross-legged while you took out something else, also in tissue paper, and unwrapped it as if it was a precious thing. One by one the other students sat in a circle. You bent over the jam jar and inside it you put my home-made daffodil. The door lock turned under my fingers.

'I'm going to tell a secret,' you said when I'd edged into a gap in the circle and sat down too. 'And afterwards it'll be your turn. Something you've never told anyone before. Something you've always been hiding.' You stared at the daffodil, your words slowed and quietened, and we leaned forward to catch them. 'Secret truths,' you said, 'are the lifeblood of a writer. Your memories and your own secrets. Forget plot, character, structure; if you're going to call yourself a writer, you need to stick your hand in

21

the mire up to the wrist, the elbow, the shoulder and drag out your darkest, most private truth.' You came forward and squatted on the floor in front of us.

'I didn't make that daffodil,' you said, nodding towards it. A couple of the petals had come off and the others were bent. I could feel the pump of blood around my body, the flush of heat up through my neck, to my cheeks.

'I stole it,' you continued. 'When I wasn't much older than some of you, my mother became very ill. She was rushed into hospital and my father telephoned and told me to come immediately because she wouldn't last the day. I lived a long way from the hospital and so I left what I was doing — writing or reading, perhaps — and jumped in my car. I had a distance to go, hours of driving, and I went fast without stopping, thinking about my mother, who I was very close to, in her hospital bed. I arrived in the early evening, parked the car haphazardly and ran in.

'My mother was an old-fashioned woman. She had rules of behaviour that had to be followed, an etiquette that we've almost forgotten now, and as I rushed into the building, even on her deathbed I knew my mother would want it done properly. I couldn't turn up without a gift or some flowers, but the small hospital shop was closed.

'So I went into the first ward I came to: a children's ward. No one questioned who I was or what I was doing there. I'd hoped to find a bunch of flowers or some chocolates that I could take, telling myself I'd replace them as soon as the shop opened, but of course no one brings flowers or boxes of chocolates to ill children. Just as I was thinking I would have to go to my mother without taking anything, I saw a home-made daffodil alone in a vase on a bedside table.' You nodded towards the flower. 'The child in the bed was asleep and he had no visitors, so I took the flower and found my way to my mother's room. We said our goodbyes and she died a few minutes after I gave it to her.'

We were silent, watching you, watching the daffodil. One of the girls opposite me sniffed and wiped her eyes. And what did I think? Your story sounded so true, so heartfelt, that I nearly found myself believing it and questioning whether it was the same daffodil. It took me a long time to work out the truth from the fiction.

I don't remember what secrets my fellow students offered up in that lesson — none of them has stuck with me. All that remains is the stunned silence when we picked up our bags and coats to leave. I gave you no secrets; I didn't stick my arm in the mire during that class or any other. It was much later that I made up a story for you. That afternoon, when I told Louise about the lesson, she said, 'That man's an idiot, you should stay away from him.'

Gil, we miss you, please come home.
Yours,
Ingrid

PS: Whatever happened to your bicycle?

3

Richard's Morris Minor was the only car on the last ferry. Before Flora set off, he had given complicated instructions about how much choke she needed to get 'the old girl' started, how the clutch was a 'little sticky', and how Flora mustn't put the car into first gear when it was rolling or she might break a tooth. Flora imagined one of her canines cracking and splitting up the middle. But the car was pretty and smelled of raspberry-coloured warm plastic, even if it wasn't practical.

The ferryman, wearing fluorescent yellow oilskins, waved Flora on and told her they were closing the service because of the bad weather.

'High winds, my love,' was what he actually said.

'But my sister is coming across tonight,' Flora shouted through the small gap she had wound in the car window, although now she couldn't remember what Nan had said about when she was coming home, and Flora thought perhaps she should have gone to the hospital after all.

'Not tonight she isn't. She'll have to go the long way round. Got your handbrake on?'

Flora got out of the car, although the ferry only took ten minutes to cross The Pinch, to the curl of land shaped like a beckoning finger where she had grown up. She stood at the front barrier, pelted by slanting rain while the engine strained and vibrated as it pulled the ferry across the short stretch of water on its chains. Flora's stomach pitched and rolled with the boat. This night there were no lights on the opposite bank and they might have been sailing out to sea. She had never been the last passenger — the only passenger — and she wondered whether her mother had recently stood here to cross The Pinch, and whether they would recognize each other when they met. As the boat juddered and struggled, Flora imagined each clank was the chains snapping, setting the little car ferry free to follow the rushing tide. The waves would roar over the ramp until the car deck was awash and the water flowed through the gap in the window of Richard's Morris Minor. She would climb the ferry's steps to the viewing platform and lean over the railings as the boat listed and its lights were extinguished one by one, until the last, beside the navigation station, stuttered and was swallowed by the sea. Black waves would lift the boat up and roll it with the swell, like mountains rising where there had been no mountains before. The air would escape from each of the cavities and pipes and human lungs, and bubble to the surface, while the ferry up-ended, nose first into the water, and she and Richard's little car and all the yellow-jacketed men would sink to the bottom.

It took two or three goes for Flora to start the car while the man waited impatiently on the ramp. He took a couple of steps towards her, but Flora swore, pulled the choke out, and with a jerk the car started and kept on going. The tollbooths on the road were unlit and the barriers were up: a free ride. The car's headlights appeared to be weaker than when she had set off, and the rain drummed on the thin roof. The wipers were unable to cut through the blur fast enough, so Flora leaned forward over the steering wheel to where the dim beams showed the road disappearing in black and white. Even with the heater going full blast, every few minutes she had to swipe the windscreen with the side of her arm.

The road from the ferry to the village cut through a nature reserve: salty wetlands criss-crossed with tracks, swampy in the hollows, rising to dusty dunes near the sea, and rocky outcrops inland. The sandy trails sliced through fields of marram grass and heather, skirted Little Sea Pond, a brackish lake lying low between the road and the sea, and passed by stands of wind-humped trees huddled together for protection.

Darkness didn't stop Flora from knowing every bend and sway of Ferry Road although she had never driven it, had always been the passenger, either in the front, beside her sister, or in the back when they were children, in her father's car. She had been almost ten when her mother had disappeared, and Flora couldn't remember ever having been in a car with her, although that must have happened. She fiddled with the radio, sliding the dial, but only got static and an occasional faraway voice.

The first bump on the car roof came when she

must have been passing the Agglestone, a massive rock eroded into the shape of a boxer's head, its broken nose flattened by the wind. It rested on a hill to her right, although there was no view of it through the misted windows. She wasn't even certain she had heard anything over the throaty noise of the engine, and the rain. Then something hit the windscreen and was swooshed away by the wipers. Flora reared back in her seat, hands gripping the thin steering wheel, her foot pressing the brake. The car slid across the wet surface to the other side of the road, and she tried to remember if she was meant to turn into a skid or away from it. Something else fell on to the bonnet and seemed to throw itself into the road, and then another, and another. The car came to a halt, stalling with one back tyre in the sandy verge and the rest on the tarmac. The gorse and hawthorn bushes pressed up against the side window as if shading their eyes to gaze in.

Flora peered forward and rubbed at the glass with her fist. The short beams thrown out by the headlights revealed objects falling and bouncing on to the road. When they stopped and she was sure the drumming on the roof was only the rain, she lifted herself over the handbrake and into the passenger seat, and opened the door. The wind in the pines was a roar, and the rain slammed against the road. Without stepping down, she saw on the slick black tarmac a fish lying on its side with its mouth open. It was the size of her palm and shone with a silvery-blue iridescence. She stuck her left foot out to flip the thing over, and even in the rain she saw that the underside was lacerated, crushed when it had hit the ground. Shielding her eyes, Flora looked in the direction of the fading headlights: hundreds of the creatures lay across the road, a handful flapping feebly. They may have been baby mackerel. The wind pulled at the open door and Flora yanked it shut, climbed back over to the driver's seat and sat staring. She wasn't sure she could bear to drive forward. She closed her eyes and turned the ignition. The engine clunked and wheezed twice, and when she tried it again it produced an old man's cough, slow, painful and phlegmy. She pulled the choke out, although Richard had said she wouldn't need it when the engine was warm, but this time the car wouldn't start, and on the fourth try the headlights went out and she was sitting in the dark.

She looked over her shoulder again; perhaps the man had been wrong about the ferry, maybe it would return once more before they closed it, but there was only the night behind her. She waited for another five minutes and tried the ignition again, but now the clunk sounded deadly. She took her suitcase and satchel from the back seat, and once more shuffled over and out of the car.

4

Dear Gil,

Of course I couldn't write the story of a marriage in one letter. It was always going to take longer.

After I finished my first letter I meant to send it straight away. I found an envelope from an old electricity bill in the kitchen-table drawer, and thought I'd walk to the postbox as the sun came up before I could change my mind. But as I perched on the arm of the sofa in the dark with the pen in my hand, there was a noise from the girls' room (the squeak of bedsprings, the creak of the door), and without thinking I grabbed a book from the nearest shelf, shoved the letter inside and pushed it back into place.

Flora stood in the doorway, the sunrise coming through the windows of our bedroom, silhouetting her skinny nine-year-old body in a nightdress.

'Is it morning?' she said.

'No, Flora,' I said. 'Go back to bed.'

'Has Daddy come home?'

'No,' I said. 'Not yet.'

I put the first letter I wrote to you inside *The Swimming-Pool Library* by Alan Hollinghurst. Appropriate, for all sorts of reasons. I've been thinking that I'll leave all my letters in your books. Perhaps you'll never find them, maybe they'll never be read. I can live with that.

So, 1976. We, the chosen four, sat in your tiny office, high up in a corner of a sixties block of whitewashed corridors, lecture rooms, thin carpets on concrete floors, strip-lighting, and metal-framed windows that let in the cold. Apart from the narrow desk overflowing with paper, you'd made your office into a cramped version of a gentleman's club: rugs, lamps, book-lined walls, an old leather chesterfield and low armchairs crammed around a buttoned foot-stool. The room had a smell — of coffee, warm upholstery and tobacco — a smell I loved to inhale, a grown-up's space. You wore a black ribbed cardigan zipped up to your chin, and you reclined in your usual chair.

'Last six lines of the final chapter,' you said, and we scrabbled for our books, found the page and stared at it. You recited them aloud, from memory. 'So what effect do they have?' you asked.

Moments passed until reliable Brian spoke up.

'Jackson's letting us know that Merricat has grown more robust. She's no longer afraid of the village children — in fact, she might even eat one. Whereas Constance has become even more dependent on her sister and most likely will never leave the house again.'

'But what do *you* think?' you said, slurping your coffee and resting the cup against your chin. Brian, looking confused, caught my eye but I shrugged. We were silent for at least a minute.

30

'Well,' Brian said. 'That *is* what I think.'

You sighed. 'What about you, Elizabeth?' You relaxed into the velvet armchair, the padded arms shiny with wear and the white stuffing coming out of the ends, like a man in a smoking jacket who has tucked his hands inside his shirt cuffs for a joke.

'I . . .' she started, clearly unsure and trying to feel around for the answer you wanted. 'I, I think, with the spiders Jackson's telling us that Constance covered up for Merricat . . .' Elizabeth paused, waiting for an indication that she was on the right track. 'Because, you know at the tea party, when what's his name, the uncle, says that Constance cleaned out the sugar bowl, because, you know, that's where the arsenic was, but the uncle, whatever he's called, said there was a spider in it.' You stretched out your legs and let her talk until she wound down and came to a stop. Even I was embarrassed for her.

'So?' you said, drawing out the word. We were silent. 'How do you interpret that?' You plonked your cup on a sheaf of papers beside you on the desk. The top page was upside down from where I sat and I couldn't read it. 'Come on, people.' Despairing of us, you ran your hands through your hair, brown, but receding, leaving a promontory of curl to flop across your forehead.

'Guy,' you said. 'Help your friends out.' I was never sure why you had included Guy in our group of four. I thought he was the weakest writer, someone who liked to string long words together for the sake of it. I'd been sleeping with Guy on and off for the previous year. Off more

31

than on, because although the sex was good, my body disturbed him. One time he'd told me it was like 'doing it' with a weird deep-sea creature, and also he talked too much and I was tired of listening.

While Guy gave his bombastic speech about what he thought of Jackson's intentions, I reduced the volume and tried to think of something to say when it came to my turn. Something that would make you sit up in your overstuffed chair and nod in agreement, something you hadn't even thought of yourself. I had no ideas. Not even a theory we could argue. Really, nothing. When Guy had finished talking, and while my heart was leaping in my throat at the horror of my empty mind, you stretched your arms up behind your head and yawned. It was a yawn so loud and so lengthy that we looked away. Once your mouth finally closed, you leaned forward and rubbed your eyes with the heels of your hands. When you took them away, the whites had a pinkish tint. I don't know how much you'd drunk the night before, but the fumes were radiating off you.

I waited with nervous anticipation for you to ask my opinion. You didn't even turn towards me.

'Look,' you said. 'Some of you, especially those tortured souls who like to think they're poets' — here you stared at Guy, who frowned back at you — 'might fantasize about the idea of scribbling away in your garret, unappreciated by the literary world until you're in your grave. But there really is no fucking point. Writing does not exist unless there is someone to read it, and each reader will take something different from a novel, from a chapter, from a line. Have none of you read Barthes or Rosenblatt?' (We scribbled down the names.) 'A book becomes a living thing only when it interacts with a reader. What do you think happens in the gaps, the unsaid things, everything you don't write? The reader fills them from their own imagination. But does each reader fill them how you want, or in the same way? Of course not. I asked you what effect those lines have, and you've all described what you think Jackson intended, what the lines do, or at least what you believe they do. In some cases you've most certainly got even that wrong.' You glanced again at Guy. 'But none of you told me what effect they have on you. What they made you, the reader, imagine in here.' You thumped your chest. 'You've missed the very essence of literature and reading. Who gives a fuck about Jackson and her intentions? She's dead, literally and metaphorically. This book' — you snatched Elizabeth's copy from her lap and flapped it in the air — 'and all books are created by the reader. And if you haven't realized that and what it means to your own work, you know shit-all about writing and you're never going to, so you might as well stop now.'

It was as if I were in my father's flat again, cowering at one of his rants about his ex-wife, my mother. Guilty by association. You leaned back once more, stretched your legs, and arching your spine put your hands behind your head and closed your eyes, as if you were reclining in a deckchair on a Sunday afternoon. I watched in fascination as your cardigan rose above the waistband of your jeans and a strip of flat stomach appeared; you weren't wearing anything underneath, and when I looked at your feet you didn't have any socks on either. You must have slept on the sofa, had likely still been asleep when Brian, always the first to arrive, had knocked on your office door at two in the afternoon.

'Yep,' you said with your eyes still closed. 'You can stop now. Go on, get out.'

Brian, sitting on the sofa beside Elizabeth, made a noise, a tiny clearing of his throat, but the rest of us just sat.

'Go on, fuck off now,' you said. For a short while more we waited, but you didn't move and I wondered if you'd fallen asleep. We gathered our notes, our copies of the novel with pages marked by slips of paper, our bags, our pens and pencils; all of us keeping a wary eye on you in case you jumped up and shouted, 'Where are you going? We've still got work to do!' But you remained in the same position in the armchair while I and my fellow students shuffled around each other like a sliding tile puzzle, one of us sitting so another could stand, Elizabeth pressing herself into your desk so Guy could squeeze past. I was the last in the queue to get to the door, Elizabeth disappearing in front of me down the corridor.

'Ingrid!' you shouted, and I jumped, turning towards the room. You were sitting up. 'Have a look at this.' In one movement you tilted sideways, plucked a book from a low shelf and

34

threw it at me. It came spinning end over end and I dropped my bag to catch it, slapping the covers between my palms to stop it just short of the bridge of my nose. 'Let me know what you think,' you said, and returned to your previous position, arms behind your head, legs out and eyes shut. I was dismissed.

Come back to us, Gil.

Yours always,

Ingrid

[Placed in *We Have Always Lived in the Castle* by Shirley Jackson, 1962]

5

Even with her head bent against the wind and the rain, Flora recognized her route through the heath. Seven years ago, the summer she turned fifteen, she had lain in a dip in the sand near this path and these woods, with her eyes and legs open beneath a boy called Cooper.

A group of teenagers — villagers and holidaymakers — would gather in the dunes if the evening was dry and light a bonfire in the sand. One night Cooper had offered Flora a drag on his cigarette and a sip of his beer, and had looked at her expectantly, waiting to see what she would offer in return. She had led him through the sandy paths of the heath to the woods at the far end of Little Sea Pond and pressed him into the muscled trunk of a hornbeam. She hadn't kissed a boy before and wasn't sure whether she enjoyed the feeling of his tongue in her mouth. She imagined withdrawing her face and him still standing there with his eyes closed and his tongue out. Flora knew no one cared where she was, not her father, who would be in the pub, and not Nan on another maternity-ward placement, who had left two plates of dinner in the fridge: a lake of stew separated from the peas by a wall of mashed potato.

After the kiss, on their walk back to the bonfire, Cooper said, 'Will you be around tomorrow?'

'Maybe,' Flora said.

The next evening they left the fire early and returned to the tree which bent its spine to the wind and crouched protectively over a sandy hollow.

Flora couldn't now bring Cooper's face to mind and she had never learned his first name, but she recalled the way the silhouetted leaves and thin branches of the hornbeam had swayed against the night sky. They didn't talk much, but there was a full moon and Flora had brought a sketchbook. She made Cooper take off his jumper and T-shirt, although he complained the night was cold, and had him rest against the tree trunk so she could draw him. She tried to look hard and not make assumptions about what was in front of her, like her art teacher had taught her, and although what she drew didn't resemble Cooper, when she had finished she liked how his face blended into the bark of the tree. Afterwards he undid his trousers and she lay back in the sand. She imagined Cooper as a faun or satyr with the legs and cloven hooves of a goat; a half-animal performing an act which came from somewhere deeper than his limited ability with conversation and his love of poorly drawn tattoos. She liked to create a picture of the two of them in her head, how they would appear to a bird or someone sitting in the top of the tree: their bodies merging and blending in the moonlight. She put up with roots digging into her spine as the boy became lost in his own rhythm and finished with two or three jerks that ran through the whole of his body.

Flora went on the pill, and she and Cooper visited the tree many times that summer, while she learned what her body was capable of and what she liked. But it was the drawings and the afterwards time she mostly did it for; when he held her and kissed her quietly, his weight still heavy, until they both felt her body ejecting the soft wetness of his.

'Chucked me out of the disco,' Cooper would say and roll off. Then he would hitch up his trousers and lie on his back beside her, their fingers entwined. Sometimes they shared a cigarette; other times he fell asleep and his fingers would go slack.

On the last night before Cooper was due to go home — to a northern city and with nothing said about love or keeping in touch or meeting the following summer — while he moved on top of her, Flora gazed upwards, watching the branches of the hornbeam slice the moon like a pie. Later that night she returned to the tree with a penknife, and to leave her mark on an object that would still be there long after she'd gone, Flora cut a nick in the trunk and pushed a human tooth into the gap, one of half a dozen she kept in an old cufflink box of her father's.

Flora trekked up the final sand dune with a puff of effort; the suitcase and her satchel were heavy. The inky sea bled out before her, mixing with the sky at an indefinable point. The rain had stopped abruptly in the way that the weather along the coast could transform from hour to hour, and the only noise was the grate of the waves and the wind rattling the trees behind her. To her left, the beach curved away out of sight around to the ferry and The Pinch. While to the right, a concave mile of sand swept into indistinct shadow, backed by more dunes and then the car park. Beyond this were a few lights from the dozen houses, shop and pub that were Spanish Green, the village where Flora had grown up. In the distance a chalky cliff rose to mark the edge of Barrow Down. But in front of her right now was the nudist beach, the place where her mother had disappeared. For the first time in nearly twelve years Flora stepped on to the sand where the sea was retreating. She took off her shoes and socks, tied her laces together, slung her shoes around her neck, and strode towards home in the shallow waves, trying to imagine who, if anyone, would be there to meet her.

6

Dear Gil,

(I've been thinking about getting a dog. Flora would love it. A red setter or an Irish wolfhound — a big dog which would bark at the wind when I take it to the beach. I know you don't like dogs. But you aren't here.)

I took my time reading the book you'd lent me. I can't remember the title now, but it was a terrible title and a terrible book, and I couldn't work out why you'd given it to me. I worried I was missing something. While I cycled to the university and home again I composed sentences in my head, sentences which were positive or at least constructive, but I couldn't find anything to redeem the book. I studied the parts you'd highlighted — the sex scenes you'd underlined and your margin notes — trying to analyse what you meant and blushing at your crude drawings. A few weeks passed, I went to several of your classes, and each time I hung around at the end, putting my coat on slowly, taking my time to pack my bag, hoping you'd ask me about the book, and although I was always the last student to leave, you never called my name, never asked me to stay behind.

I thought you must have forgotten, so one

40

afternoon when I had a free period, I went over to your office. He won't be in, I told myself, although that morning I'd put on my yellow crocheted dress, the one which never failed to get comments. He's a rude bastard and he won't be in, I repeated. But when I walked down the footpath you were hanging out of your office window four floors up, smoking a cigarette. You saw me and smiled, and gave me a kind of salute, which I took to mean come up, so I went through those echoing stairwells and corridors to your office, half terrified, half expectant.

As I lifted my hand to knock on your door, it opened. You stood there, holding the glass jug of your coffee percolator, and, from the surprised expression on your face, I immediately realized that the wave from the window had been a hello, not an invitation.

'How lovely,' you said. 'Were you coming to see me?' You moved past, and there was that smell again, which made me close my eyes for a moment so I could concentrate on inhaling it. 'Go in,' you said. 'Make yourself at home.' You held up the jug. 'Water,' you said, and went off along the corridor.

I stood in the small space between the sofa and the armchairs, breathing you in, tugging at the bottom of my dress and regretting my choice. A brown Smith-Corona sat in the middle of your desk with a piece of paper curling out the top. I leaned over it and, hooked by the word 'Guy', straightened the page and read about a man on a beach waiting for a woman. I read until I heard a cough behind me.

'Sorry.' I jumped back.

'It's OK.' You laughed at how flustered I was. 'Although maybe you should wait until a later draft to read it.'

You put the coffee on and flapped a newspaper around the room. 'I make coffee because I hate the smell of cigarettes. I'm trying to give up,' you said. 'But then I always want a cigarette to go with my coffee. Know what I mean?'

'Absolutely,' I said. I'd never smoked a cigarette, and in England my coffee came out of a jar.

'So, what can I do for you?' You paused and looked at me, your unshaven chin tucked down and your eyes up. 'Ingrid.' You were twice my age, a university professor; my university professor.

'I came to return your book,' I said, sitting in the middle of the sofa.

'Book?' You said from behind me, where you were flinging coffee dregs from the window. The machine rumbled and hissed on the desk.

'Sorry I took so long. I hope you haven't missed it.' I fished the novel out of my bag and held it flat across my white legs where my dress had ridden up.

You put the cups down and, sitting on the arm of the sofa, took the book from my lap. I pulled again at my hem. You flicked through the pages, stopping at several points and smiling to yourself.

'I found your notes very helpful . . . ' I trailed off.

'What?' you said, looking at me, as if only then

42

remembering I was there. You shook your head.

'Your margin notes,' I said.

'Margin notes? You didn't think they were mine?' You laughed, head tilted back, showing your teeth, an infectious laugh, so that, despite feeling young and stupid, I smiled.

'Oh Christ, they're not mine. I was trying to show you another reader's interpretation — that we all take different things from books. I may have underlined a few phrases in my time, folded over some corners, but I can honestly say I've never drawn a cock and balls in the margin of a book.' Heat was rising up from my neck. You bent back the page you had open and held it up to me. 'Juvenile marginalia,' you said. 'Drawn by a boy, about fifteen, a virgin, never been kissed, masturbates frequently. Cocks aren't ever drawn by girls. And they are always drawn by their owners — have you ever seen a frenulum in a margin?'

I shook my head because that seemed the correct response. I'd no idea what a frenulum was. I knew my face was red, but you were gracious enough not to comment.

After a moment you said, 'I take it you didn't like the book?'

'No, I didn't,' I said. 'It was one of the worst books I've ever read.'

'You read it all?'

I nodded.

'Oh dear. You weren't meant to read it — it is dreadful. I shall have to make it up to you.' You stood and put the book on a different shelf from where you'd taken it, stuffing it into a gap. 'How do you like your coffee? Actually, don't bother to answer that, there's no milk and no sugar.'

'Black would be fine.'

'I know . . . ' You turned once more and sat again on the sofa's arm. 'Let's not have coffee; let's go out and get a proper drink.' You slid over the rounded arm of the chesterfield and landed beside me in a puff of dust. 'You didn't have any other plans, did you?'

I'd never been so close to your peppery smell before. 'I have to go to the library,' I said, 'but I can go later.'

The side of your leg, your jeans, was touching my bare leg. In that moment after I replied, you looked down at my knees, my short dress, and your legs, wide open, pressing against me. And you jumped up.

'The library?' you said, staring out of the window, although there was nothing to see except blue sky. 'I have some library books that need taking back. They're here somewhere. I don't suppose you could return these while you're there, could you?' You picked up a pile of folders and a stack of papers and dumped them on the floor, uncovering six plastic-wrapped books. 'They've been on at me for ages to get them back.' You put them in my hands. 'God, I need a cigarette,' you said.

There was a queue in the library, and I swore at you under my breath, and I swore at myself for being so ridiculous, for reading every signal wrong and for coming so close to embarrassing myself. 'He's an idiot,' I said, and realized I'd spoken aloud when the plump woman in front of me in a grey cape swivelled her pigeon head.

At the front of the queue I handed your books over.

'Eight pounds forty,' the librarian said. Eight pounds forty. That was forty-six loaves of bread, or about forty boxes of eggs, or twenty-eight glasses of Cinzano in the Duke of York. It was more than I'd ever had in my purse.

'They're not mine. I'm returning them for a . . . ' I stopped. 'Someone else,' I said. The librarian scowled, and the queue behind me shuffled and muttered. I found my chequebook in my bag and the woman stood over me while I wrote, signed and tore out the slip. I wasn't sure it wouldn't bounce. I should have stormed into your office, demanded you pay me there and then, but I went to the bike shed, deflated, all the anticipation gone out of the day, and cycled home.

I didn't see you again properly until my next tutorial. One of your classes had been cancelled and another covered by the deputy head of the English Department. There were rumours you were ill, that you'd been suspended for drinking, that your wife had died. Wife! How that made my heart lurch. Everywhere I walked — around the English block, the library, through the streets of Bloomsbury — I looked for you. Once, I saw you at a distance, hands shoved in trouser pockets, walking away from me, head lowered and stooping handsomely near the history rooms. I turned and raced around the building, slowing on the final corner so I could saunter towards you, but by the time I got there you were talking to the bird-lady from the library You laughed at something she said, touched the top of her arm, and I could see the pleasure in her face from your attention. The two of you walked away. I wanted to pluck that old woman's feathers out.

For a week I didn't check my pigeonhole so I could claim ignorance if you cancelled my tutorial. Although I was still cross with myself for paying your library fine and with you for not knowing I had, I wore the yellow dress again.

Like before, the window to your office was flung wide, but this time you weren't leaning out. Upstairs, your door was ajar, and when I knocked on it, it opened further but you weren't inside. I stood on the threshold, smelling you, and looking at your disorder.

'Ingrid,' you said from behind me. I turned, you held that coffee jug full of water and you smiled. You were wearing espadrilles and creased linen trousers which you'd rolled up to reveal your ankles and a bit of tanned calf. Your big-collared short-sleeved shirt with its wide, off-centre stripe was open at the neck. You looked like a rich American from the 1950s, holidaying on the Italian coast. If I'd gone to the window and glanced down, I'd have seen a beautiful woman in a headscarf and sunglasses waiting for you in an open-topped sports car.

'I wasn't sure you'd come,' you said. 'You've missed some classes.'

'I haven't missed any,' I said.

'Well, sit down.' You manoeuvred past me into your office and set the coffee machine going. I

46

sat on the edge of one of the armchairs.

'So.' You spun your desk chair around to face me. 'How's it been going?'

'Fine.'

'Well, that's good.' Behind you the percolator's stomach rumbled. Neither of us looked at each other. 'So, I suppose we might as well get straight to it.' You slapped your thighs, and pushed off against the floor with a foot so that the wheeled chair slid along a well-worn track in front of your desk. You stopped it at a stack of papers, which you searched through until you teased out my assignment from halfway down. My first name was trapped inside the brown circle of a coffee-cup stain. 'Did you bring your own copy?'

'No,' I said, folding my arms.

'No,' you said.

'No,' I said again.

You flicked through the pages on your lap. 'I take it this is set in Norway?'

'The Oslo archipelago.'

'Is that where you're from?'

'My father's family.' I crossed my legs.

'Right,' you said, glancing up and flicking through the pages again. I could see red writing on the white sheets. 'The sense of place is very well developed.'

'I've never lived there.'

'Well, I liked it very much, but I was confused about where you were going with the ending.'

'It isn't finished.'

'No,' you said, 'I could see that.' You looked at me with a half-smile and your head cocked while

47

I stared, willing myself not to smile back. In my head I repeated 'Eight pounds forty pence', over and over, so that I could hate you, dislike you, not like you quite as much as I already did.

'Maybe we should have a coffee,' you said, swivelling round and standing up to pour. 'Black?'

'Fine.'

You handed me a cup with a saucer and sat in your armchair beside mine. 'Ingrid,' you said patiently, 'you might get more out of this tutorial if you say something other than fine and no.'

I took a swig of coffee. It was scalding and I had to force it down.

'Are you all right? You're not looking very well,' you said. 'Pale.'

'And you're looking very well fed and tanned.' It was the sort of thing Louise would have said.

You laughed, that big bold laugh, and swept your hand through your hair. 'How about that proper drink I promised you last time?' I was surprised you'd remembered. 'We can discuss this.' You patted the assignment on your lap. I must have appeared undecided. 'A working drink?' You glanced at your watch. 'We'd better be quick.' You stood up and took my cup. 'Come on, come on.' You hurried me out of your office and down to your car. If you'd held the door open for me like my father used to insist on doing, I wouldn't have gone with you, but you got into the driver's seat and turned the ignition before I'd even closed my door. The interior of your car was the smell of leather and your office, concentrated, as if it had been

48

reduced to your essence.

You drove east along narrow London streets, overtaking black taxis and appearing to know your way as well as any of their drivers. You pulled up outside a scruffy pub which looked more like a butcher's — brown tiles on the outside. There were no lights showing, and when you pushed the door it didn't open.

'Shit!' you said and slapped the tiles with the flat of your hand. 'Seems we can't have that drink after all.'

'Cup of tea?' I said.

'What?' You were like a sulky child who pretends not to hear the offer of an apple after the ice cream van didn't stop.

'Let's go and get a cup of tea,' I said.

We sat opposite each other at a tiny table in the window of a cafe which smelled of the overripe bananas from the fruit-and-veg shop next door. You had coffee and I ordered tea from a surly waitress, which she brought to us in a metal pot. You chose an iced bun. Neither of us ate it. The cafe was full of yellowing spider plants, some lined up along a ledge which ran the length of the room, and others hanging from macramé baskets above our heads. I had the excited feeling that I was on the cusp of something and that at any moment my life could spin off in a direction I'd never intended or anticipated. We examined each other's faces but didn't speak, and I was giddy with vertigo. We were the only customers. A fly buzzed against the front window, and the waitress tuned in and out of stations on a portable radio, a burst of dance music followed by static and something orchestral, then a return to white noise. You leaned towards me as if to tuck a length of my hair behind my ear but it was to put your hand around the back of my head and pull me to you until your mouth was at the side of my face. It was the smell of you that kept me there, stretching over the cups and plate. The bristles on your chin were against my cheek. 'I'm sorry about the library fine,' you whispered. You moved your face so your lips touched the corner of my mouth and I panicked, suddenly not clear what I wanted after all. I pulled away from you and stood up in one motion, so you pitched forward across the table, upsetting your coffee on to the bun, brown liquid spilling. The waitress, now paying us attention, stopped the radio at a station that was playing 'Big Bad John', and stared at me as I reversed out of the door and on to the street.

'Ingrid, stop, I'm sorry,' you said, following me out, but I fled. You were called back by the waitress, and as I glanced over my shoulder you were standing in the doorway, both hands resting on the frame as if you alone were keeping the building from collapsing.

Your loving wife,

Ingrid

[Placed in *Swiss Bakery and Confectionery* by Walter Bachmann, 1949]

7

By the time Flora reached the bottom of the chine — the narrow track up to the village — her shoulders and arms ached no matter how she held the suitcase and satchel. There had once been a path which zigzagged from the beach up to the Swimming Pavilion's garden, but now the only way to reach the house was via the chine that ended at the bottom of Spanish Green. Even in the hottest summer the overhanging trees made the path shady, and the ferns and grasses dripped moisture which oozed out of the rocky sides.

She took a few deep breaths and tilted her face to the sky. The clouds had cleared, blown away inland, and the stars were appearing. Once, years ago, her father had taken her hand and said that some people believed Ingrid was up there amongst them, shining in the dark. But Flora, who had been eleven or twelve, still watched Ingrid inside her head, as if a short scene from a film had caught in a loop: her mother turning away from the front door of the Swimming Pavilion again and again. In her long pink evening dress with its beads catching the sun, she endlessly repeated the steps from the veranda, turned her head to take in the lawns, the flowerbeds and the view down to the sea, then turned back so her eyes swept across the gorse bush Flora was hiding in, before she walked out of the garden for ever.

Flora had pulled her hand from her father's. 'They're wrong, Daddy,' she said.

'It's difficult to live with both hope and grief.' He spoke to her in the adult way he always had. 'To keep imagining that we might come home one day and she'll be waiting for us on the veranda, and at the same time living with the idea that she's dead. A balancing act. It's OK if you believe your mother's gone, you can tell me and no one will blame you.'

'Do you do the balancing act?' Flora asked.

'I do,' her father said.

'Then I will too.'

Gil had taken her hand again and squeezed it.

It was the thought that Nan may have brought her father back early and that her mother could be at home that kept Flora walking up the chine, her bare feet knowing the way even in the dark, but when she reached the lane the idea that Ingrid might be around the corner made her hesitate. For years she had practised what she would say to her mother when she saw her again. There were plenty of choices — 'Where have you been?' 'How could you leave us?' — but mostly she came back to 'Why?' Flora wasn't certain she wanted to go on, and yet she found herself running along the short stretch of tarmac, clasping the suitcase to her front, and holding her breath when she reached the drive. But as soon as she came around the corner she saw there were no cars beside the house, not even Nan's, and there were no lights on. There were just the silhouettes of the unrestrained bushes and trees in the neglected garden, and the low shape of the house.

Flora's feet also recognized the three steps up to the veranda, the depth of each tread, where the wood was smooth, how the top step was never quite as high as expected. Her right hand reached out to the square pillar and, beside it, the railing, even in the dark her fingers knowing the heart-shaped chip in the paint; touching it for luck. Two paces forward took her to the front door. She put down her shoes and suitcase, and fumbled inside her satchel for her keys. She put the key in the lock but it wouldn't turn. She tried the handle and the door opened.

Inside, the house smelled the same as always: old books, damp in the bathroom, fried eggs; home was the colour of toasted fennel seeds — a warm speckled brown.

'Hello?' Flora whispered into the unlit hall. 'Daddy? Nan?' She stretched a hand forward, and called out, 'Mum?' The house was silent. She flicked the light switch and the overhead bulb came on.

'My God,' she said.

8

Dear Gil,

Yesterday afternoon I decided to do some clearing. I went through the wardrobes and the chest of drawers in the girls' room to collect clothes they'd outgrown. On Flora's side I found your old dressing gown, a formal shirt you'd spilled red wine over which I thought had been thrown away, and that pair of reading glasses which went missing about a year ago. When Flora came in and saw me, she clutched the things to her, saying I was throwing away her 'hair-looms'. We fought and I slapped her calf hard enough to leave the red print of my fingers on her skin. She didn't cry, instead her face became stony, an expression I recognized in myself, and she strode outside. I was the one who ran to my room and wept into my pillow. Later, I turned out that suitcase of old papers kept under the bed. I was meant to be sorting, but each out-of-date passport, hand-drawn Mother's Day card, and photo delayed me. They gave an impression of the perfect family: picnics on the beach, children digging in their flowerbed patch, doting parents — like a photograph album flicked through by a distant relative, oohing and aahing at the happy times, without knowing about the hundreds of pictures which had been discarded.

And then, at the bottom of the suitcase, your letter.

I sat on the floor with everything spread around me and imagined you all those years ago in your writing room at the end of the scrubby, gorse-filled field you called the garden, bashing out the letter on your typewriter. You might have been wearing those old shorts you loved so much and flip-flops with sand between your toes, and your hair standing stiff from the saltwater after a swim. I reread the letter and felt again the presumptuousness that you could write about love when we hadn't declared it, the absurdity of mapping out our whole lives when we'd only just met, the shock of you mentioning ageing when I wasn't ever going to grow old, and laughing at how wrong you were about children; and I remembered too my secret pleasure that you'd chosen me. I was just twenty then, a different woman from the one I am now.

I read that letter so many times, wondering what you hoped your reader's reaction would be. Rereading it yesterday made me cry for when we were starting out, before I'd come to this house, and because nothing turned out like you said it would. Well, maybe one thing; perhaps I shouldn't have laughed so readily at the idea of children.

Flora came in while I was sitting on the floor.

'Don't be sad, Mummy,' she said. 'What's the worst that could happen?'

I love who we were then and who we might have become.

Yours,
Ingrid

Spanish Green, Dorset, June 1976

Ingrid,

If I could, I would turn our love on its head: we would get the anger, the guilt, the blame, the disappointment, the irritation, the work-a-day and the humdrum over and done with first. We would have everything to look forward to.

At the bitter beginning, when I am old and many parts of me don't work like they used to and other bits have fallen off, you will return. You, so much wiser, will make me wait a long time. Years, perhaps, or maybe even until I'm dead.

After that you will leave. My friends will not be surprised. In public I will be vitriolic, I will get drunk, vomit on the front of my suit and fall over in the street, but in the privacy of my bed I will let the tears fall down my moth-eaten face.

But you too, Ingrid, will be old: your corn hair blanching to silver, the backs of your hands livered, your skin looser, yet more beautiful. In the decade after you leave me, you will insist we switch off the bedroom light before we undress, and when, accidentally, you see me naked, you will sigh and wonder why you hadn't taken a younger man; one who still had flesh on his backside.

A year after that, you will move out for a week to your sister's, telling tales of pissing in the nettles at the bottom of the garden, too many books, and toothpaste smeared around the end

56

of the tap where I have sucked the water from it. You will complain that I drink too much and don't write enough. Your sister will agree about what a shit I am and that you deserve better. Neither of you will speak to me for months. (Tell me, do you have a sister?)

Five years later I will try, and fail, to mend the hole in the Swimming Pavilion's roof and you will refuse to hold the ladder because you have better things to do. You will ask our neighbour's 34-year-old son to nail on a new corrugated sheet, and as you hold tight to his ladder you will look up with regret and thoughts of the different life you could have had in the city. In the evening we will shout at each other; one of us will slam doors.

In our middle years, we will travel together: I will take you to Emerald Lake in July and hire a boat so you can trail your hand in the water, stirring the blue mountains that pass beneath us. You'll hum a tune about the lakes of Canada and I'll put down the oars so I can kiss you; we will hire bikes and cycle across the Golden Gate Bridge on a cloudy day and the next morning our faces will be pink with sunburn; we'll travel through Turkey by public transport, standing on the buses and ducking like locals when the driver shouts, 'Police!'; in Sweden we will slip duty-free gin into glasses of tonic that we've bought in a bar, and discuss our children, all six of them.

We will drive up to London for the launch. As we grow younger, I will write a successful novel and dedicate it to you. I will sit at my window typing, happy to see you stroll to the sea for an afternoon swim. When you return, we'll take armfuls of books out to the unmown lawn and lie on a blanket with them spread about us. We will read to each other and watch the gulls wheeling above. If we are shat upon, you will teach me to swear in Norwegian.

Then one day I will borrow a more sensible car than the one I own now and arrive outside your room in London at five in the morning. I will toot the horn with excitement until you put your sleepy head out of the window above me and we will both laugh, and I will be full of desire for you. We will pack my sensible car with your belongings: your grandmother's velvet chair, a box of diaries, and suitcases of clothes that you won't need when you live beside the sea.

After you come to live with me, we will go to the supermarket and I will press you up against the blackcurrant jam shelf in the preserves aisle and kiss you full on the mouth so that old ladies smile at us, remembering. You will beat me at Monopoly and I will lose my temper and hide the Mayfair card between the sofa cushions. We will take a picnic to the nudist beach and stay there until the sun goes down, and when the sea is lit by the moon we will make love on the sand.

The last time you come to my house it will be stormy and the noise of the rain drumming on the tin roof will be so loud we will have to shout to make ourselves heard. There will be a power cut like there often is here, and we will light candles and I will hold your face in my hands and kiss you again, and when I lead you to my bedroom we will know that everything is as it should be and that we will always feel this way.

Near the end I will say that I want you to see my house beside the sea, and the next day I will drive us down and both of us will know what will happen after we have had dinner. We will cook eggs and bacon and move around my kitchen as if we have been choreographed, and we will eat at the table amongst the books.

The day after that, I will take you to lunch on Candover Street for hot salt beef and a warm beer. I will walk you home and we will kiss for the last time at your front door, on the street where anyone can see, but neither of us will care. Your lips will taste of mustard and cloves.

I will write you a letter.
Gil

[Both letters placed together in *Prophecy: What Lies Ahead* by Oswald J. Smith, 1943]

9

In the hallway, towering piles of books lined the walls all the way to the kitchen. Precarious columns of paperbacks and hardbacks, cracked spines and dust jackets, rose like eroded sea stacks, their grey pages stratified rock. Many were higher than Flora's head, and as she walked between them it was clear that one bump might have them tumbling in an avalanche of words. The house had always been full of books, far too many for one person to get through in a lifetime. Her father didn't collect them to read, to own first editions or to keep those signed by the author; Gil collected them for the handwritten marginalia and doodles that marked the pages, for the forgotten ephemera used as bookmarks. Every time Flora came home he would show her his new discoveries: left-behind photographs, postcards and letters, bail slips, receipts, handwritten recipes and drawings, valentines and tickets, sympathy cards, excuse notes to teachers; bits of paper with which he could piece together other people's lives, other people who had read the same books he held and who had marked their place.

Flora hadn't been back for a month or two, and in that time it was as if the books had spawned. When she looked into the sitting room it was the same: nearly all the surfaces — the side tables, coffee table and sofas — were covered. A second wall of books, as high as her waist, had always leaned against the outer one, but now that had grown, sagging in places, collapsing in others like a rockslide on a mountain road, and a third buttress was in development, encroaching on the diminishing space. She was surprised Nan hadn't said anything; her sister would surely have been worrying about their father's state of mind before now.

From the doorway, Flora saw that the record player was clear of books and a record had been left on the turntable. Just for the sound of something, so she wasn't alone in the house, she made her way across the room and switched it on, and a guitar started, a man singing. She picked up the album cover, one she hadn't seen before amongst her father's collection, showing a man sitting at a kitchen table, pots and pans hanging above his head. 'Townes Van Zandt' was written along the bottom. She turned the volume up so she would be able to hear it through the house, and then she flicked the sitting room light off and went down the hall. There were fewer books in the kitchen, but they still hugged the walls, cluttered the table and roosted on the counter. These had strips of newspaper, hanging out like loose grey tongues, marking pages. Flora picked up a brick-red hardback without a jacket, its cover worn in places to brown suede: *Queer Fish* by E. G. Boulenger. She flicked through it and one of the home-made bookmarks fluttered to the floor. She stopped somewhere in the middle and held the book up to her nose

— dust, memories, and the smell and colour of vanilla. She found a pen, and at the bottom of the page drew a phalanx of fish dropping from a raincloud. She closed the book, replaced it and checked in the fridge: a bottle of milk in the door, four eggs in a box, an opened packet of smoked bacon secured with a pink elastic band that the postman must have dropped. Flora sniffed the milk, filled the kettle and spooned leaves into a teapot.

Using the telephone in the kitchen, she called her sister's mobile — Nan had programmed the number into Gil's phone — and let it ring until the message service kicked in and Nan's infuriatingly calm voice, the one she must use for women in labour, invited the caller to leave a message or, if it was an emergency, to call the maternity ward. Flora tried Nan's house: no reply. She scrolled through the telephone's contacts list, searching for her father's mobile number, but when it wasn't there she was almost pleased that Nan hadn't thought of everything. Flora considered phoning the hospital to ask about Gil, but told herself that if there was something urgent Nan would try to find her.

With her cup of tea, Flora walked back down the book-lined hallway, running her fingers along the spines as she passed: an Italian phrase book, *How to Breed Cats for Profit*, *Jaws*. She stopped to flip the record and then went into the bedroom. For the first nine years of Flora's life it had been her mother's, filled with her mother's things, and although her father had occasionally spent the night there rather than sleeping in his writing room, Flora still thought of him as a visitor to the house. The bedroom was on a front corner, with two side windows facing the sea and one looking out on to the veranda. She put the light on and saw this space too was full of books, against the walls and stacked beside the bed. A glass of water stood on top of a pile on the bedside table, and on the other side the digital alarm clock that had stopped working years ago perched on another stack. The bed, an ancient giant which used to dominate the room, was now overshadowed and reduced by paper. The blankets and cover were rumpled, and one of the pillows still bore the indent of a head as if someone had got up a few minutes ago. Flora put her nose to it, smelling the khaki colour of unwashed hair. She wasn't sure what she had been hoping for. If her mother had come home it was ridiculous to think she would have got into bed. Flora opened the wardrobe, half hoping the greatcoat would be hanging there. She remembered the odour of it, thick and heavy like the stems of nettles and tangled undergrowth. She had liked to hide things in the pockets. No greatcoat. Just Gil's shirts, all facing the same way, pairs of trousers folded over the hangers with the creases crisp, a jacket, a suit Flora couldn't remember him wearing and two pairs of slip-on shoes. They might once have been stylish: soft Italian leather, hand stitched, but now split around the seams and the heels worn down. She realized her father must have moved back into the house.

When she was fourteen, just over four years after Ingrid had disappeared, Flora had come home early from school to discover Gil and Nan clearing away her mother's clothes. As soon as she opened the front door she heard Nan talking in the bedroom.

'It's time, Dad,' Nan was saying. 'Having this stuff around isn't healthy for Flora. You know she comes in here all the time, dressing up, playing with the jewellery, spraying Mum's perfume. I can smell it on her.' Her father mumbled a reply.

Flora didn't wait to hear more. 'What are you doing?' she said as she burst through the bedroom door.

Gil stood in front of the dressing table holding open a bin liner, his face turned towards the sea as Nan tipped in all the lacy silky things that Flora liked to stroke.

'We're having a clear-out,' Nan said, opening the bottom drawer, which Flora knew contained jumpers because when her sister was at college and the house empty she took them out, pushed her face into them, then refolded each one and put them back. Gil said nothing, just continued to hold the bag open and stare out of the window.

'But what will Mum wear when she comes home?' Flora made a grab for the bin liner and the plastic ripped, underwear falling on to the floor.

'Now look what you've done,' Nan yelled, scrabbling about, scooping everything together. Flora joined her sister on the floor, snatching as many pieces as she could, stuffing them under

64

her body and lying on top of them while Nan tried to drag her off. Flora let go of the bundle with one hand and lashed out, clawing at her sister's face. Nan drew back, her fingers against her cheek, and when she lifted them off, blood oozed from a long scratch. She struck Flora across the face. The two of them stopped, shocked into silence.

'Sit on the fucking bed, Flora,' her father said, 'and don't make this harder than it already is.' She sat in silence and watched her mother's 1940s shirtwaist dresses, woollen palazzo pants and A-line skirts being lifted from their hangers and folded into boxes. The cheesecloth tops and yellow crocheted minidress were squashed under the pairs of Oxfords, pumps, the make-up from the dressing table, the cheap necklace with the paste stone like a bird's egg, and the perfume. And on top of them, the pink chiffon evening dress. And then the boxes and the bin liners were loaded into Nan's car. Flora didn't think about where they would end up; they were gone.

Two weeks after Nan had taken everything away, Flora went with her father into Hadleigh, and while he flicked through the second-hand books in the charity shop, she wandered to the back to rummage through the old tweed jackets and wide-collared shirts. A girl of about twenty came out of the changing room in Ingrid's chiffon dress — the skirt dragging on the carpet tiles, the neckband too tight. The girl stood in front of a mirror and twisted sideways, stretching around to look. Flora grabbed on to a clothes rail to keep herself upright, and glanced at the girl's reflection. She remembered the day she'd seen her mother wearing the dress, a sandy-coloured towel draped over one arm and a book in her hand. There was a waft of coconut — the colour of golden honey again, and Ingrid turning and stepping, turning and stepping, out into sunlight.

'It doesn't fit right,' the girl said to her friend, plucking at the gauzy fabric. 'And there's a rip in it.' She held up the bottom.

'It's old-fashioned, but not in a good way,' her friend said, lifting the skirt and sniffing. 'And it smells of dead people.' The girl wearing it twirled in front of the mirror and pretended to choke. They both laughed and returned to the changing room together. At the front of the shop Gil was still busy flicking through the books. His daughter slipped a cheap and ugly bead necklace off the display and dropped it into her coat pocket.

Flora shut the wardrobe door and went into the bedroom she shared with Nan. It had a single window with a view of the tangled garden and Gil's writing room and, from Nan's side, since she was the elder sister, a glimpse of the sea. Nan's teddy bear was propped up against her pillow, her bed made with sheets and blankets, hospital corners tucked under. A chest of drawers stood between both beds. Long ago Ingrid had painted a wide white band across the top, down the front of the drawers, and inside them. In her anger, desperate to stop her daughters arguing over which side belonged to whom, Ingrid hadn't removed any of the contents when she yanked out the drawers and painted, so that for years afterwards Flora had worn clothes streaked with white. Now she opened the deep bottom drawer and looked inside. On the left, a pile of Nan's winter jumpers, neatly folded, and on the right a knot of laddered tights, jeans that Flora had never got round to taking in and bras with their under-wire sticking out. She burrowed through her clothes, flipping the heap over, moving aside her father's empty cufflink box, searching for a flash of pink chiffon. The day after she had seen the dress in the charity shop Flora had left school during morning break, stuffed her tie in her pocket, turned her blazer inside out and walked the two miles into town. Using her lunch money she had bought the dress and taken it home, keeping it hidden at the back of the drawer. Flora found it now, took off her damp clothes, leaving them on the floor where they fell, and then pulled her mother's dress over her head, reaching behind herself to do up the clasp, and stood facing away from her wardrobe mirror. The man in the sitting room was singing about a woman with yellow hair. Flora held the handle of the bedroom door and half turned, staring over her shoulder at her reflection. She was the same age as her mother had been when Gil had bought her the dress, shortly after Nan had been born; to celebrate the birth, Flora presumed. Many of the sequins and silver beads had gone from the bodice, leaving hanging threads, and the skirt was stained and still ripped, but in the mirror, an image of Ingrid and her heart-shaped face looked back. Only the towel and the book were missing.

10

Dear Gil,

They say that insomniacs are at their most creative in the middle of the night. It doesn't feel like that to me, although these letters do come out in a rush of words that fly from the end of my pen, and when I read them back the handwriting is so poor many of the sentences are hard to decipher. I remember hearing about a poet (a famous insomniac) who would hire five hotel rooms and sleep in the middle one to guarantee complete silence during the night. What was her name? You would know if you were here. There'll be a book of her poetry somewhere in the house, although even you wouldn't be able to lay your hands on it. Some of the walls are two books deep. That poet, whatever her name was, wrote *The Letter*, and said her handwriting was like the legs of a fly and her heart chafed for the want of her lover. How appropriate. How easy it is to imagine the worst. I would prefer to know where my lover, my husband, is; who you're with and what you're doing. Maybe that's why I never really became a writer of fiction. I am a writer of truths, a factualist. No more lifting of carpets or turning of blind eyes; what we'll have here, in these letters, are bald, bare facts.

69

Flora and I aren't designed for sleep. Our eyelids are too thin, our bodies too light, to stay weighted down in a bed, and our ears too sensitive. We wake at any noise, whether it's real or imagined: the rain on the roof, the creak of the floorboard in front of the cooker, or the rattle of the window frames already dulled by chocks of ripped-up beer mats. When the windows are opened, scraps of card with the words 'Old Speckled Hen' and 'Henry's Original IPA' litter the floor under the sills.

Your letter arrived in my university pigeonhole a week after I'd run out of the cafe. Although I carried it with me everywhere and tried out all sorts of replies in my head, the letter was too huge to know how to respond, so I never did. And I didn't tell Louise any of it (the tutorial, the cafe, the near kiss), and I didn't show her the letter. I knew she'd have warned me off, made a joke about older men, initiated a conversation about children and why neither of us would be having any. I went to your class sick with excitement but didn't say much and you didn't ask me any questions, avoided my eye. Like when you'd lent me the book, I lingered just long enough for you to ask me to stay behind, but you didn't. I found out where you lodged in London when you were teaching, and I walked past your house, guessing which window was yours. I scanned the streets for a mustard-coloured Triumph Stag, but didn't see one. When I was supposed to be writing, or working, or revising, I found myself doodling the words 'Gil Coleman' and would have to black them out with my pen, pressing hard enough to mark the desk with tiny oblongs of redaction. I joined my nearest public library, but the only books I borrowed were the two you'd written. I sat on a bench in St George's Gardens and consumed them both in a day, trying to tease the author out from the words on the page, like a winkle from its shell. I've never told you that I loved them. I loved them.

For that week I replayed our time in the cafe so often the memory became grey through overuse, and I thought you must have given the letter to the wrong person (the wrong Ingrid). Then, in my pigeonhole I found my short-story assignment about a girl, a boy and a box of matches. You'd marked it, underlining the words 'now and again he would glance at the undulation of her top lip and imagine pressing his thumb into that narrow channel', and in a scrawled hand, you'd written, 'Please see me.' Reading your handwriting brought you back into Technicolor and so I told Louise.

She said the things I'd been expecting her to say: that you had a reputation, that you were a misogynist, an old man preying on young students, that it was sick, I should report you, the letter was an outrage, and I would be more of a fool than she ever could have imagined if I saw you again.

One wet Saturday lunchtime on the way back from Levitt's my bike got a puncture. I was worrying that the jarring of the flat tyre against the pavement would prematurely crack the two

71

eggs which were wedged into the corner of the bike's front basket with four rashers of streaky bacon wrapped in greaseproof paper. Louise and I had slept in late and I'd volunteered to go and buy breakfast. When I looked up, you were leaning out of the window of your car.

'Hello,' you said.

I carried on walking, the bicycle limping through the puddles.

'Ingrid.' Your voice was raised. 'Don't be so fucking difficult.'

I stopped and pushed back the hood of my raincoat with the inside of my wrist. Trickles of cold water ran over my cheeks and dripped from my chin. 'Just get in the car,' you said. 'So we can talk.'

I indicated my bike and made to carry on walking, although we were beside the railings outside my house.

'Ingrid,' you said more quietly, 'I want to wind up the window, I'm wet. Please get in.'

I propped my bike against the railings, taking a long time about it and trying to look nonchalant. When I got in the passenger seat you turned on the car's ignition and for a moment I thought you were going to drive us away, but instead you stretched across and adjusted the vent until warm air blew over me.

'Are you ill?' you said. 'You shouldn't be out in the rain. You're so pale.' Your fingers touched my cheek, but I continued to look straight ahead at the blurred shops and houses of Goodge Street while trying to work out what I should say about your letter. 'Let's go and get a drink,' you said.

'We can talk, that's all. I promise.' You smiled your winning smile, which was already chipping away at the cold hard core of me.

You put the windscreen wipers on to clear the glass and peered out at the Jekyll and Hyde. 'How about that place? Come on,' you said. I'd never been inside before, but I'd heard the drinks were overpriced and I already knew the clientele were cheap; I'd often sat at my top-floor window opposite watching the drunks at closing time, fighting, groping or vomiting their wages into the gutter.

Eleven men's heads twisted towards us as we went in. They sat in a line at the bar on top of their owners' necks, while their hands alternately lifted pints of beer and cigarettes. A watery sun slanted in through tall Victorian windows, highlighting eddies of smoke which swirled into the pub's brown corners. You bought me a port and lemon. Did you have a whiskey? I don't remember, but I can still recall the smell of cigarettes mixing with the greasy odour of pastry kept for too long in a pie warmer on the bar. A yellowing sign taped to the side of the glass read, 'Topless Bar Maids Every Wenesday Lunchtime'.

'There's a girl in the novel I'm writing who looks like you,' you said after we'd sat opposite each other in a vinyl booth. 'I keep trying to get her to eat, to fatten her up and give her a bit of colour. I'm worried she's going to fade away.'

'Would that be a problem?'

You considered the question. 'I think the whole plot might collapse without her,' you said. 'She's central to the protagonist's well-being.'

'So she's not the protagonist?'

'No, I've never been good at putting myself inside women's heads. Far too complex.'

'Have you tried?'

'Many times.' You gulped at your drink.

'I'm sure your character is perfectly capable of looking after herself.'

'Oh, I know that, but she keeps surprising me. I haven't quite pinned her down yet.'

'Maybe you should give her a subplot of her own,' I said, and sipped my drink. 'What's that cliché? The one all creative-writing lecturers come out with at some point?' You gave me half a smile. 'Let them be, and you'll find that after a while your characters will write their own story.'

'But I think this girl is heading for an unhappy ending and that would be a shame.'

'There's a man in the story I'm writing,' I said, and paused, took another sip.

'Yes?' you said.

'He doesn't look anything like you.'

You laughed, chin up, loud, so the heads at the bar turned ninety degrees to stare at us again. 'What does he look like, this man in your story?' you said.

'Actually, I lied.'

'He does look like me, after all?'

'There aren't any men in what I'm writing, only a woman.'

'Isn't she lonely?' You finished your drink, put your glass on the table.

'She has plans, things to do, places to see.'

'And a man would stop her?'

'Yes.' I finished my drink too.

'I think you're wrong. Would you like another?' You held up my empty glass.

'Yes, please.'

You eased yourself out of the booth and stood at our table. 'Maybe they could do those things together. No one wants to read a novel with just one character.' You fished in your trouser pocket and took out a crumpled pound note.

'*The Old Man and the Sea*,' I said. 'Hemingway.'

You shook your head. 'What about the boy, Manolin? Will you get the drinks? I'll be back in a moment.' You headed towards the men's toilets. Before you went through the door you shouted, 'And don't forget the marlin.'

At the bar, the landlord lifted my glass, saying, 'Another port and lemon?' He put the drink on a bar towel in front of me, picked up your glass and then, not to me, but to his front-row audience, said, 'And the same again for your father, love?' One of the men at the bar snorted into his pint and a flush rose up from my neck.

'No, nothing,' I said, my insides clenched.

'Nothing for you or nothing for your father?' The landlord winked at his regulars. Another snort.

'Nothing at all.'

'Make up your mind, love. I've poured the port and lemon already, you'll have to pay for it now.'

I slammed the money on the counter and left the pub, laughter following. Outside, the rain had stopped, a warm lunchtime sun had emerged and London steamed. I took lungfuls of the city air as the pub doors swung open behind me and you were out on the pavement too, my raincoat over your arm.

'Where did you go?' you said. 'What happened?' You took my elbow. 'Are you all right?'

'Do you have a pen?' I said through gritted teeth.

'A what?'

'A pen, or a pencil?'

From your jacket pocket you produced a red pen. I took it and marched back into the pub. The heads at the bar were still laughing with the landlord, but all rotated for a final time as I appeared. I went up to the pie warmer and uncapped your pen. On the poster taped to the side I wrote a giant red 'd' in the middle of 'Wenesday' and turned on my heel. Back outside you gave me a crooked smile and didn't ask for an explanation. A bit more of the rock inside me crumbled.

'Would you like some lunch?' you said. 'There's a little place I know around the corner.'

'Louise was expecting me with breakfast half an hour ago.'

'Really?' you said, disappointed.

We waited for a car to pass and then crossed the road. 'This is where I live,' I said. 'Up there.'

'I know,' you said, and I remembered your letter and how you wrote that you would pull up outside my house and I would put my sleepy head out of the window, and I realized you'd found out where I lived, just as I'd done with you.

'I can't invite you in.' If I'd let you come upstairs, Louise would've been outraged that I'd had a drink with you, she would've accused you of taking advantage of your position, and she would've caused a scene. So instead, I leaned towards you and, keeping my eyes open, pressed my lips against yours. You drew away to look at me, hung my raincoat over the railings next to my bicycle and moved forward again. I saw your hands come up to my hair, I watched your eyes close and your brow soften as you kissed me, and I also watched Mrs Carter from the university's Arts Faculty office walk past us, a tiny dog trotting at her heel. The clear plastic scarf tied over her styled hair was beaded with raindrops, and it was me, with my open eyes, who saw her glance at us and hurry on.

When we broke away we were shy, surprised. I fumbled in my bag for my key, and when I unlocked the door you were right behind me. I manoeuvred myself so I was inside the hallway while you were still on the step.

'Well, goodbye,' I said. 'Thanks for the drink.'

Your hand was on the door, pushing.

'Wait, Ingrid,' you said and I paused. 'If you won't come to lunch, come to a party to celebrate the end of term. Next weekend. Saturday.' You looked like a hopeful boy; you might have been sixteen and me the older woman.

'Maybe,' I said, and shut the door.

I ran up the three flights of stairs, and with Louise standing behind me saying 'What? What? Where's the bloody eggs and bacon?' I shoved

up the sash window at the front of the flat and leaned out. You were three houses down already.
'Yes!' I shouted.
I need you.
Yours,
Ingrid

[Placed in *The Complete Poetical Works of Amy Lowell*, 1955]

11

The loose floorboard in front of the kitchen cooker creaked while Flora lay in the cooling bathwater. The music in the sitting room had come to an end and she gripped the sides of the bath, bringing her knees up to her chest without sloshing the water. She turned her head towards the door, waiting, listening again for the creak, but there was only the gurgle of the underfloor pipes. Pressing with her palms against the rim of the bath, she lifted herself up and pushed her bottom against the cool of the wall tiles and her head against the ornate mirror saved from a long-ago house. Now hung on its side, the frame was lopsided and flaking gilt into the water.

The towelling curtain which hung around the bath to keep out draughts was pulled open, and Flora saw a shadow pass across the crack under the door, and she shoved herself further backwards as if hoping the mirror and the tiles could soften and envelop her. The doorknob twisted and Flora screamed, her heels slipping on the enamel so that she plonked down and a wave of water flowed over the side of the bath. Her sister stood in the doorway.

'For goodness' sake, what's all the screaming about?' Nan said, coming into the room and flapping a towel she picked up from the floor. She held it out for her sister, and pushed the bath mat into the puddle of water with her foot.

'I've put the kettle on.' She turned to go.

'I'd rather have something stronger,' Flora shouted. And then to herself, 'Maybe a whiskey.'

* * *

In the kitchen Nan had tidied up and pushed the books to one end of the table. 'I thought you weren't coming until tomorrow,' she said.

'And I thought you were Mum,' Flora said. 'I heard the creaky floorboard, and I really thought you were her.'

'Which creaky floorboard?'

'The one in front of the cooker.'

Nan looked at her blankly.

'How can you have forgotten?'

'There's never been a creaky floorboard. It's just your imagination running away with itself again.' Nan stood in front of the cooker and rocked back and forth. There was no squeak.

'I thought you were Mum,' Flora repeated, tying her towel around herself more tightly.

'You must have fallen asleep in the bath. You left the record player on and your bags and shoes were on the doorstep. Didn't you hear me come in?'

'No, I suppose not.' Flora felt like she'd been cheated. Nan put two cups of tea on the table. 'How's Daddy?'

'He'll be discharged tomorrow, hopefully.' She looked at her watch. 'Later today.' She sighed and poured milk into her cup. 'But he's weak, he'll need looking after. I've arranged for some compassionate leave from work.'

'Isn't that for when someone's dying?' Flora said. 'He's just got scrapes and bruises, a black eye, that kind of thing, hasn't he?'

'Yes.' Nan didn't look up as she spoke. 'That kind of thing. He was very lucky.' She blew across her tea, rippling the brown surface, pushing back the tide. 'Goodness, I'm so tired.'

Sometimes Nan surprised Flora: when she moved her head a certain way, or if soft lamplight caught her, she could be beautiful for a moment, like sunlight on the peak of a wave, there and gone. But more often, Nan was out of proportion with her surroundings, broad shoulders, and hands large and muscular enough to catch a slippery newborn. She was wearing her uniform, dark blue patches showing under her armpits, the fabric tight across her large chest.

Nan started to say something, but changed it to, 'Aren't you going to put some pyjamas on?'

'Probably not.'

'You must be cold.'

'Not really.' Flora sniffed the bottle of milk, put it down and stirred her tea with the end of the pen that had been lying on the table.

'Please use a teaspoon. For my sake,' Nan said wearily.

Flora stood and the towel, which had come loose from under her arms, remained on the chair. She strode naked to the cutlery drawer and yanked it open, Nan huffing behind her.

'What?' Flora said. 'I got the spoon, didn't I?'

'Flora,' Nan said, and put her head in her hands in exaggerated distress. Flora opened the

81

cupboard under the sink to hunt for her father's whiskey. She opened several more cupboards. The fourth, in the corner above the toaster, was packed with tins of dog food, all of them lined up with their labels facing outwards. Flora stared for a moment, then closed the door and sat at the table. She wrapped the towel around her again as a concession to modesty. She tried to think of a way to shift the subject around to who their father had seen in Hadleigh, but she couldn't work out how to do it without Nan dismissing it as nonsense.

Her sister yawned. 'I've got to go to bed. It's been a long day. The ferry had stopped running when I got there because of the weather. I had to drive all the way round.'

'Oh my God!' Flora interrupted, rapping her forehead with the bowl of the teaspoon. 'I forgot to tell you. It rained fish when I was driving along Ferry Road.'

'Driving?' Nan put her tea down.

'They fell out of the sky. Dead fish all over the tarmac.'

'Flora, you haven't bought a car, have you? You're an art student. You can't afford a car.'

'I would have taken a picture if I'd had a camera, or drawn them if it hadn't been raining.'

'The insurance must be astronomical.'

'It's not my car,' Flora said. 'It's Richard's.'

'Who's Richard?'

'Shit! Richard's car.' Flora jumped up. 'It broke down and I just left it there.' She rushed from the kitchen into their bedroom and pulled on her knickers and a sock.

82

'Where?' Nan said, following. She sat on her bed.

'I told you, Ferry Road. Can we get someone to tow it?'

'Now? It's nearly one. We'll sort it out tomorrow.' Nan was speaking in that voice, not the sister or the mother one, but the calm sensible one, which Flora sometimes found herself listening to.

She pulled her sock off by the end of its toe. 'OK,' she said, and saw that she had forgotten to wash her feet and ingrained dirt still crusted her toes.

'What do you think Gabriel's doing right now?' Flora said into the dark of the bedroom. 'What do you think he looks like? Maybe he has a moustache.'

'Not now,' Nan said, rolling over in her bed.

They were silent until Flora said, 'Do you remember when I found a life-sized plastic whale's head washed up on the beach?'

Nan gave a small laugh. 'You insisted we drag it home.'

'You would only help me some of the way and then you dropped your end.'

'There was a bad smell about it. It was slimy and full of water. It must have been in the sea for ages. It was disgusting.'

'I carried on pulling it though.'

'You could have only been about six. You got it all the way around the point to our beach. I think it was the rocks at the bottom of the chine that defeated you.'

'I remember asking Daddy to hang it on the wall of the sitting room like a big game trophy. He said we could borrow Martin's wheelbarrow and go back the next day.'

'That was Mum,' Nan said.

'No, it was Daddy. I remember.'

'Dad wasn't even there.'

'Yes, he was.'

Nan sighed. 'He wasn't, Flora.'

'Where was he, then?'

A few seconds passed before Nan said, 'He was just away.'

'Well, whoever it was, the next day the whale's head had gone,' Flora said bitterly. She still wanted it, still wanted someone to blame for its loss.

They were both silent, and when Nan's breathing slowed and deepened Flora whispered, 'Do you ever think you see Mum walking along the street?'

Nan didn't reply.

12

The Swimming Pavilion,
8th June 1992, 7.05 a.m.

Dear Gil,

This morning, a little before six, I gave up trying to sleep and went to the sea for a swim. I was halfway down the chine, wrapped in a blanket and wearing a pair of flip-flops which had been left in the hall, when I heard someone running behind me. I turned and there was Flora, bare-foot and in just a towel, coming after me.

'Mum! Wait!' she called. 'I'm going to swim too.' Flora is like a cat, everything is done on her terms. If I'd asked her to come with me for a swim, she'd probably have said no. Occasionally she'll allow me to stroke and pet her, but if I put out an uninvited hand she'll often scratch and claw, and run away.

There was no one on our beach: too early for joggers or overenthusiastic dog walkers. The tide was going out, sucking at the sand, rattling the loose stones, and the sea was the colour of wet denim. Above it, the palest lemon yellow stained the sky. We dropped the blanket and the towel on the rocks and stood at the edge of the water. Flora put her hand in mine.

'What's the worst that could happen?' I said and she squeezed my fingers, and my heart was so full of love for her. She counted to three and

85

we ran into the water, high-stepping through the wavelets, laughing and shrieking at the cold. And when the water was up to Flora's thighs we plunged forward and under. The coldness, as ever, was thrilling, breathtaking, a shock to every nerve. We came up gasping and Flora stuck her nose out of the water like a seal as she bobbed about in the waves. She's a fine swimmer, strong shoulders, with an even stroke. Her swimming coach is already saying good things about her. Flora's a different child in the water, calmer and more self-aware. No, that's wrong: she becomes one with it, literally in her element. You should see her.

She says, 'When Daddy watches me swim in the gala . . . ' or 'When I look up from the pool and see Daddy . . . ' or 'When I win the competition . . . ' What shall I tell her, Gil? When are you coming home? She needs you, we need you.

In 1976, on our way to the party, you drove us south-west, the noise of the road a roar in your little Triumph. We crossed the Thames twice, and it wasn't until the terraced houses which pressed up against the sides of the dual carriageway yielded to playing fields and then countryside that I understood the party wasn't in London. I'd never been out of the city before, except when I'd had to catch the train from Liverpool Street to Harwich and then a ferry to Oslo to visit my father once a year until he died.

I watched your profile as you drove, and once, when we stopped at a red light, you leaned over and with your hand around the back of my head pulled me towards you and kissed me until a car horn sounded behind us. Somewhere near Basingstoke you said, 'A slight detour. We have to pick Jonathan up from the station. It won't take long.'

Jonathan. It's difficult now to recall my first impressions. Tall, of course, and something off-centre in his clothes, his Irish accent, his face. I worked it out a while ago: he's like one of those Michelangelo figures high up in the Sistine Chapel (Ezekiel or Jeremiah), their perspective perfect when viewed from the floor, but see them up close and they're distorted, out of alignment. Despite the cigarette permanently hanging from his lips, Jonathan is the healthiest-looking man I know: muscled, ruddy and freckled, as if he spends his time working outdoors instead of hunched over a desk. That day, do you remember, he was wearing plus fours and mustard-coloured socks with brogues as though he was on his way to an Edwardian round of golf. Beside him on the pavement was a porter's trolley loaded with a barrel of beer, a milk-bottle crate of spirits, and, dangling from his raised hand, a full-sized human skeleton. He held it high so its feet were flat upon the pavement and it appeared to stand beside him.

We got out of the car.

'What in God's name have you got there?' you said. Passers-by (porters and businessmen, a woman with a child wearing reins) turned to stare.

'Annie, meet Gil,' Jonathan said. 'Gil, Annie.'

He jiggled the skeleton so its bones clattered.

'Surely you didn't bring it all the way on the train?' You shook your head and laughed.

'You told me I should bring a guest.' Jonathan squinted through his cigarette smoke. 'And I see you have too.'

'This is Ingrid.'

Jonathan bowed and the skeleton dipped with him. While the two of you loaded the car boot with the alcohol, I held Annie, her knees on the pavement as if begging or praying, and saw a look pass between you both. I couldn't interpret it at the time; it's only with hindsight that I know Jonathan's raised eyebrows were questioning the wisdom of bringing me to the party. And your quick shrug to him, how shall I decode that now: recklessness, bravado or a master plan?

In the car, Jonathan folded himself into the passenger seat while Annie and I lounged in the back.

'She's been very well behaved,' he said. 'She sat beside me for most of the way until the guard wanted me to buy a ticket for her too, on account of her taking up a seat. After that she was happy to sit on my lap, and fell asleep actually. I think she might have been at the booze when I wasn't watching.'

'Did you get the whiskey?' you asked.

'Of course,' Jonathan said. 'How many people have you invited?'

'Just a few. The regulars from the pub, neighbours. I thought we'd keep it small.'

'Oh,' Jonathan said. 'And I might have invited a few more than a few.'

88

'Hang on,' I said, my head in the gap between the two front seats. 'Invited?'

'Bloody hell, Jonathan. Not all those old hippies you're always picking up?'

'You know they're very friendly.'

'This is your party?' I said.

You smiled, winked and tweaked my cheek for reassurance.

Do you ever get that memory trick, where you think about a place and realize you are already there? It happens to me often now when I'm remembering, sitting here in the early mornings. Memories unwind: the high blowsy hedgerows of summer, walkers in shorts standing on the verge to let the car go past, the sweet tang of cowslip, the village sign for 'Spanish Green only', the flash of the sea through a farm gate, and apprehension and excitement building inside me. I can see the view through the windscreen as you turn the car on to the drive. I can remember my gasp at that first proper sight of the land (grass and gorse) dipping away towards a wide expanse of sky, and the busy water, shining. I hadn't imagined there could be English views as beautiful as those I'd seen in Norway. I can recall getting out of the car and turning towards the house (low and wooden, single-storeyed, with a tin roof) and the veranda, its paint peeling, and a circular table at one end. A cricket pavilion, I thought. And with a jolt I realize I'm on that same veranda, I'm sitting at that memory-table writing this letter. That house from sixteen years ago is my house now.

The cars and camper vans boxed each other in on the drive, and people crowded the veranda, the hall, sitting room and the kitchen. Men shook Jonathan's hand, a few slapped you on the shoulder, and the girls kissed you, embraced you for slightly too long, and seemed disappointed, I thought, when you introduced me. Someone turned up the music, opened the French windows, and four girls in orange jumpsuits danced. The people squashed in to see, sweating in the summer evening, shouting above the music and conversations. The bottles Jonathan had brought were poured, glasses lined the window-sills, the air filled with smoke, the pub up the road closed and the party swelled. And when your house was bursting with dancing and shouting and people drinking, I lost sight of you.

In the sitting room you'd introduced me to Martin and George, and left to get me another drink. Maybe you thought I'd be safe and occupied talking to those two. Every now and again I stood on tiptoes to check your whereabouts, only half listening to their conversation. A ring of people had drawn away from the dancers and I glimpsed you being pulled by one of them into the group. I saw your head dip towards hers, heard whistles and claps, and the gap through the people closed. I craned my head.

'They'll be troublemakers, mark my words,' George was shouting over the noise. 'Campfires on the beach, broken glass . . . '

'New holiday homes mean more people. And that means more business,' Martin said.

'. . . used rubber johnnies . . . ' George said.
'More shandies, more pints pulled.'
'Village girls being pulled, more like.'
'Good for business,' Martin said. He rubbed his thumb and fingers together.
'Get them pregnant and then bugger off to Blackpool or wherever they've come from.'
'It won't be people from Blackpool. They've got their own beach,' Martin said.
'It'll be like the GIs all over again.'
'I don't think the new holidaymakers are likely to leave used rubber johnnies on the beach,' I said, still looking through the crowd for you, '*and* get the village girls pregnant.' I left them to continue their argument, and pushed my way through the packed room. The slower music had been replaced with something more rhythmic, the beat thrumming up through the wooden floor to my bones. I stood at the edge of the circle of men watching the dancing girls, just three now. One of them had taken her arms out of her jumpsuit and rolled it down around her waist. She wasn't wearing a bra. She danced by rotating her hips; and her breasts, small and tipped upwards at the nipples, were surprisingly solid. I asked a man if he'd seen you, and without taking his eyes from the girl he said, 'Who's Gil?'

I edged out of the sitting room and put my head around the door across the hall (your bedroom). On the four-poster bed a man and a woman were jumping, shrieking and flinging themselves backwards like five-year-olds. The room next door had two single beds in it, both of which were occupied. I watched for a while, but none of the five people in the room were you. I joined a queue of women waiting for the loo; I stayed long enough to see someone who wasn't you come out of the bathroom.

In the kitchen, two spiders (one of them the fat, pendulous-bodied kind, the other thin and quick) were waiting to see what prey might come by to tease before they gobbled it up.

'And who have we here?' The man slurred his words as he ground out a cigar in the sink. Joe Warren was still fat then, the fattest man I had ever seen, with the belt of his trousers hoisted up over a protruding stomach, larger than a pregnant woman's.

'Have you seen Gil?' I said, reversing accidentally into Denis, standing behind me. I spun around.

'Gil?' Denis said, looking over my head. 'Do you know anyone called Gil, Joe?'

Joe laughed, deep and throaty. 'I don't think I do,' he said. I turned back towards him. People pressed past us, some leaving the kitchen, others coming in looking for drinks. A girl in a maxi-dress fell off a chair, lay on her side on the floor, tucked her hands under her head and closed her eyes. A baby slept in a carrycot on the table amongst the bottles.

'I don't know why you would want Gil when you could have me,' Denis said. I looked at him over my shoulder. The tip of his tongue came out and licked his moustache; too red, obscene. 'A bird in the hand and all that.' He reached down and pawed at my bum. I took a step away from him and towards Joe. Denis closed in behind me.

'A little uptight this one, I think,' he said.

'Are you Gil's new secretary?' Joe asked, pushing himself away from the kitchen counter and swaying like a skittle.

'No, I am not,' I said. 'I'm his . . . ' But I didn't know how to finish and the chatter in the kitchen was too loud anyway.

'Your glass is empty,' Denis said, pressing himself forward. 'Find the young lady a drink, Joe.'

Joe checked through the bottles and glasses on the kitchen table. 'What'll it be?' he said.

'I'm fine,' I said. 'I don't want another drink.'

'Cinzano Bianco?' Joe said, finding a bottle with something left in the bottom and pouring it into my glass.

'What's that old philanderer Gil got that we haven't?' Denis said. 'Apart from looks of course, and physique.' When Joe laughed, his stomach laughed with him.

'I think this one likes to take dictation,' Denis said.

'She can take my dictation,' Joe said.

'Bottoms up.' Denis drank from his glass and at the same time gave me another squeeze. I turned, reached down and held Denis's balls tightly in my hand. He stopped laughing.

'Ingrid?' An Irish voice behind me. Jonathan.

'Have you seen Gil?' I let go of Denis and stood up straight. The spiders withdrew.

'He had to go out. Come on.' Jonathan took my arm, steered me from the kitchen, down the hallway and outside. A small group was sitting at one end of the veranda and I smelled marijuana. Some of the cars had gone from the drive, but I could still hear people indoors, dancing and laughing as we sat side by side on the wooden steps. The sky in the east was deep blue above a black strip of water. Jonathan took a packet of cigarettes from his pocket; I accepted the one he offered. He fiddled with his box of matches and didn't meet my eye as he held the flame up.

I inhaled tentatively and on the exhale said, 'Where's he gone, then?' and Jonathan flicked his eyes up at me, the fire reflected in his pupils.

'I haven't known you for long,' he said, 'and I can tell you're a nice girl. But I'm not sure if you're the right kind.'

'The right kind of girl for what?'

'For Gil.' He stared into the night as he spoke. 'He's not an easy man.'

'Who said I'm looking for an easy man.'

'And . . . ' He trailed off.

'He's twenty years older than me and my university lecturer,' I finished for him.

'I was going to say he's only looking for two kinds of women and I don't think you fit into either category.'

'And what categories are those?'

Jonathan inhaled, blew smoke out through his nostrils. 'The first sort are women he'll sleep with for a week or two until someone else takes his fancy; women who won't make too much of a fuss when he doesn't return their calls.'

'And the second sort?' I took another tentative drag on the cigarette.

'A wife,' Jonathan said. I coughed out the

94

smoke in my throat and he laughed. 'See, I said you didn't fit either category.'

But I wasn't coughing at the shock of what he'd said, I was remembering your letter. 'Maybe he'll make someone the perfect husband.'

'I don't think so.'

I waited for him to go on.

'We have different views of marriage, Gil and I. We were both brought up Catholic, did you know that? Although none of it's stuck with him — he shucked it off years ago.'

'And you still believe?'

'Oh, I pick and choose. Sleep with who you like, but one at a time.' He laughed again. 'And that goes for married people too.'

'Gil doesn't hold with that view?'

'Perhaps it's him you should be asking.'

'You're not painting a very nice picture,' I said. 'I thought you were friends.'

'We are. He's funny and charming, good-looking and a bloody fine writer.' Jonathan put his hand over his heart. 'But I think you should know what you're getting into.'

'And do you warn all his potential victims in this way?'

'No, you're the first,' he said.

'Oh.' I was glad it was dark and he couldn't see my consternation. I stubbed my cigarette out on the step beside me.

I wasn't worried about Jonathan's warning; I was thrilled by it. I imagined a third category I'd create. Gil Coleman would fall in love with me but I wouldn't fall in love with him; I'd make love with him for the summer, and when the

95

autumn came I'd go back to university and at the end of my final year I'd leave to do all the things Louise and I'd planned.

'Can you see the beach from the end of the garden?' I said after a few moments of silence. I stood up, took a couple of paces off the path into the long grass. There was a flickering light at the bottom, a lamp or a candle shining through a window. 'What's that?' I said. Jonathan stood beside me.

'Gil's writing room.'

'He's writing? Now? I thought you'd said he'd had to go out?'

I took a step forward. Jonathan sighed. 'Well, yes. Probably writing.'

I couldn't see his features, couldn't make out his expression.

'That's ridiculous. He's having a party.' I flung my arm back towards the house. 'Which he invited me to. And he's writing?'

'He does that. Sometimes. You won't want to be disturbing him now.' Jonathan took my hand, led me up the steps. 'Come on, time for another drink, and a dance — you do dance, don't you?'

I looked over my shoulder at the yellow square of light.

This morning, as I write this letter, the garden is missing the tap, tap, tap of your typewriter.

We love you.

Ingrid

[Placed in *The Cocktail Party* by T. S. Eliot, 1950]

13

In the morning when Flora got up, Nan was already in the kitchen making breakfast.

'Glad to see you managed to put some clothes on,' Nan said. Flora was wearing Ingrid's pink chiffon dress again. Nan set a plate on the table. 'I phoned the hospital. I thought we could go and see if you can get that car working and then you can follow me there.'

'Can you pass the marmalade?' Flora said.

'I've already put marmalade on your toast.'

'Don't worry,' Flora said. She got the jar and a knife, and took them to the table.

'Flora, there's something . . . ' Nan sat down opposite her.

'What?' Flora looked up. Nan stared at the toast. 'I've always liked my marmalade to go right up to the edge.'

'Yes,' Nan said.

Flora saw purple shadows beneath her sister's eyes. She took a bite of toast, and after a while Nan stood and began to tidy the kitchen, eating her own breakfast as she wiped the surfaces.

'When did the number of books in the house get so crazy?' Flora said.

'You know he's been buying them for years,' Nan said.

'Yes, but it's never been this bad. You can hardly walk down the hall.'

Nan sighed. 'It was even worse a few weeks

ago. I popped over one morning and Dad had spent the night pulling nearly all the books off the shelves — mountains of them in the sitting room and the bedroom, like there'd been an explosion. He said he was looking for something.'

'What?'

'Goodness knows. He became all evasive. "Letters" was all he would say. It seemed he'd been up for the whole night, flicking through every book. The ends of his fingers were red raw.'

'What letters?' Flora yawned.

'I have no idea. All the books are full of letters and bits of rubbish.'

'You should have called me. I would have come down.'

'It was all right in the end. I got him into bed, and when he was asleep I put most of them back. But I did manage to fill a few carrier bags to take to the shop in Hadleigh without him knowing. Viv was really pleased to have them.'

'Viv?' Flora said.

'She bought the bookshop a couple of months ago. She's trying to turn it around.'

'I bet she was pleased to have them,' Flora said sarcastically. 'Daddy bought most of them from her in the first place.'

'It's a lovely bookshop now. Viv's very choosy about her stock.'

'I remember the smell of it. Old brown wood and smoke, like the smell of a country house with open fires. I haven't been in it since Daddy took me years ago. I must have been about eleven or twelve.' Gil had told her to choose any book in the whole shop — whatever she wanted. Flora had picked out *Lady Chatterley's Lover* without knowing fully what it was about, but somehow understanding it was a dangerous choice. Gil had raised one eyebrow but let Flora take it to the desk to pay.

'Does your father know you're buying this?' The previous shopkeeper looked at her over his glasses.

'Of course, Harrold,' Gil said, appearing from behind the Local History section. 'It's not up to you what my daughter reads.' He handed over the money. Outside the shop Gil took the book from her and slipped it into his jacket pocket. 'You won't be reading this for a while.' He laughed. 'Let's go and get an ice cream.'

In the kitchen Nan said, 'Oh, you should go again. Viv is so welcoming and happy to show people around and recommend things.'

'You seem to know a lot about her.' Flora licked marmalade off her knife. She looked up at Nan. Her sister's cheeks were flushed. 'Really?' Flora said, smiling, her head on one side.

Nan rinsed a dishcloth under the tap and wrung it out. 'She's just . . . she's just a very nice woman.'

'That's wonderful,' Flora said. She got up and hugged her sister, whose arms hung limply by her side, the dishcloth still in one hand. 'I'm so pleased for you.'

'I think you should change out of that dress,' Nan said.

Once more Flora sat in the driver's seat of the

Morris Minor. Nan leaned in through the open passenger window. There was no sign of last night's storm and no fish on the road. The sky over the heath was blue and cloudless. Cars disgorging from the ferry streamed past, and the road verges were packed nose to tail. A queue had built up in front of the Morris Minor, impatient motorists wanting to pass to catch the ferry. Flora, picturing her father waiting for them in hospital, wanted to get going too. 'Can't we just go in yours?'

'We can't leave this car here,' Nan said. 'It's blocking the road. Try the ignition one more time.'

'It's not going to start.' Flora felt like weeping.

'Aren't you meant to pull out the choke or something,' Nan said.

A driver in one of the cars in the queue tooted a horn.

'It's broken.' And to prove it, Flora turned the key once more. The awful clunk sounded again.

'I'll call the garage and you'll just have to wait with it. I'll go and get Dad on my own.'

'But I want to come.'

'You shouldn't have driven then. You should have come down this morning by train like I suggested.' Nan took her phone out of her handbag, looked at the time, rolled her eyes and called the garage.

In the cab of the tow-truck, Flora stared out of the rear window over the roof of the Morris Minor as they drove away from the ferry and the hospital, towards Hadleigh. The line of traffic heading in the opposite direction stopped to let them out and she saw on the road a single fish that must have been under the car, its scales winking in the sunshine.

'Fan belt,' the man said as he withdrew the top half of his body from under the bonnet.

'Is that important?' Flora said.

He laughed. 'It's not going to go without it. Take a walk, get yourself a cup of tea and come back in three hours or so. We should have her all fixed by then.'

The route from the garage to the sea took Flora through the public car park. Halfway across, she noticed her father's car, a parking ticket stuck to the windscreen. When she peered through the window she saw that all the footwells and the seats, apart from the driver's, were full of carrier bags spilling out second-hand books.

She took an alleyway to the sea and walked the length of the promenade. At the town end she leaned on the railings and tried not to think about her father tumbling over them; how he could so easily have died from the fall. She ducked under the bottom bar and sat on the lip of the concrete for a moment, her legs dangling over the rocks, before she jumped down. Maybe her mother had been there; perhaps she had been the one who called the ambulance. Flora clambered across the rocks close to the promenade, out towards the rounder boulders next to the sea — searching without knowing what she was looking for. She found a jelly shoe

— slimy with age, its buckle permanently fused shut by saltwater — five rusty beer-bottle tops and a plastic toy soldier wedged in a crevice that her mother might have crouched beside. The soldier stood sideways on its base, legs akimbo, one arm raised as if waving on an invisible army. Most of its green pigment had been leached by the sea so that when she held it up to the sun it was almost translucent.

Flora climbed back up and sat on a bench on the promenade overlooking the water. The view was so familiar she barely noticed it. Below, people rested in deckchairs and three hardy children ran about in swimming costumes. She held the soldier close to her face and shut one eye so that the little man became huge and out of focus, balancing on the horizon, and she imagined her mother sitting on this bench, in this spot, and wondered what she had been thinking.

After Ingrid disappeared, neighbours and friends had searched the nearby coves, walked over Barrow Down, tramped through the heath with sticks and dogs, and dredged Little Sea Pond. Jonathan and, later, her mother's old university friend, Louise, came down to Spanish Green, although there wasn't much they could do, and they spent their time in the pub avoiding the reporters who massed around the village like swarms of wasps. They took two rooms above the bar and didn't come to the house. One evening, when Flora went to the pub with her father — who bought her a Coke and a bag of crisps and told her she could stay, as long as she sat in a corner and kept quiet — Jonathan suddenly remembered a conversation he'd had with Ingrid about Ireland, and Gil shouted, broke a barstool and was asked to leave. Sometime later Louise resigned from Parliament.

Gil refused to give up hope. He went to Ireland, but returned alone. He had posters made and placed adverts in the local papers. Flora and Nan spent their weekends in the car, sleeping, eating and watching the countryside and towns speed by, chasing possible sightings of their mother.

Flora asked someone the time and was disappointed to find that only an hour had passed, so she crossed the road into town. She got a window table in Sea Lane Cafe and read through their menu. She ordered toast, the cheapest item, and a cup of tea. The waiter's hair was gelled forward as if he were in a constant battle with a backwind, and Flora would have liked to make him sit so she could draw him, but the cafe was full and he was busy. When he brought the food over she said, 'Did a woman come in here yesterday? On her own, I think.'

'A woman?' the waiter said, raising an eyebrow. 'Don't get many of those in here.' He smiled. His teeth were the size of a baby's, small and square with a gap between the front two. 'What does she look like?'

'I'm not sure.' Flora blushed. 'Straight hair, maybe. Light coloured. Pale skin.'

'How old?'

'Forty-eight . . . no, forty-seven.'

103

'A bit old for me.' He winked. When Flora frowned he said, 'Do you have a photo?' He put down her plate of toast.

'No.'

The man set her cup of tea on the table. 'Get a lot of work as a private detective, do you?' Another wink.

'I'm in great demand,' Flora said. She picked up her knife and a pat of butter, pleased they hadn't spread it on for her, and suddenly starving.

'I'm afraid it was my day off yesterday, I wasn't even here.' He seemed like he wanted to carry on talking, but he was called to the kitchen for another order.

When she had finished eating, Flora pulled the toy soldier from her pocket. The small man stood in heavy boots, a pair of binoculars hanging around his neck. She thought about the child who must have lost him on the beach. How long had it been before they realized the soldier was missing, and did they blame themselves for not noticing when it became buried in the sand, was swept out to sea or fell from a boulder into the crevice? And did the child remember it every time they returned to the beach? Flora balanced the soldier on the crust of toast she had left, took her sketchbook and a pencil out of her satchel and stared at the tiny man with his arm raised. But when the waiter came over and asked if there was anything else she wanted, Flora realized she had drawn her mother standing in front of the Swimming Pavilion. In her mind the tin roof shimmered in the heat and the long dress flowed around her mother's ankles.

'It rained fish last night,' Flora said to the waiter, when he returned with the bill. 'On the road from the ferry.'

He looked over her shoulder at her drawing and at the soldier propped on the toast. 'I like a girl with a vivid imagination,' he said. 'It makes a change,' and he smiled his baby smile. He left the bill, and Flora put some money on the table and packed her sketchbook and pencil into her bag. As she glanced up, a woman walked past the cafe window, gone in an instant, but leaving an impression of fine hair the colour of ripe wheat. Flora cried out and jumped up, knocking her chair into the man sitting at the table behind. She snatched up her satchel and was nearly out of the door when she turned to grab the little plastic soldier.

'I've got another day off tomorrow,' the waiter shouted after her, but she was gone.

And so was the woman.

Flora ran along the pavement, stepping into the road to dodge slow walkers, along past the library, the supermarket, the butcher's with the closing-down notice, the estate agent and two hairdresser's and another estate agent, and once she was around the corner and on the road beside the promenade again she stopped and bent forward with her hands on her knees to catch her breath. The pavement was empty, so she turned around and went into each shop she had passed. There were a few customers in each — no one like the woman. In the small supermarket, Flora worked her way up and down the aisles towards the checkouts. The woman wasn't there.

She hesitated outside the library. The last time she'd been inside she was eight and on a junior-school trip. Now, she put her hand in the pocket of her jeans and rubbed the soldier between her thumb and finger, lifted the strap of her satchel over her head and pushed through the glass doors.

The smell inside took her back to when her family was complete: saffron-yellow upholstery and warm 1970s orange wood. A man sat behind a desk in front of a wall of exposed brick-work. He looked up at Flora and smiled encouragingly as if he knew she hadn't been in a library for thirteen years. She had been a voracious reader until her mother was lost. Overnight, on the 2nd of July 1992, she had stopped reading. She tried to rearrange her expression into that of a regular library-goer and strode towards the shelves, ducking down an aisle and removing a random book from the row in front of her. She opened *The Heart is a Lonely Hunter* and flicked through the pages until she was sure the librarian must have gone back to his work. When she had replaced the book, Flora searched the room for the woman with the long hair. After she had been into the children's corner, down each row and glanced at every browser, she took the stairs up to a mezzanine floor which had racks of magazines and newspapers and study tables, most of which were empty.

The woman sat at a table furthest from the stairs with her back to Flora, her hair touching the top of her chair. She was flicking through a large book, and before she turned each thin page the woman licked a finger and stuck it to a corner. Flora thought that might not be allowed in libraries. She stared at the woman's hair, remembering how she used to beg to be allowed to play with her mother's, to brush it and plait it, but that when she did, Ingrid would complain Flora was too rough, that she was catching her fingers or tugging on purpose. And sometimes, Flora knew, her mother was right.

She moved towards the woman until she was a foot away from the chair and leaned forward. She closed her eyes and breathed in through her nose. The woman's hair smelled of lemons, a bright eye-blinding yellow.

When Flora looked up, her eyes met those of the man sitting across the table, a newspaper in front of him, and she became aware of other people at other tables turning to stare at her. Flora straightened and, as she did so, the woman raised her head and must have caught the expression of the man opposite. She twisted around slowly, as if nervous of whom she would find standing behind her. Flora held her breath, milliseconds seeming like minutes.

14

Dear Gil,

Yesterday evening the phone rang and Flora answered it before I could get there. She was in the sitting room playing your records.

'Hello?' she said.

'Who is it?' I asked, going in.

'Hello?' Flora repeated, louder. I went up to her, close enough to know the person at the other end was talking perfectly clearly. 'I can't hear you,' Flora bellowed.

'Flora, who is it?' I asked again, trying to take the receiver from her.

'Nope,' Flora shouted. 'I'm sorry, whoever you are, but no one in this house is listening to anything you have to say.' And she put the phone down.

'Flora, you mustn't do that. Who was it?'

'Louise,' she said.

I was worried she'd worked it out, overheard something I shouldn't have said, but I'm sure now there hasn't been anything for her to over-hear; she's picked up on a feeling she doesn't fully understand. I couldn't help myself: I laughed. Flora laughed too, standing on the sofa arm and leaping on the cushions. 'No, we can't hear you,' she yelled. She turned up the volume on the record player: Cat Stevens singing 'Rubylove'. We

108

both started dancing, doing a little shimmy on those Greek guitar bits, spinning each other around. Nan came in — of course she wouldn't have been able to avoid the noise — but instead of switching it off like I thought she would, she danced. Moving her feet stiffly at first, clicking her fingers, until Flora grabbed her and soon they were both jumping on the sofas. I stopped to look at them, laughing and making up the words they didn't know, and I was strangely removed from the scene, as if I were watching a film about somebody else's children.

The day after your party I woke to the sound of women's laughter and the front door slamming. A car revved on the drive, reversed on to the lane and sped away. The house was silent. I lay on the sofa, still dressed, with someone's left-behind coat thrown over me. Bright sunshine poured through the open French windows and struck the empty bottles and dirty glasses, fracturing the light. The place smelled like a pub: stale booze and cigarette ash. My watch said it was a little after two. There was a hiss and a repeated click from the corner of the room where the record-player's needle had come to the end of an album possibly hours ago. When I sat up I saw the skeleton, Annie, reclining in an armchair, her grotesque head tilted at a crazy angle and her arms hanging over the sides as if she had flopped there, too drunk to move. And I saw what I hadn't taken in the night before with the crush of people: your books. Every wall was lined with shelves, and every shelf was crammed with books, jammed in any way possible. I scanned some of the titles, fiction mixed with non-fiction and reference. There was no order and no way of judging your taste: *Anna Karenina* wedged under *Secrets of the Jam Cupboard* and *The Country Companion: A Practical Dictionary of Rural Life and Work*; *Green Eggs and Ham* by Dr Seuss sandwiched between Roth's *Portnoy's Complaint* and *The Missing Muse and Other Essays* by Philip Guedalla.

I wandered into the hallway. 'Gil? Jonathan?' I called out. There was no reply. I knocked on your bedroom door and, after a moment, opened it. The place smelled of you, musky and male. (Bedrooms always smell of their owners.) The bouncing couple from the previous night had gone. I hadn't appreciated the bed then, but I saw now that it was huge. Four intricately carved oak posts rose up from each corner as if they should have supported a missing canopy. I ran my fingers over the nearest — scrolls, leaves and vines entwined. A cover had been smoothed over your bed, or perhaps the bed hadn't been slept in. It was made of faded silk, embroidered by hand in a Japanese style, willowy plants, flowers and exotic birds against a pale blue background. Many of the stitches had come apart through age and use, and the whole thing looked like it was in the wrong house, like it ought to be in a much bigger, grander room. I ran my hands over the cover too, wondering about the person (surely a woman) who'd had the patience and the time to create every tiny stitch. I pulled back your wardrobe doors and inhaled you. I opened your chest of drawers and looked at the neatly curled ties. I lifted the lids on dusty pots containing matching cufflinks and a watch that was silent. Your things. I peered at the oil paintings in gold frames hanging on the wooden walls — fishing boats heading out of a harbour on a violent sea; a girl in a white dress with a veined turquoise necklace at her throat and a dog on her lap. I examined the books in this room too, on the shelves and stacked into precarious towers on the bedside table. They were topped with half-drunk glasses of wine and an empty whiskey bottle. I sat on the edge of the bed and watched four bars of sunlight drift across the front of the chest of drawers and on to the wall opposite, and I listened to the noises of your house: water glurping in the pipes; the wooden walls moaning and creaking where the afternoon sun warmed them.

The party debris continued into the second bedroom and the kitchen: dirty glasses cramming every surface, overflowing ashtrays and used cups. I drank three glasses of water one after the other while I gazed out of your kitchen window at a washing line slung from a corner of the house to a metal pole. A dozen clothes pegs clung like birds on a wire and a sock dangled from one of them. No woman lives here, I thought. I went to the toilet, tidying myself in the mirror over the bath and using a toothbrush I found in the cabinet, hoping it hadn't been used to clean anything other than teeth. And then I went out of the front door and into the grass where I'd stood with Jonathan the night before. Everything was still. Your car was on the drive, but all the others had gone.

There was a path through the grass, one I hadn't seen in the dark, a trampled route from the house to your writing room at the far end. I can turn my head and see the room from where I sit now, with the morning sun lying on its tin roof. I thought then, and it still makes me think, that the tiny room with its two long metal legs to keep it level was balancing at the very edge of the garden, where the zigzag path I made now leads down the bank to the bottom gate and the beach, as if at any moment it might fling off its wooden walls and roof, and leap into the water far below. The stable door to your writing room faces the house, and that morning I sidled up to it with a sense that I was trespassing. I stood on the bottom step and knocked. No reply. I knocked again and pressed my ear up against the wood. I turned the handle. The door was locked. I moved up a step and, shielding my eyes from the glare of the day, looked inside. Nothing has changed since that time: I saw the double bed built into the far end with its drawers underneath, the wood-burning stove just big enough to boil a kettle, and a folding desk with your typewriter facing a window which over-looked the sea. You weren't inside.

I was trying to angle my head to read the title on the sheaf of papers lying beside the typewriter when you called my name. I turned to see you standing in front of your wooden house with two shopping bags in your hands. You waited for me to walk to you.

'I don't let anyone go in there,' you said, and

you were smiling, but I knew I'd been warned off. There was a moment of embarrassment until you held up a bag and shook it.

'Would you like some breakfast, or perhaps we should call it lunch?'

You fried bacon and eggs, I started on the washing-up, and made coffee and toast, and we ate on the veranda in the sunshine. Afterwards you packed a bag for the beach (rug, apples, cheese), and led me down the chine to the sea.

The beach was crowded, a boiling Sunday afternoon in early July with the tide out: damp towels hanging on striped wind-breaks, sun-faded folding chairs, terry nappies drooping with seawater, hand-dug sand holes with little boys inside, tiny crabs overheating in buckets, and curling sandwiches in greaseproof paper. You rolled up your trousers and we waded out up to our knees amongst the air-beds and beach balls, and kissed, and the idea that people who knew you were watching thrilled me. We walked around Dead End Point and past the beach huts where the families would soon pack up for the day and get into their hot cars to wait in the queue for the ferry. We walked past the car park and the ice cream van, along the perfect curve of the bay, and at the sign for the nudist beach you raised your eyes and I laughed when we passed it. We undressed and neither of us was shy, only curious. I didn't think about how old you were: your body was tanned that summer, and still firm. You held my hand and we tiptoed together, wincing, into the water. Walkers turned to watch.

Something about the two of us together has always made people look: our bodies suit each other, look right together. I remember thinking that the air and then the water on every part of my body was like a lover; a new, fresh, cold lover.

We didn't stay in for long. We lay on the rug and ate the apples, but you had forgotten a knife so we took the cheese from its waxed paper and bit chunks off with our teeth. You told me that when you were a child sometimes whole summers would go by and you'd realize you hadn't been in the sea, and I told you about the summers spent next to the icy waters of the Norwegian island where my father had lived.

I waited for you to kiss me again or suggest we take the rug into the dunes after everyone had left, but instead you put your hand on my skin and said, 'Let's get dressed and go back.' We dragged our clothes on over our sandy arms and legs, and walked home through the dunes and along the road.

Late that evening, when we were sitting out on the veranda, you said, 'I don't think we'll ever have to shout to make ourselves heard over the noise of the rain drumming on the roof. I don't think it'll ever rain again.' You kneeled in front of me, took my face in your hands and kissed me again. Then you stood and led me to your bedroom.

Yours, always,
Ingrid

[Placed in *I Am the Cheese* by Robert Cormier, 1977]

114

15

The woman in the library was Flora's age, perhaps younger, and from the front her hair had that look of having been artificially straightened in the way it poured from her centre parting. Her eyes narrowed. 'Can I help you?'

Flora stuttered an apology and backed away, stepping into someone standing behind her.

'Flora?' The person held her by the elbow to stop her from falling, and when she turned it took her a moment to recognize the man out of context, clothed and vertical: Richard. She pulled away from him and ran down the stairs to the ground floor, her face burning. Out on the pavement he caught up with her.

'Who was that?' he said. 'What were you doing?'

'Nothing. It was nothing.' She marched past the cafe, up the high street, Richard jogging to keep up. 'Anyway shouldn't it be me asking you questions? Like what the hell are you doing here?'

'I came to find you. You weren't answering your phone.'

'It's broken.'

'I had to get a train and then the bus — no idea where to get off. I went into the library to ask directions.'

'So you were stalking me.'

'I was worried about you.'

'There's no need. I'm fine.'

'Flora,' he said, touching her arm. 'Slow down. Who was that woman?'

Flora stopped walking, flung her arms up in the air and let them flap to her sides. For a moment her voice wouldn't come, but she swallowed the lump inside her. 'I thought she was my mother. OK? But she wasn't. Happy now?'

'I'm sorry,' Richard said.

'For following me or because she wasn't my mother?'

'For both.'

'Well, you don't need to be sorry. As you can see, I'm fine.' Flora was aware she was shouting and that people walking past were staring. 'You can go home now.' She opened her satchel and groped in it for Richard's car key and then remembered that the Morris Minor was in the garage. 'I had an accident, last night. In your car.'

Richard's eyes widened. 'Were you hurt? Are you all right?' He dropped the small rucksack he'd been carrying and put his arm around her; she let it stay.

'I'm fine. But your car . . . '

His arm fell away.

'It's the fan belt. I got it to the garage. They're mending it now. It should be ready in a couple of hours.'

'As long as you're OK,' he said. 'Come on, let me buy you a cup of tea.'

'I'd bloody well rather have a proper drink,' she said.

Richard and Flora sat on the veranda drinking Gil's whiskey as the sun went down. Richard had found it under the kitchen sink behind a box of tools after she had sent him into the house without her. She'd also got him to drag the cover off the bed so they could wrap it around them. The tide was in, and the deep water crashing against the cliffs boomed where it hit hollows in the rock, the sound like distant thunder.

'This used to be a swimming pavilion?' Richard said.

'Changing rooms to you and me,' Flora said. 'When Daddy sold the big house up the road, this was all that was left. I think there were debts and death duties when my grandfather died. Daddy doesn't talk about it.'

Headlights swung around into the drive, illuminating the gorse flowers, yellow jewels in the black. Nan's car pulled up.

'Where have you been?' Nan said as soon as she got out and saw Flora standing at the top of the steps.

'Where have you been, you mean,' Flora said. 'You were meant to be home hours ago. How's Daddy?' She went towards the car.

'He's sleeping. Leave him.' Nan blocked Flora's route to the passenger door. 'I've been calling the house phone and your mobile all afternoon. There was some stupid delay with the doctor wanting to see him again. Why didn't you pick up?'

'I thought I saw Mum in Hadleigh,' Flora said. 'But it wasn't her.'

'Oh, Flora,' Nan said, her puff gone in an

instant. She stepped forward as if to take her sister in her arms.

Deflecting her, Flora said, 'This is Richard.' She turned towards the veranda, and Richard moved out of the shadows and down the steps to shake Nan's hand.

'How do you do?' Nan said, unable to resist her natural inclination to be polite no matter the circumstances.

'I'm sorry to hear about your father. Is there anything I can do?'

'Well,' Nan said, running her hands through her hair, 'perhaps you could help me get him into the house. I think he might need to be carried.'

'Carried?' Flora said. 'Why can't he walk?'

'I've told you,' Nan said. 'He's tired. Why don't you go and put the lights on so we can see what we're doing.'

'There's a power cut.'

⋆   ⋆   ⋆

Flora stood close by with a candle while Nan woke their father and introduced Richard. In the end Gil struggled out of the seat by himself, brushing off any helping hands, but allowing Richard to tuck his arm under Gil's elbow as they walked around the car.

'Oh, Daddy,' Flora said, her hand going to her mouth. The candlelight showed butterfly stitches across Gil's left cheek; the eye above it was dark and swollen shut. A graze speckled his forehead. He looked smaller, thinner, than when she had last seen him.

118

'Flo,' Gil said sleepily. 'Do you have the book?' He reached out for her hand with his right, and Flora saw that his left arm was held in a sling.

'He keeps going on about the book he had with him when he fell,' Nan said to Flora. 'We don't have it, Dad.'

Flora pressed her father's hand, the skin as soft as sand-papered wood, the bones inside fragile. She kissed him on his good cheek, smelling the sour breath of sleep, and under it his familiar odour: pepper, dust and leather, otter brown.

Nan helped Gil into bed while Flora held the candle. The light hollowed out his good eye-socket, gouged craters into his cheeks and cast distorted shadows on the wall. Under his coat Gil was wearing the pyjamas that Nan must have taken into the hospital. He winced when his bandaged arm was touched, but then sank into the bed with a sigh.

'Love you, Daddy,' Flora whispered in his ear, although he was already asleep.

In the kitchen they sat with Richard and talked in the half-light, working out who would collect Gil's car from Hadleigh, and drinking tea made with water boiled in a pan on the gas hob. Flora had hers black, not trusting the temperature of the fridge. She had seen Richard take note of the books in the hall, the sitting room and the kitchen, but he made no comment about them. Instead, looking straight at Nan, he said, 'What did your father say about seeing your mother?'

Although it was the question Flora wanted to

ask, she was shocked at Richard's audacity.

Nan's fingers tightened around her cup. 'He was mistaken,' she said stiffly.

'You mean he's changed his mind about what he saw?'

'Richard,' Flora said; a warning.

'I mean what he saw isn't possible,' Nan said.

'But — ' Richard began, and Flora put her hand on his and squeezed. 'Is he going to be all right?' he continued.

Nan made a low hum, her mouth closed. Flora caught a glance from her sister before she looked away again.

'You're worrying about his wrist, aren't you?' Flora said.

'He has a urinary tract infection. It probably explains some of his confusion, but . . . ' Nan paused.

'What?'

'Things have become' — she chose each word carefully — 'potentially more . . . complicated.'

'What do you mean?' Flora said.

'He'll be fine at home, Flora. We'll do everything we can to make him comfortable.'

'You think his wrist is broken, don't you?' Flora put her cup down on the table and tea slopped over the edge. 'We should take him back in. Get another X-ray.'

Nan and Richard looked at each other, the light from the candles moving across their faces so she couldn't read their expressions.

'No,' Nan said softly. 'He should stay at home with us. If he's here I can keep an eye on him.'

The three of them sat in silence, sipping at

120

their tea, until Richard said, 'It's late. I should get going.' He stood up.

'Tonight?' Nan put her cup down. 'I thought you'd be staying.'

'Would you like me to stay, Flora?'

'Richard's got to work tomorrow,' Flora said.

'I could leave in the morning.'

'You'll have to get up at a ridiculous time.'

'I wouldn't,' Richard said. 'It's Sunday, the bookshop doesn't open until eleven.'

'It's far too late to go now,' Nan said. 'You can sleep in the writing room.'

'If he's going to stay, one of the sofas will do,' Flora said. 'It's only Daddy who sleeps in the writing room.'

Richard looked from one sister to the other.

'The sofas are full of books,' Nan said. 'And it would mean making one of them up.'

'It won't take a minute to throw a sheet over a sofa,' Flora said.

'Dad isn't sleeping in his writing room now.' Nan stood. 'Come on, I'll show you the way.'

Flora narrowed her eyes at Richard, but he didn't appear to notice. He followed Nan out of the kitchen.

Flora thought about sleeping with Richard in the room at the end of the garden, but there was something about the two of them being there, using her father's private space, that made her uncomfortable. So when she woke with the early light creeping through the window, it was Nan's bed she saw with its covers thrown off and the sheets showing. There were voices across the hall

121

— her father's and her sister's. Flora got out of bed and put on a spare dressing gown of Nan's.

'Give me the phone,' Nan was saying in her midwife's voice.

Nearly all the lights in the house were lit. The power must have come back on in the middle of the night, and the lamps in the sitting room glowed orange. Gil was perched on the arm of one of the sofas in his pyjamas, the telephone receiver pressed between his shoulder and his ear. He held the index finger of his right hand up at Nan, as if telling her to wait while he finished his conversation.

Gil nodded. 'Yes, yes, of course.'

'Dad,' Nan said. 'Give me the phone.'

'Who is it?' Flora said, yawning. 'What time is it?'

'Half past five,' Nan snapped. 'Go back to bed.'

'But who's he speaking to?'

'Shh,' Gil said to Flora, and then down the phone, 'OK, I'll pass you over. It's been lovely to speak to you, finally.' He paused, listening. 'Me too,' he said, and Flora felt she was intruding on a private moment. Gil pressed the receiver against his pyjama top.

'It's for you,' he said to Flora.

'Dad,' Nan said, exasperated.

Flora frowned at her sister, shrugged and stepped forward to take the phone from him. She was nervous about holding the receiver up to her cheek, as if something dreadful might slide out of the earpiece.

'It's your mother,' Gil said. 'She wrote and

122

told me she would call.'

'Oh, Dad,' Nan said, the exasperation gone and her voice now full of pity.

But on his face Gil wore an expression of just-you-wait-and-see, and Flora's stomach jolted with an excitement she couldn't control. She hesitated, looked at Nan and her father, and lifted the phone to her ear. She heard a fuzz of white noise and then the multi-toned dial sound. 'There's no one there,' she said.

'Come on,' Nan said to Gil. 'Let's get you back to bed.' She shepherded their father, who went willingly now, saying to Flora over his shoulder as he left the room, 'She must have hung up.'

Flora moved some hardbacks and sat on the sofa. She dialled 1471 and listened to the recorded announcement: 'You were called at five twenty-six. The caller withheld their number.' She returned the phone to its cradle and pulled her legs up to her chest, although the night was warm. The piles of books surrounding her collapsed, hedging her in.

The one time she could remember speaking to her mother on the telephone was when she had been made to stand in the school office a few days before Ingrid disappeared. Her headmistress — backcombed hair and tweed suit — had spoken to Ingrid first, explaining that Flora had been discovered standing on the side of the main road with her thumb out when she should have been in school. And that it was only luck that Mrs May, who taught craft and home economics, happened to be passing or who knows what would have happened. The headmistress passed the phone over and Ingrid's voice buzzed with suppressed anger in Flora's ear.

'What were you thinking?'

Flora shrugged, although Ingrid couldn't see her.

'You could have been picked up by God knows who,' her mother said. 'Abducted, disappeared or worse.'

Flora stretched out on the edge of the sofa, making a prop for her head from four books. She stared at the paperbacks squashed under the coffee table: *The Pursuit of Love, Valerientje aan Zee, Room at the Top, The Cocktail Party*, until the titles blurred and she heard Nan return.

'Do you think that was Mum on the phone?' Flora said.

'Of course it wasn't Mum. He's imagining things. There wasn't anyone on the other end, was there?' Nan sighed, ran her fingers through her hair, and Flora saw streaks of grey at the temples. She tried to remember how old Nan was; her birthday had only been a couple of days ago. Twenty-six? Twenty-seven? Too young to be going grey. Nan switched off the lamps in the sitting room. 'You should come back to bed too,' she said. 'We could all do with some rest.'

When Nan left, Flora couldn't resist picking up the handset and listening again. The dial tone murmured at her. She put the phone down and went over the conversation she'd had earlier with Richard and Nan, trying to work out if there was something she'd missed.

124

16

Dear Gil,

Yesterday morning when we were having breakfast Flora told Nan and me she didn't go to school on Friday.

'The school pool was closed,' she said. 'So what was the point?'

'To learn stuff?' Nan said, shaking her head.

'I have to practise. I went down to the sea and swam there.'

'Flora,' I said, clenching my stomach muscles, and my throat. 'You must go to school. And you mustn't swim in the sea on your own. It's too dangerous.'

Flora picked up her spoon, sank it carefully into her bowl of cereal so it filled with chocolatey milk and slurped like it was soup.

'You do,' she said.

After the party we were on our own for almost a month, in bed with the windows open and the sound of the sea in our ears, sleeping, talking, eating toast and making love amongst the crumbs. You liked to look at me when we'd finished; you would lie at the end of the bed with your head propped up and watch me while I fell asleep. It was too hot even for sheets, but I wasn't shy. You said everything was beautiful.

125

Sometimes when I woke you'd drawn parts of me in the margins of your books. (Juvenile marginalia.) Everything *was* beautiful.

Or we lay front to front, no space between us, our skin fused by sweat. 'Promise you won't die before me,' you said, your face pressed into my hair. 'I couldn't live without you.'

'Don't worry.' My lips were against your ear. 'If I do, I'll come back to haunt you. I'll call you in the early morning; I'll wake you from your bed and down the telephone wires I'll tell you that I love you.' You laughed.

When we got up, our bodies would be marked by the imprint of creased sheets and speckled with crumbs. We'd have a bath, me leaning back against your chest and you whispering, 'Tell me what it is you want me to do. Anything.' I didn't know what you meant the first time you said it. Afterwards we would lie in the grass in the garden like you'd said we would, surrounded by books and the hurrying of insects. It was still a field then, the old pasture for your mother's long-dead horses; scrubby gorse bushes, clumps of deergrass, rowan, hawthorn and hazel grew on the southern edge above the chine, a nettle bed at the sea end.

We picked up paperbacks and read to each other: a chapter from Barbara Comyns, a paragraph or two from *As I Lay Dying*, a line from *Lady Chatterley's Lover*.

''What the eye doesn't see and the mind doesn't know, doesn't exist,'' I read aloud.

You put your hand on my thigh, stopped me from going on. 'That's not true,' you said. 'You existed for me before I'd ever set eyes on you. I knew I'd find you, it was only a matter of waiting.'

'I don't think that's what Lawrence means, is it?' I lowered the book and stared at you over the top of my sunglasses.

'It doesn't matter,' you said. 'It's what I mean.'

We took the phone off the hook, didn't switch on the radio, and the newspapers piled up in the hall. If visitors arrived uninvited, you scared them away by shouting over the closed gate that we were quarantined because of smallpox. Once, remember, you made me stagger out of the house, dotted with lipsticked spots.

We played your records, drank red wine and danced in the sitting room until late. We took picnics to the beach, and when night came we made love in the sand dunes, and again you said, 'Tell me what you want me to do,' and this time I knew what you meant but I'd nothing to tell you, all that I wanted I already had. We must have spent most of that time without clothes when we were indoors; do you remember me surprising the postman as he stood at the front door with a letter to be signed for? After I returned to bed I told you how his gaze had started on my face and slid downwards at the same rate as his eyebrows went up. You asked if I liked him looking.

The envelope stayed where you dropped it, unopened on the floor, another document marking time with the rings of coffee cups. (Later I found burned pieces of it amongst the nettles, and it was years before I understood its

127

significance.) I thought Jonathan had been wrong when he warned me about you, and I'd been right. Things would be different for us.

You didn't pick up a pen or go to your writing room for almost four weeks. The path which had snaked through what we optimistically called the lawn began to disappear as the grass sprang up, even while it yellowed in the sunshine. I wrote, though, to Louise in London to say I was staying with a friend on the south coast for the summer and not to worry, and to my aunt to say London was hot and I was working hard. I blocked October and the beginning of term from my mind.

One day when we were lying out in the garden, my head in your lap, we heard an Irish voice.

'I thought you were dead,' it said.

Jonathan.

You stood up, my head dropping on to the ground with a bump, and I remember a stab of something like anger that the day had been interrupted by your friend. You opened the gate for him, and when I stood up the two of you were hugging.

'Ingrid,' Jonathan said. 'I didn't know you were here.'

'Ingrid's been teaching me how to live the Scandinavian life,' you said, turning towards me. 'Did you know she's half Norwegian? It's been a smorgasbord of delights.' He slapped Jonathan on the shoulder. 'How about a drink?' he said, leading his friend into the house.

'It's not a smorgasbord,' I said to no one. 'The word is koldtbord.'

That first evening you and Jonathan sat out late, drinking on the veranda. I couldn't keep up with the whiskey intake and went to bed. The next morning, when I walked past the spare room I saw the chest of drawers gaping and Jonathan's suitcase open and empty on one of the beds, and I understood that our time alone together (yours and mine) was over.

I tried to freeze Jonathan out, not speaking to him unless I had to answer a direct question, leaving the room when he came in, letting the two of you go to the beach without me, saying the sun was too harsh. I thought about packing up and returning to London.

After a week there was one morning when you were gone from the bed, and when I pulled open the curtains the world outside had gone too, hidden by the mist that had come up from the sea in the night. I opened one of the windows in the bedroom and heard the tapping of your typewriter, dulled and distant, and considered whether I might have misidentified my enemy — it wasn't other women, or Jonathan, but your writing. Perhaps, I thought, during our month alone you'd been waiting for someone else to come and entertain me, to take me off your hands so you could go back to your room and the people in your head.

I packed my belongings into a small blue case I found under the bed, not that I had many — some clothes you'd bought for me in Hadleigh, a sun hat and a toothbrush. Outside, the mist obscured everything like the light in an overexposed Polaroid. I walked blind out of the drive and stumbled to where I thought the lane must be. The silence was a thick blanket, and even the normal morning crockery clinking and shouts from the kitchen staff in the pub were muffled as I passed. By the time I reached the bus stop on the main road, beads of water clung to my clothes and in my hair.

The headlights showed first and then the bus crawled out of the fog, pulling up a little way past me. The door opened and Mrs Allen, the pub cleaner, got off. She looked at me shivering in my summer dress and sandals.

'Reckon this haar will blow over in an hour or two.' She gave my arm a pat. 'Then the sun'll come out, just you wait and see. Don't you go running off so fast now.'

'You getting on, young lady?' The driver was hanging out of the bus. 'Only it's a bit miggy with the door open.'

And as I picked up my case, there were footsteps running up from the lane. Jonathan appeared out of the mist. 'She's not going,' he said, panting.

'Did Gil tell you to come?' I said.

'What do you take me for? He's still typing. It's me who wants you to stay.' Jonathan took the suitcase from me. 'Come on, will you?'

I looked at the driver, undecided.

'You don't get an offer like that every day,' he said, and disappeared inside his bus, the door closing behind him.

As Jonathan and I walked down through the lanes, Mrs Allen was right, the sun glowed over our heads and by the time we reached the drive the sea mist had cleared and I felt I was coming home.

After that, Jonathan and I spent every day together, swimming, and walking through the heath to Little Sea Pond. Post came for him sometimes, with writing commissions, and when he agreed to them there would be telephone calls a week later asking where his articles were. We went out in the morning before the holidaymakers, or in the dusk, when our only company was the bats. Occasionally we persuaded you to come with us for a swim or a picnic, and of course you always emerged in the evening for the food I'd cooked and the whiskey Jonathan provided in payment for his board and lodgings. It was Jonathan who explained, while we tramped across the heath and around the Agglestone, that you'd grown up in the big house down the road with your ill and controlling father, and beautiful Catholic mother. You'd watched the disaster of their marriage, escaping to London as soon as you were old enough, and vowing that you wouldn't make their mistakes. It was Jonathan who told me the real version of the story you'd given in that first creative-writing class: that your father didn't tell you your mother was ill, instead sending a telegram when it was too late. 'Your mother's died. Funeral Friday' or some such thing. And he'd made you see her body, so changed in death that you found it difficult to remember what she'd looked like alive. He told me your mother left you a small amount of money in a trust fund, but how, when your father died of lung disease, there were debts so large the house had to be sold. I

131

like to imagine the Swimming Pavilion being rolled on logs through the lanes of Spanish Green, men levering it along with giant poles, and cart-horses pulling it, until it rested in its current position overlooking the sea.

Once Jonathan went up to London and returned with people he'd picked up on his travels: hitchhikers with guitars, Dutch girls with dusty feet. Bums and hangers-on you called them, but I knew you didn't really mind. They camped in the grass, not bothering with tents, and I got used to seeing strangers in the kitchen spreading jam on dry Weetabix or sitting around the table like it was their home. I liked the house busy with people and music. There was an impromptu party that started in the pub, had a stop-off in the Swimming Pavilion and ended at dawn around a campfire in the dunes. And there were one or two girls who I could have made friends with, but after a couple of days they were gone. Even while these people slept in your garden, used your bathroom, cooked in your kitchen, you locked yourself away in your writing room. Sometimes you came out for the drinking and the food, and occasionally you came out to spend the night with me in the four-poster bed.

Then, at the beginning of September, when the fog rolled in from the sea once more, I realized I was pregnant.

Yours,
Ingrid

[Placed in *Small Dreams of a Scorpion* by Spike Milligan, 1972]

17

When Flora got up she was surprised to see her father dressed and sitting at the kitchen table, a cup of coffee and a plate smeared with egg in front of him. Two rashers of bacon lay on the edge, untouched. His left eye looked grotesque in the morning light, puffed and purple like a rotten aubergine. Another bruise spread out under his bottom lip and over his chin, which was stubbled with grey hairs. His left arm still rested in its sling. She was even more surprised to see Richard sitting in the chair opposite.

'Morning,' Flora said, bending to kiss her father on the top of his head. Gil patted her cheek absent-mindedly. As she sat, Nan put a plate in front of her — a fried egg, flipped once but with the yolk still soft, two slices of crisp bacon and a piece of toast, each with their personal space intact. She tried to catch Richard's eye so she could frown at him, but he was concentrating on Gil.

'Take this, for example,' her father was saying. Gil tilted his chair to stretch for a slim volume from the top of a stack of books beside the cooker.

'Careful, Dad.' Nan stopped squirting kitchen cleaner over the cleared surfaces and passed the book to him.

Gil moved it backwards and forwards, squinting to try and focus. 'God knows what I did with my glasses. I couldn't find them in the bookshop either.' His hand stopped. 'By the way,' he said to Nan, 'did that book ever turn up, the one I was holding when I . . . ' he paused ' . . . fell?'

'No one mentioned it,' Nan said. 'I don't remember seeing it in the hospital.'

'Perhaps you could call them for me?'

'About a lost book? Surely it's not that important?'

'Maybe Viv has it,' Flora said, in a way that made Nan glance at her. Flora raised her eyebrows, smiled and gave her sister a private nod.

'I'll give the hospital a ring,' Nan said.

Gil adjusted the book in front of his face again. '*Rood-Lofts and Their Remnants in Dorset* by E. Z. Harris,' he read.

Richard patted the papers on the table, moving books. A pair of glasses with black frames appeared from under the side of a plate. He picked them up, opened the arms, and Gil bent forward so Richard could slip the glasses over the old man's ears. The action was like a familiar habit, as if they had known each other for years. With her knife, Flora worked at freeing her egg yolk from its white without breaking it or having it touch the bacon. Gil let the book fall open at a page marked by a scrap of newspaper. Flora ate a piece of egg white with an edge of toast.

'This writing was done by a woman,' Gil said, waving the pages.

'How do you know?' Richard said, peering at it upside down.

134

'Purple ink, for a start.'

'Spending their pensions on brandy and summer gloves?' Richard said.

'Setting a good example for the children.' Gil and Richard laughed together. 'It's women who underline and write words in the margins,' Gil continued. 'Men doodle and scribble obscenities.' Gil handed the book over to Richard, who examined the writing, turning it sideways to decipher it. Now he had an attentive audience Gil leaned backwards for another book.

Nan topped up everyone's coffee.

'Thanks,' Richard said, and Flora saw that her sister was wearing an apron which had belonged to their mother, and she had put on lipstick.

'Oh, yes, thanks,' Flora said to Nan. Gil picked up his cup and drank, still looking at the book.

'I can't read it,' Richard said. 'What's this word?' He squinted.

'Now this is wonderful,' Gil said. He pressed the book against his chest so he could open it one-handed, and Flora saw the cover: *Queer Fish* by E. G. Boulenger.

'A first edition?' Richard said. Flora and Nan made eye contact and smiled.

'Richard,' Gil said, as if he were teaching a five-year-old. 'Forget that first-edition, signed-by-the-author nonsense. Fiction is about readers. Without readers there is no point in books, and therefore they are as important as the author, perhaps more important. But often the only way to see what a reader thought, how they lived when they were reading, is to examine what they left behind. All these words' — Gil swung his arm out to encompass the table, the room, the house — 'are about the reader. The specific individual — man, woman or child — who left something of themselves behind.' With Richard's help, he opened the book and revealed a paper napkin lodged in the pages. It was folded into a square — yellow and brittle with age. Flora looked over his arm. The napkin had an emblem on the front with an M in the middle, and underneath, in an ornate font, *Hotel Mirabelle, Salzburg*. Below that some handwriting.

'*Suzannah, room 127,*' Flora read aloud. With her knife she spread egg yolk over the now crust-less toast and ate it together with the bacon, using her fingers. Nan tutted.

'A whole story is contained in those three words,' Gil said, stroking the text with his thumb as if to pick up some smell or particles of Suzannah. 'Did she write her own name and room number, or did a man overhear it?'

'Maybe he visited her in room 127 and had to pay for her services,' Nan said.

'Or perhaps it wasn't a man who visited her, it was a woman.' Flora raised her eyebrows again at her sister.

'I'd rather know the truth, though,' Nan said. 'I'd like to know what really happened.'

'Not knowing is so much better, isn't it, Daddy?' Flora said. Gil took his eyes off the napkin and looked at her as she continued. 'I don't want to discover that the writer was actually the chambermaid and Suzannah was just a guest in room 127 who needed fresh towels. Or that room service got Suzannah's

136

request for eggs on toast but couldn't find the order pad.'

Gil was slow to answer, looking down at his uneaten bacon.

'Daddy?' Flora said.

'Perhaps,' Gil said. 'But I'm beginning to think it's better to know, one way or the other. It's taken me a long time to realize, but I don't think it's good to have an imagination which is more vivid, wilder, than real life.'

'But you've always said we should hope and imagine. You can't just suddenly change your mind.' Flora sounded petulant.

'I agree with Nan,' Richard said. 'Better to live with the facts even if they are mundane.'

Gil closed the book, put it on the table, and Nan turned back to the sink. Richard, oblivious to the atmosphere, picked up *Queer Fish* and flicked through it, stopping at a different page and holding it open. 'What about this doodle? Black biro, obscenity rating unclear. A man, would you say?'

Gil took the book again and inspected the drawing of a cloud with fish falling from it. Frowning he said, 'You're catching on quickly. Yes, definitely a man.'

Flora folded her arms, said nothing.

18

Dear Gil,

Annie died yesterday. It was unclear whether Nan or Flora was responsible, but there was a terrific noise from their bedroom (wailing and shouting) and, when I ran in, the skeleton was on the floor, most of its ribs in bits, the skull in several pieces like a broken teacup, and the teeth scattered. Nan said she'd hung Annie on the back of the door and that Flora, knowing the skeleton was there, had thrust the door open against the side of the wardrobe and then stamped on the bones. It sounds too vicious an attack even for Flora, but she was wearing your greatcoat and heavy boots, seven sizes too big for her. Whatever happened, Flora was in there, kicking and shouting, while Nan wrung her hands and asked if we could glue Annie back together. I knew she was past repairing. Flora stopped her noise and said, 'Daddy will be able to mend her.'

She ran outside to your writing room and we watched her standing on the top step and beating on the stable door with her fists.

'Daddy! Daddy! Annie's bust!' (Bust — where did she learn that word?)

She knew you weren't in there, that you haven't been here for months (I've just worked it

138

out and you've been gone for three-quarters of a year), but perhaps Flora liked to imagine your door opening, you sweeping her up, striding over to the house and fixing everything. Nan tried to catch my eye, to share an expression with me. I turned away but not before I saw those raised eyebrows, that adult understanding of where her father might be — too many things guessed at without any real knowledge, even for a girl of fifteen. Of course, you aren't here to fix Annie; you aren't here to fix anything any more.

'Daddy's in London doing things with books,' Nan called out to her sister, and Flora stopped her hammering and gave the door a kick instead. Later, when I kissed her goodnight, she asked whether you'd be home in time for her swimming gala and I didn't know what to say. What shall I tell her, Gil? And what do I say to Nan when she raises her eyebrows again with that knowing look? That I'm tired of forgiving you? That I'm not sure I want you back this time?

So, Annie. I couldn't bear to just sweep her up and tip the pieces into the dustbin (jaw against ankle, hip touching skull), so late yesterday we piled all the bones we could find (Flora crawling in the dust under the beds — I'm sure several teeth have vanished) into the old Silver Cross pram I found under the house, and bumped it down the chine to the sea. Every time a wheel hit a stone Annie's remains jumped and rattled.

We carried the old Silver Cross over the sand, up to the far end of the beach where it tapers away under the cliff. As the sun went down

139

behind the village, the children helped me dig a hole, the three of us excavating rocks for half an hour, then we laid Annie to rest and toasted her with flat lemonade. We put the picnic rug over the top of her grave and ate jam sandwiches.

'I think we should say a prayer,' Nan said.

'Don't be stupid,' Flora said. 'You don't believe in God, none of us do.'

'But a prayer is still a nice thing to say and sometimes it makes you feel better,' Nan said patiently. She bowed her head. 'To dear Annie. We will miss you. May your bones be washed by the saltwater, your spirit return to the sand and the love we had for you be forever around us.' (Nan can be quite poetic when she puts her mind to it.)

'Amen to that,' Flora said.

'Amen,' I said.

Later, after the children were in bed, I went again to the beach. I lay on the grave with the stars shining above in the huge arc of the sky, and wondered where you were lying, and I thought about all the things which have gone wrong and whether we will ever be able to put them right.

It was Jonathan I told first about the pregnancy. Not you, not Louise, and actually for a while I denied it to myself — the frightening idea that something alien had set seed inside me. I wanted Jonathan to make it go away. I wanted it to never have happened. But perhaps there were other things Jonathan didn't want to face, because he said I had to tell you.

'You should make the decision together,' he said.

I tried to tell you that I didn't want it, wasn't ready, might never be ready, but you put your finger on my lips and said, 'Marry me,' and all those plans of creating my own category and giving you up after the summer disappeared like a wisp of sea mist under the relentless energy of your sun. You stroked my stomach. 'One down, five to go,' you said and took me to America to celebrate.

Do you remember the yard sale we stopped at, on the road between Sebastopol and Guerneville, after we'd driven north from San Francisco? And those three grown-up brothers, selling the contents of their grandmother's house: everything laid out by the side of the road for any passing tourist to rummage through? Heaps of tarnished cutlery, books, threadbare linen piled on decorating tables, and a leather three-piece suite set out in the front yard.

'Let's buy it,' you said, bouncing on the cushions.

'Gil, get up,' I said, pulling on your hand. 'Don't be silly. It's horrible and how would we get it home?' You gave me a tug so I fell into your lap. You held me by the waist and kissed me, and we toppled sideways, you manoeuvring until you were lying on me in full view of the house.

'Tell me what you want me to do. We can do anything — anything at all,' you whispered.

'Gil! Someone will come. Someone will see,' I said. And then as a final attempt to get you off, 'The baby!'

141

'Who'll come? The Three Brothers Grimm?' Your hand was under my skirt and your mouth pressed against my neck.

'Gil!' I struggled, but I was laughing too, twisting my head to move your lips from my ear. I think you might even have got as far as unzipping your fly when a shadow fell across my face.

'What the fuck?' said the man looking down on us. From where I lay I could see the bottom of his belly hanging over the cinched belt of his jeans.

Still on top of me, you reached down to a box of books beside the sofa and picked up the top one. 'How much for this?' You smiled your most handsome smile. I pushed hard against your chest with my hands and scrambled out from underneath you, pulling my skirt over my knees, sitting up straight and blushing like a teenager caught by a parent who's come home earlier than expected. You sat up too and flicked through the book, stopped at a page and read. The margins were filled with notes and drawings. 'In fact,' you said, 'how much for the whole box?'

Later, I learned the cost of that holiday. Everything, including the box of books, bought with money we didn't have.

Yours,
Ingrid

[Placed in *Hand Crocheted Creations for the Home: Bedspreads, Luncheon Sets, Scarfs, Chair Sets* by Bernhard Ullmann, 1933]

142

19

After breakfast, Flora brushed her teeth and got dressed, and when she returned to the kitchen Gil said he thought he would go back to bed for a while.

'But you just got up,' Flora said. 'I thought we could go to the beach. Or for a walk, show Richard the heath and the Agglestone since he doesn't seem to have to go to work today. You'd like to see the Agglestone, wouldn't you, Richard?'

'Perhaps later,' he said, helping Gil to his feet and leading him out of the kitchen. Flora went to follow, but Nan grabbed her arm and pulled her back.

'Dad has asked Richard to stay a bit longer,' Nan said.

'What?'

'He asked Richard if he can take some time off work.'

'Why?' Flora said. 'He does work full-time, doesn't he?'

'I mean, why would Daddy want Richard to stay?' She glanced towards the hall and hissed, 'He's just some guy I'm sleeping with.'

Nan rolled her eyes. 'Well, I like him and Dad does too. He says he can talk to Richard.'

'But you both barely know him. And anyway, why can't Daddy talk to us?'

Nan shrugged and went into the hall. Flora followed.

Gil lay against his pillows in the front bedroom. Richard had eased off the old man's shoes and Nan was fussing, making sure he had a glass of fresh water. He appeared small in the bed, as if the mattress were growing around him so that in a few days or weeks he might be absorbed by it, in the way that trees will grow around iron railings. Nan opened the curtains and a window, and the smell of the sea came into the room, billows of Cambridge blue.

'What a magnificent bed,' Richard said.

'It belonged to my grandparents,' Nan said, smoothing the cover. 'When they lived in the big house down the road. I was born in it, and Dad was, weren't you, Dad?'

'It's a fucking ridiculous bed.' Gil sank backwards and closed his eyes.

'Well, it's the wrong height for nursing.'

'You're not at work, Nan,' Flora said. She went around to her mother's side and lay down next to Gil.

'Do you want me to read to you?' Richard pulled up a chair to Gil's bedside. All the thousands of books in the house, and Flora realized she'd never heard her father read any of them to her. It had always been her mother.

Flora opened her eyes to a stack of books on the bedside table and a cold cup of tea balanced on top. She shut them again when she heard Richard and her father talking behind her back.

'I used to follow Ingrid sometimes, in the dawn,' Gil said. There was a catch in his voice that surprised Flora. She tilted the side of her

144

head that was against the pillow so she could hear better, and smelled the khaki whiff of unwashed hair again. 'She was a poor sleeper,' Gil continued. 'And I spent most nights in my room at the end of the garden.'

'And is that when you did your writing?' Richard said.

'Writing?'

'At night?'

'No, I didn't use the night for writing, although I should have. It was Ingrid who wrote in the night, well, the early morning — she sat for hours on the veranda.'

'I didn't know Ingrid was a writer. Did she have anything published?'

'No,' Gil said sharply. 'She wrote letters.'

'To her family?'

Too many questions, Flora thought, and her father must have thought so too because he didn't answer. Instead he said, 'She would go swimming as well, although her doctor advised her against it.'

'Against swimming?' Richard said. 'I thought it was meant to be good for you.'

'I followed her to Little Sea Pond once. It's a pool behind the dunes, a beautiful place, secluded. I sat in the bird hide and spied on her while she shed her clothes. She was so slender and pale, almost transparent. She stepped into the pond and turned; she might have been looking straight at me, except I was hidden. She lay back and it was as if the pond cradled her; she didn't have to move her arms or her legs to stay afloat, she just reclined in the dark water, her hair spread about her head. I watched as the sun rose — a naked Ophelia.'

'Like a creature native and indued unto that element,' Richard said.

'But long it could not be till that her garments, heavy with their drink, pulled the poor wretch from her melodious lay to muddy death,' Gil finished, and was quiet for a moment, remembering perhaps. 'But I should have shown myself, should have waded in, a lumbering old fool, to tell her I loved her. Too late now.'

'Perhaps she knew, in her way.' Richard's voice was soft. Flora held her breath, straining to listen.

'She had no fucking idea.'

'Perhaps you'll have another chance to tell her, soon.'

Gil snorted. 'Nan's told you about that Catholic rubbish, has she? I very much doubt Ingrid will be in the same place as the one I'm going to.' Flora felt Gil's position in the bed change. 'Flora, are you awake?'

She stretched and opened her eyes as if she had only just woken up. And Flora knew it was because Gil thought she'd been listening that he said abruptly, 'Don't start with that religious shit, Richard.' And the younger man, shocked, withdrew into his chair.

20

Dear Gil,

Yesterday afternoon as soon as the girls got home they started arguing. When I went into their room Nan's face was filled with horror and Flora was huddled on the bed, clutching your old cufflink box tight to her chest.

'Oh my God!' Nan cried. 'She's killed someone! She's actually killed someone and kept their teeth.'

'They were on my side of the drawer,' Flora said, tears running. 'You shouldn't be looking. They're mine.'

'You're sick, Flora,' Nan said. 'Something's wrong in here.' She tapped the side of her head.

'They're Annie's. You know they're Annie's!'

Nan made a surprise attack, snatched the box and shook it in the air like a rattle. Flora jumped up at her sister's arm, pulling on the sleeve of her school shirt and screaming for her to hand them over.

'Stop!' I shouted. 'Both of you, stop it!'

The shirt ripped. Nan wailed, flung the box on to her bed and ran out of the house, slamming the front door behind her. Flora grabbed the box of teeth and locked herself in the bathroom. I sat on Nan's bed, feeling useless, and gazing out at the sea where ragged clouds tore themselves to

147

shreds against a knife-sharp horizon.

Later, when Nan had gone to a friend's house to do homework, Flora and I sat together on her bed. She rested her head against my chest and I stroked her hair, breathing in the sweet smell of my child. Without lifting her face she said, 'Why are blackbirds called blackbirds and not brownbirds, when the ladies are brown? And dogs . . . ' She pulled away to look up at me. 'Why aren't they all called bitches? And foxes should be vixens. That would make it fairer.'

I was starting to answer, but she carried on.

'And why is it mothers have to stay at home to look after the children? Why can't that be the father's job? Because they *are* better at it, aren't they?'

Louise stopped calling you by your first name when I told her I was pregnant, and used 'that man' instead. You and I were back in London; me living at the flat with Louise, and you staying in your old lodgings.

'He'd better be there when you get rid of it,' had been the first thing she'd said.

'I'm not going to get rid of it.' I was sitting on the sofa, my handbag on my lap. 'Gil and I are engaged; we're going to be married. On Tuesday. I was hoping you'd be a witness.'

'What?' Louise banged a saucepan of beans on the stove. 'Are you mad? Married? For God's sake why? What about everything we're going to do?'

'I love him.'

She made a *phh* noise. 'I thought we were

148

going to see the world. I thought we weren't going to end up like our mothers.' Her tone was as dismissive as I'd imagined it would be.

'I can go later.'

'And what about me?' Louise said.

'You can still go. They say you meet more people if you travel alone. You can send me postcards — let me know what I'm missing.' I tried to laugh, but it came out strangled.

'You've changed. It's those baby hormones making you stupid. Bloody hell, Ingrid, just get rid of it. There's nothing to be ashamed of. That man's the one who should be ashamed.'

'I'm not ashamed. I'm excited.' I didn't sound it, even to myself.

'You have no idea what it'll be like, do you?' She sat beside me and took my hand, trying another tack. 'You're too young, Ingrid. Think what your aunt would say. Have you told her?'

'Not yet.' I withdrew my hand from hers.

She looked me up and down. 'You're not showing — well, the boobs maybe a bit. How far gone are you?' Her hand was on my knee. 'We could go to the clinic together.'

'I'm keeping it. This is what I've chosen, with Gil.'

'What that man has chosen.'

I didn't say anything.

'Think about what you're giving up,' she said.

'What do you mean? I won't be giving anything up. I'm going to finish university.' It hadn't occurred to me that I wouldn't. I'd avoided thoughts about the birth or what life would be like afterwards. I'd been to the GP in

149

Hadleigh and then to an appointment at a London hospital where I was weighed and measured and examined by a doctor who didn't bother to tell me his name. He'd given me a date when the baby was due, but it seemed so far in the future, like thinking about Christmas in April, that I couldn't imagine it ever coming round. I'd been given leaflets on antenatal classes and weaning, but the sketchy drawings of grown-ups holding babies and smiling seemed to have nothing to do with me, and I'd thrown them away.

'When's it due? April, May next year? Term won't have finished and you'll be enormous. Think what people will say.'

'When did you ever care what people said?'

'What will you live on?'

'Gil has something in trust from his mother and some money from his novels . . . '

'So you're going to live on the money given to you by a man?'

' . . . and there's his teaching.'

'His teaching!' She spat out the words. 'He won't be in that job for long when they find out.'

'They won't be bothered. They've seen it all before.' I pulled away from her and stood up.

'It's an abuse of power,' she said. 'You're his student. It's disgusting.'

'I love him,' I said again, angrily this time.

'And you think he loves you? You think he hasn't done this before?'

'We're getting married. I know he wants this — a family.'

I sat again and we were both silent for several

150

minutes. After a while I said, 'I think I can smell the beans burning.'

I wore the yellow crocheted dress to our wedding. Louise, however, arrived at Caxton Hall registry office on the 5th of October 1976 in a long white dress, high-necked, with lace sleeves. 'Second-hand,' she said. 'What do you think?' She twirled on the pavement. She wore it to annoy you and had no idea how much it hurt me.

Inside, waiting in the lobby, Jonathan tried to defuse the atmosphere. 'Diana Dors and Orson Welles got married here,' he said. You and Louise looked in opposite directions and I sat on the only chair. 'Not to each other, of course.'

'Actually,' Louise said to no one in particular, 'this is where the suffragettes held their first meetings.'

The registrar appeared, picking food out of her teeth and wiping her hand across her mouth. And it was you and Louise, in her mock wedding dress, that the woman greeted and ushered forward to be married.

★ ★ ★

In the end, of course, Louise was right: the university did find out and they did care. I never discovered who told them — perhaps it was Mrs Carter, who'd seen that first kiss; perhaps it was Louise, so angry with me for deserting her that she didn't think about the consequences. Whoever it was, on the 29th of April 1977, when

151

the baby was nearly due, you received an invitation for a chat the next day with the Dean. 'It'll be fine,' you said. 'A slap on the wrist. 'Just don't do it again, Coleman,' with a nudge and a wink. Really, nothing to worry about.'

Neither of us had been wearing our wedding rings on campus, and when I attended your classes we carried on as if we were still only lecturer and student. At the beginning of the autumn term, when I still wasn't showing, Guy had invited me to his lodgings for a 'bedroom shuffle' (as he called it), and I delighted in telling him that I was seeing someone else, and watching his face fall.

'Who is it?' he asked, and when I wouldn't tell he pressed me further. 'It's someone I know, isn't it? He's married, isn't he?'

I knew there was gossip. Sometimes rumours went round like Chinese whispers: you were having an affair with the Vice Chancellor's wife, or his secretary, you were a homosexual, you'd been discovered with your pants down in your office. Up until Christmas the latter was nearly true; we just hadn't been caught. The number of private tutorials I had that first term grew until I was being requested by you almost daily, but we never discussed my work. Instead, you asked me again and again to tell you what I wanted you to do, until I had to come up with something.

'I want us to make love in your writing room,' I said, although I was perfectly happy with your office, the Swimming Pavilion's bed, or the dunes. 'I want to lie back on that velvet cover. It's night and the window's open.' I was

152

beginning to enjoy myself. 'We can hear the sea lapping at the sand. I want you to kneel between my legs and push my thighs apart.'

'Only Professor Coleman is allowed in, miss,' the porter said, blocking my entry to the administration building with his suited bulk. He was more like a bouncer than a porter, and I reckoned if I couldn't match him pound for pound, our waist measurements would be similar.

'Mrs,' I said.

The man would look me only in the eye.

You, Gil, placed your hand against my neck. 'I'll be fine,' you said. 'What's the worst that can happen?' You smiled a brave smile.

Louise was standing behind me, and I knew she would have that concerned expression on her face, the one where her eyebrows met, below her wrinkled forehead. That morning during a 'chat', she'd pulled the same face and said, 'Someone has to be there for you. This isn't all about Gil.' I'd told her I was perfectly capable of looking after myself, but she'd insisted.

You pushed through the glass swing door into the university while Louise and I waited, leaning against the wall like girls skiving school. In front of us was that famous metal sculpture: tubes and beams criss-crossing each other and a circular plate resting at the end of a pole.

'What do you think it's meant to be?' Louise said, tilting her head.

'The skeleton of an arthritic elephant,' I said.

'A line drawing by a left-handed octopus.'

'A climbing frame for rectangular children.'

153

The porter had been posted by the door as a sentry, as if they were worried we might storm the building. (A pregnant girl and her skinny friend rushing past him and demanding that Professor Coleman be allowed to keep his job.) After a while he went inside and came out with a chair. I was determined to refuse it, although I could feel the downwards pull and stretch of things inside me. But the man set it beside the door and sat on it himself, tilting it back, waiting for the show to begin. He stretched out his legs and rolled a cigarette, lighting it in the cup of his hand even though there was no wind, and smoking it with the lit end tucked under his fingers.

You came out of the building smiling, with bravado, I suppose.

'So,' I said when no one spoke. 'What happened?'

Louise read your face faster than me. 'Have you considered adoption, Ingrid?' she said with a laugh.

'Just shut up,' you said. 'I'm not even sure why you're here.'

'I'm here to look after Ingrid's best interests.' She folded her arms across her chest.

'Stop bickering,' I said, 'and tell me what happened.'

'Listen.' You took me by the elbow as if to lead me away. 'Fuck Louise, fuck the Dean. In fact, fuck the lot of them.' You put your arm around me. 'My next book will sell. I know it.'

I stepped away. 'But surely you apologized.'

'It's a bit late for that.'

154

'They can't throw you out. Don't you have tenure, or something?'

'They haven't thrown him out,' Louise said, still leaning against the wall. 'I think he's saying he's resigned.'

'Not exactly,' you said.

'Why?' The muscles of my stomach contracted and hardened painlessly. Braxton Hicks contractions, you told me later. 'Why would you do that?'

'I wasn't really given an option. The Dean blabbered on about avoiding a scandal in the papers and an imminent visit by the university funding committee, blah, blah, blah.'

'Perhaps he's behind on the payments for his modern art collection,' Louise said.

'But you can get another job, can't you?' My hand was on my stomach, as hard as a rock. 'At a different university.'

'I wasn't going to give him the satisfaction of letting him recommend me. He can fuck his job and any other up his arse.'

The porter dragged on his cigarette, listening and watching, a smirk on his face.

'No, Gil, tell me you didn't.'

'Come on,' you said, taking my arm again. 'It'll be fine.'

'I'm going to speak to him,' I said, pulling away. 'You need that job — we need that job.'

The porter jumped up as I approached and threw down his cigarette to open the door for me. He gave a little nod of the head as I passed, perhaps with some respect for the angry pregnant woman.

155

I walked straight past the Dean's secretary sitting behind her desk. Despite my size I was too quick for her, and I was in the Dean's office before she'd even stood up.

He was older than I'd expected. I'd seen him from a distance of course, from the high seats at the rear of the main lecture theatre when he gave us a five-minute pep talk at the beginning of each year about not letting the university down, or our parents, or, most importantly of all, ourselves.

'Miss Torgensen,' he said, as if it were he who'd requested a meeting. 'Please, take a seat.' He indicated the chair in front of the desk he was sitting at. Perhaps I shouldn't have been surprised that he knew my name.

'I'd rather stand, thank you,' I said, although my knees were shaking.

'May I offer my congratulations on your expected arrival?' He nodded at my bump. 'When is the little bundle of joy, as they say, due to arrive?'

'The week after next.' I said.

I was pleased to see a brief expression of shock pass across his face before he composed himself. 'My goodness.' He came around to hold out the chair. 'Then please do sit. I wouldn't want anything to start in my office.'

I remained standing, and he let go of the chair and went back to his own.

'Have you thought of a name yet?' The Dean was all smiles.

Do you remember, Gil, our weekends by the sea when I was so pregnant I couldn't move? You

156

would stuff me into the car in London on a Friday afternoon and drive south, your hand on my stomach whenever you weren't changing gear. At the Swimming Pavilion I undressed and collapsed on the bed. My skin was stretched tight over my belly, which you said sat like a white beach ball caught in the branches of an aspen. My tummy button popped out and I developed the faintest linea nigra (as you told me it was called) — the ghost of a ginger line — as if you could have peeled me open to reveal six babies packed together in segments. My areolae darkened to salmon pink and enlarged as my breasts swelled. You said the new constellations scattered over my nipples were called Montgomeries, and I didn't question how you knew all the words. You crouched between my knees, pressing your lips up against my distended stomach, whispering to our unborn child, telling it stories about seahorses, cuttlefish bones and the tangled nets of fishermen. Or you opened my legs to gaze at me, and to exclaim at the width of my boyish hips and wonder how our baby would make it into the world through that narrow passage. When I tried to pull you up and into me, you said it wouldn't be right now I was almost a mother. You wanted to look, but you no longer touched. Instead you lay beside me, reciting names to see which one would stick: Fyodor, Saul, Wallace. Don't you know any female writers apart from Shirley Jackson?

'We haven't decided,' I said to the Dean. I knew what he was trying to do. 'I want to talk to you about Professor Coleman's job,' I said.

157

'I'm afraid I can't discuss the personal information of an employee of the university. That's private.'

'He's my husband.'

'So he told me.' The Dean straightened the blotter in front of him. 'The information about his employment is still confidential.'

'But we need that job.'

'Perhaps something he should have considered earlier.' The Dean looked at my stomach. 'Actually, Miss Torgensen,' he said pointedly, 'it's rather useful that you've come to see me now.'

'So you'll reconsider?'

The Dean put his head on one side and frowned. 'No, no, it's your own position I'd like to discuss. I was hoping to invite you in for a chat next week, but since you're here . . . Are you sure you wouldn't like a seat?'

My belly tightened again and I shook my head.

'It's a question of standards, you see. I'm sure you understand that the university has a reputation to uphold. You might think we can turn a blind eye to relationships between professors and students, but I'm afraid that isn't the case. It's a matter of trust, expectations are changing . . . ' The Dean continued, his voice a monotone. I swayed on my feet, his words coming back into focus when he said, 'I've already had a word with the Head of English and he's happy for you to take some time off from the university, get some rest, or whatever it is mothers do.'

'But my finals start next week,' I said.

'You shouldn't worry about those. No, no. I suggest you go home and look after your husband and your baby. That's where your place is now.'

'My place is here. I want . . . I need to finish my degree.'

The Dean pushed his chair back from under his desk and smiled. 'Perhaps something you also should have considered earlier.' He stood, his arm extended as if herding me out. 'Now, if you don't mind, I've another appointment.'

I turned and left, marching past his secretary and slamming the door behind me.

And that was the end of my education, in the Dean's office, one week before I would have finished anyway.

Yours,

Ingrid

[Placed in *Advice to a Wife: On the Management of Her Own Health, and on the Treatment of the Complaints Incidental to Pregnancy, Labour and Suckling* by Pye Henry Chavasse, 1913 edition]

21

In the afternoon when they returned from collecting Gil's car, Flora took Richard down to the beach. A breeze was blowing in from the sea, a tang of military-green weed, and things half buried. A group of gulls circled the up-currents, banking and turning, waiting for something. She'd found a pair of old swimming trunks in the airing cupboard but Richard had refused them. He sat on his towel, running the fine dry sand through his fingers. Flora pulled her shirt over her head; she was wearing a bikini underneath. Goose pimples rose across her legs and arms.

'Are you coming in?' she said.

'With a skeleton inked on me? That'd get your neighbours talking.'

She'd forgotten about the drawing. Flora went to the water and was in up to her thighs before she turned to look back. Richard had come to the edge, his jeans rolled up, his feet lapped by waves.

'It's freezing,' he called.

'Don't be such a baby.' She took a lungful of breath and launched herself out. Like always, the coldness of the water shocked her, but within two strokes or three, the rest of the world was forgotten and she was transformed from a person who breathed air to a thing of the sea, an underwater creature where everything was the smooth action of bone, muscle and moving forward. Flora opened her eyes. The water was the colour of mint tea, and sometimes if she listened hard enough her mother's voice sounded amongst the swish of the weed and the tumble of the sand, telling her to straighten her legs, to keep her lead hand in motion, to swim against the current so that it was always easy to return, even when tired. She dived to where the waves churned the bottom, aware of her arms and thighs, the bubble of air she held inside her. She touched the seabed and surfaced with a fistful of sand: a good-luck charm. When she glanced towards the beach, Richard was still standing, watching for her. Flora turned away and moved into a front crawl, her arms slicing through the water, her hips, shoulders and head rotating as she lifted her mouth above the chop. She glanced up at the buoy in the distance, her usual sight, and swam straight for it. The swell tossed her, but she found its rhythm, breathing in the dips, pushing through the waves. She kept her head low so her bottom and legs rose, and let her body work with the water's flow. When the tips of her outstretched fingers touched the buoy she pulled up her legs, flipped, pushed off with the balls of her feet, hearing the heavy underwater yaw and slap, and headed back to the beach.

When she was within her depth, Flora stood and waded. Richard was on his towel again.

'Impressive,' he said.

'Mum taught me how to swim.' She flopped

161

down beside him, chest heaving. 'It was about the only thing we could do together without arguing.' She wrung out her hair and wrapped her towel around her.

'Was she a good swimmer too?'

'Very. She could go a long way beyond the buoy. It's further than it looks.'

'I'm sure.'

'I know everyone thinks she drowned. That's what the police and the journalists and everybody assumed. I found an old newspaper cutting once. The headline was something like 'X-rated novelist's wife drowns off Dorset beach'. They didn't even bother to name her; she was just a wife.'

'But she wasn't a writer. It probably wouldn't have made the papers if she hadn't been married to Gil.'

Flora knew that her story, or rather her mother's story, trailed along behind her family like a second shadow, reminding the people who saw it to repeat what they knew to the people who didn't. Once, when she was eleven, Flora had been choosing an ice cream in the village shop when she overheard a woman, a tourist, say to her husband, 'Wasn't it one of the beaches here where that Swedish girl drowned? Didn't she put stones in her pockets or something, or am I getting muddled? You know, that famous author — or was it his wife?' Flora had lifted her head from the chest freezer and seen Mrs Bankes, the shopkeeper, frown and shake her head. The husband had paid for his newspaper and hurried his wife away.

Flora had wanted to shout 'Norwegian!' after them, but instead she had licked the tips of her fingers and pressed her skin against the icy inside of the cabinet.

'Are you going to ask your father who he thinks he saw in Hadleigh?' Richard said.

'No.'

'Really? Aren't you curious?'

'We don't talk about that stuff. It's not what we do.' She rubbed the tops of her arms with the towel.

'Your father thinks he saw his dead wife, your mother, and you're not going to ask him?' Richard was incredulous.

'I told you, she's not dead.' Flora's voice rose. Ingrid turned again from the front door of the Swimming Pavilion, the towel over her arm, the dress showing off the pale skin of her neck and shoulders. Flora probed the memory like a tongue poking at a bloody gap left by an extracted tooth. When the skin healed over and the remaining teeth moved together to fill the hole, she was still aware of what was missing.

'OK, OK.' Richard held his hands up, palms flat towards her, as if she were attacking him.

'If you're so interested, ask Daddy yourself. You seem to be very pally even though you've known him for all of two minutes.' Flora yanked her shirt over her head, her damp arms sticking in the sleeves. 'Richard, remind me again why you're still here?'

'Gil asked me to stay. I like to think I might be able to help.'

'With what exactly?'

163

Richard looked disconcerted. 'With everything that's going on.'

'And what do you think is going on?' Flora rubbed her goose-pimpled legs with the towel and stared at the sea. The waves were getting bigger, cresting and foaming, slapping on to the beach and racing back. A mother called her child in from the water.

'Flora, I know this is difficult for you — your dad's . . . ' he stopped. 'All those memories of your mum that must be resurfacing — I know you haven't had the easiest time, but why are you trying to push me away?' He put a hand on one of her chilly knees. 'Why do you do that? Really, I only want to help you — all of you.'

'Because we barely know each other,' she said, and shoved at him. A family sitting near them — a mother, father and two young girls — were eating sandwiches and staring. 'What?' Flora shouted and the parents turned away, busying themselves with blowing sand off fallen grapes. When she looked at Richard again, he had slipped his feet into his shoes and was standing up.

'I'm going back to the house.' He waited, then said, 'I don't think this is working.'

She was aware of his Converse trainers, black with white laces, on the periphery of her vision.

'See you later, then,' he said.

She clenched her jaw. The shoes stayed a couple of seconds longer, and when she didn't reply they disappeared from view.

22

Dear Gil,

After our meetings with the Dean you insisted we drive back to the Swimming Pavilion. You checked that I was well, kissed my tight-stretched skin and went to your room to write. I didn't mind: I wanted you to finish your novel, we needed the money. I stood at the window and watched the light wink out in your room and thought you should get some rest — what was the point in both of us being awake? A period-like cramping pain came, low in my back, nothing I couldn't cope with. It passed. Another arrived twenty minutes later when I was in the kitchen getting a glass of water; I bent over the sink and hummed with my teeth clamped together. It faded and I brewed a pot of tea, sitting at the table in the unlit kitchen to drink it, thinking how it was impossible and ridiculous that I had grown a human being inside me and soon it would arrive, fully formed, from my body. The next pain came as I stood up, so that I had to clutch at the back of a kitchen chair to stop myself from dropping to my knees. 'Gil!' I called through gritted teeth. 'Gil!'

I used the toilet and returned to the bedroom, curling on my side under the covers and kicking them off when the pains gathered strength. I didn't want to move; if I lay there for long enough they might go away. It was too soon to have a baby — I wasn't ready, I wouldn't ever be ready. But the bursts of pain made me arch and cry out, and struggle from the bed. A few minutes before six, when the sky was lightening and I was on all fours on the bathroom floor, my waters broke with a pop. I crawled along the hall, too afraid to stand; if I stood, the baby would fall out of me. Still on my knees I opened the front door and, sitting on my bottom, levered myself down the three steps to the path. That was where you found me.

'Why didn't you shout?' you said. 'Why didn't you come and get me?' You helped me up, took me into the bedroom, put a nightie over my head. 'Have you phoned anyone? Have your waters broken? Ingrid, we're going to have a baby. He's coming.'

'I don't want to do this,' I said before another contraction overtook me. 'I've changed my mind. I'm meant to be travelling with Louise. I was meant to get a degree.'

'You're going to be an amazing mother. It'll be wonderful. I know it.' You tried to prise my fingers from where they were clamped around your forearm, turning the skin white.

'Don't go,' I cried. 'Please don't go.' I was being dragged under again, tossed upside down and scraped along the bottom.

'A minute, Ingrid,' you may have said. 'I'll just be a minute.'

There was the sound of someone screaming and there was pain and when I was dumped on dry land there was exhaustion.

You held a bowl for me and pulled my hair out of my face while I sat on the edge of the bed and threw up. Your red hands smelled of soap. I wondered if you'd been a surgeon in a previous life.

'Can you stand?' you said after you'd wiped my mouth. 'We need to go now.' You had hold of my elbow, guiding me upwards, but the wave came again, a tsunami of pain that picked me up and tossed me. I must have climbed on to the bed, pressing my face into the pile of blankets and pillows at one end. 'Ingrid,' I remember you saying before a groan, deep and guttural, escaped.

'Fuck off,' I said into the pillows, then I was on my back, pushing and panting, and you were looking between my legs and smiling.

'I can see him, Ingrid,' you said. 'He has dark hair.'

'She,' I said in between strains.

'Whichever. It doesn't matter. It's here.'

'I don't know how to do this. I can't do it!' I could hear myself shouting in panic, and with a searing red-hot pain the head was delivered.

'Wait,' you said. 'Breathe, she's turning, she's coming.' And with one final heave the baby was out. You scooped her up, put her over your knee and smacked her tiny blue bottom until she cried and pinkened. She was your colouring — dark hair, her skin brown next to mine. At some point while I was under or resting you'd fetched clean towels from the airing cupboard, and a bowl of hot water. You wrapped her so only her face was

167

showing. 'We've got a girl,' you said, kissing me, putting the baby in my arms and wiping damp hair from my face. Our daughter was as plump and creased as a Shar Pei. Her eyes were glassy and looked straight through us. 'The first,' you said. And I laughed; I felt hysterical.

The midwife arrived an hour later, bumping a wheeled tank of gas and air up the veranda steps. The placenta had been delivered, the cord cut, and you were holding Nanette.

'My goodness, what a bed,' the midwife said, and then, 'Looks like I wasn't needed after all.' She sat on the edge of the mattress and took hold of my wrist. She was tall and thin, with the blue belt of her uniform pinching her waist.

'Waspish,' you said later.

A round white hat was stuck on the back of her head, behind a severe middle parting. 'I'll need to carry out a quick examination,' she said, lifting up the sheet covering my legs. 'Mr Coleman, I'd be obliged if you'd leave the room.'

I could see you were about to argue. 'A cup of tea, Gil,' I said. 'Please?'

'And leave baby with us,' she said.

The midwife tutted as she examined me. 'I always prefer it if my ladies are shaved before delivery,' she said. 'It makes everything so much neater. Did you lose a lot of blood?'

'I don't know.'

'Have plenty of pilchards and Guinness, just to be sure. Well, you'll do. Legs together, please. Let's have a look-see at baby now. You don't have to breastfeed, you know.' She took Nanette from me, unwrapping her. 'Lots of women are

168

bottle-feeding these days. Formula's got everything in it, and more.' She inspected the umbilical cord and seemed satisfied. Nan was weighed on portable scales, wrapped up again and handed back.

I felt nothing. I waited for the rush of love I knew was supposed to come, and I wondered what my mother had thought when she looked at me for the first time. A few days later, when I was still forgetting there was a baby in the next room and would only remember when the front of my dress became wet, I telephoned my aunt. She was delighted to hear she had a great-niece, said she would visit as soon as she was able, and, when I asked, she told me my mother had loved me from the moment she saw me. I believed then, but didn't say, that there had to be something wrong with me. My aunt never made it over from Norway; she died a week later.

I woke a little while ago to see Flora sitting beside me in her nightie. The sun was up and there was dribble on my cheek where I'd laid my head on the table to close my eyes for a few moments; it seems my little sleep had become a couple of hours.

'What are you doing?' Flora asked.

'I'm writing,' I said.

'But you're not a writer. Daddy's the writer.'

I paused, thinking about all the things I could tell her. 'Yes,' I said. 'Daddy's the writer. I just write letters.'

'In your sleep?'

'I was writing before I fell asleep.'

'Who do you write letters to?'
'Daddy.'
'What do you put in them?'
'All sorts of things.'
'Do you write about me?'
'I haven't got to the bit where you were born.'
'Does Daddy write back to you?'
'No.'
'Why not?'
'Because he hasn't read my letters yet.'
'Why?'
'They'll be waiting for him when he gets home.'

Flora huffed, as if the idea of writing anything was ridiculous and exhausting.

'Why don't you just talk to him?' she said.

Why don't I just talk to you? Because you aren't here, because even if you were you wouldn't listen.

Yours,
Ingrid

[Placed in *Egon Schiele* by Alessandra Comini, 1976]

23

When Flora returned from the beach, Nan was on her knees wiping the kitchen floor, wringing a sopping cloth into a bucket. The chairs had been lifted to stand amongst the books on the table, and Richard was washing something under the tap.

'What happened?' Flora said, standing in the doorway.

Nan looked up, pushed her hair out of her face with the back of her wrist. 'The washing machine leaked. Some kind of blockage.'

'Found the culprit,' Richard said. He placed the little soldier on the counter beside Nan's head.

'How on earth did that get in the wash?' Nan stretched her neck to look at it.

'It's mine.' Flora stepped forward and snatched it up. They stared at her. 'I found it,' she said, 'on the beach in Hadleigh,' and she backed away across the hall and into the bathroom. Behind Flora's eyes, Ingrid turned from the Swimming Pavilion, the towel over her arm and a book in her hand.

Through the gap in the door Flora heard Nan say, 'For goodness' sake,' her voice breaking.

'Come on,' Richard said. 'Up with you. Come on.' There was the sound of a chair being placed on the floor and Nan sniffing.

'I can't do it any more,' Nan said. 'I just can't do it.'

'You don't have to.'

Flora had to lean forward to catch what Richard was saying.

'If I don't, then who will?' Nan said.

'People will manage. You're not Gil's wife, and you're not Flora's mother. These aren't your roles, Nan.'

'Things would fall apart if I wasn't here.'

'So let them,' Richard said, his voice calm and soft. 'It's time to start your own life.'

Nan sobbed, a peculiar noise Flora couldn't remember ever hearing before, although it was muffled as if Nan was holding her head in her hands. Suddenly the bathroom door was pushed open, knocking Flora backwards so she had to catch hold of the sink, just managing to keep upright. Richard stared at her and then tugged off a length of toilet roll, and left, pulling the bathroom door shut behind him.

Flora tore off her own piece of toilet paper, wetted it and, looking in the mirror, scrubbed at the smudged mascara under her eyes. She stripped off her wet bikini, put on Ingrid's pink dress, which she had left hanging on the back of the door, and went into the kitchen.

'I thought we could have dinner in the bedroom,' Nan said as if nothing had happened. She glanced at what Flora was wearing and looked away without comment. 'Then Dad won't need to get out of bed.'

Gil was sitting up again, this time in his pyjamas, a pillow on his lap ready for his plate. The skin on his face which had taken the impact of the fall

172

was now like a plum at its peak of ripeness — stretched tight, as if with one touch it would split open. The other side was waxy and yellow. Nan had made a quiche Lorraine.

'That was the dress I bought for your mother,' Gil said, reaching out a hand to touch it as Flora sat again on her mother's side of the bed. 'Years ago.'

'I keep telling her to take it off,' Nan said.

Gil rubbed the fabric between his fingers.

'I've worn it before, Daddy. Loads of times.'

He looked at her. 'Have you? I never noticed.'

Nan served the food, picking the cucumber and tomatoes out of the salad for Flora and leaving a space around them on her plate. She chopped up Gil's food so he could eat it with a fork.

'Martin said he would call in sometime,' Nan said. 'See how you are.'

'Surprised he has the time with his golf and that bloody dog.'

'Martin has a dog?' Flora sat up. 'What sort?'

'Small and too yappy,' Gil said.

'There's a cupboard full of dog food in the kitchen,' Nan said.

'I was thinking of getting one as well,' Gil replied. 'A bloody big dog. I might call her Barbara — or no, wait, Shirley.' Gil laughed.

'How about Charlotte?' Richard said.

'Or Simone?' Flora said.

'Carson?' Gil said.

Nan rolled her eyes.

'Harper?' Flora asked.

'Yes, Harper. Definitely Harper,' Gil said, laughing.

173

'But you don't like dogs,' Nan said, watching Flora slice between the quiche's egg mixture and the pastry.

'You're not really going to get one, are you?' Flora said.

Gil leaned forward to pat her hand, still laughing. 'Sorry, Flo.'

She scraped off the eggy filling and pushed the pastry to the side of her plate. She could sense Nan's disapproval without having to look up.

'So, you work in a bookshop,' Gil said to Richard. 'Second-hand?'

'New, I'm afraid. It's just temporary, until something better comes along.'

'What kind of temporary job lasts two years?' Flora said.

'I am surprised,' Gil said. 'My youngest daughter being courted by a bookseller. It's not often we see her holding a book unless it has drawings in it. There was a time when Flo was a great reader.'

'We're not courting!' Flora snapped, and then under her breath, 'It's Nan you should be asking about that.'

'Although I'm not exactly sure what I'm looking for,' Richard said. 'Teaching perhaps. Or maybe I'll do a bit of travelling first.'

Flora stabbed a piece of cucumber with her fork.

'A very good idea,' Gil said. 'Don't let yourself get side-tracked by relationships or having children.'

'Daddy!' Flora said.

Richard looked flustered, but Gil continued,

174

'Give yourself some time to work it out. There's no need to settle down too young. How old are you? Twenty-two, twenty-three?'

'Twenty-nine.'

'Ah,' Gil said.

Flora sliced through the cucumber flesh in one smooth motion.

'I called the hospital about your book,' Nan said. 'I spoke to someone in A&E and they put me through to the ward, and then I talked to someone in charge of ambulances and they suggested I call the lost property office. But when I rang again the woman on the switchboard said they didn't have a lost property office. No book, I'm afraid.'

'Perhaps it got left on the beach,' Flora said. She looked at Gil, whose eyes were watering. He blinked and the tears were sucked back in.

'I'll check with Viv,' Nan said. 'Maybe someone handed it in at the bookshop. But you've got plenty to be going on with here, haven't you?' Her voice had taken on that sing-song tone of patronizing encouragement.

'If I don't go soon, this house will be more paper than wood.'

'Daddy,' Flora said, 'don't say that.'

'What?'

'About going soon.' She put her knife and fork on top of her pastry — a child's trick of hiding the food she didn't want to eat.

'In fact,' Gil said, glancing between Nan and Flora, 'there's something I've been talking to Richard about.'

Richard shuffled on his seat, looked down.

'I've asked him to burn the books.'

Nan's head jerked, a mouthful of food in her cheek.

'After I'm dead,' Gil said. 'Whenever that may be.' He smiled at Flora.

Nan swallowed. 'Which books? What do you mean?'

'All the books in the house,' Gil said.

'And you've agreed?' Flora said to Richard accusingly. He didn't answer.

'You girls aren't interested in them,' Gil said. 'The collection has got out of hand. I know it's something your mother would have wanted.'

'Mum! How do you know what Mum wants?' Flora kneeled up on the bed, her plate tipping, the quiche crust sliding off.

'But I thought you loved them,' Nan said.

'Why don't you sell them back to Viv?' Flora shifted on the bed, unaware that her knee was resting on the pastry. 'Or give them to her? Viv would take them, wouldn't she, Nan?'

Gil put his hand on Flora's arm and she sat down.

'You're sure?' Nan said.

'Absolutely fucking sure.' Gil put his fork on top of his uneaten dinner.

176

24

Dear Gil,

Jonathan warned me not to go into your writing room because I might find things I wouldn't like. When I raised my eyebrows, he said, 'You know, scrappy bits of paper with bad words written on them, screwed-up pages with everything crossed out, first drafts. Apparently first drafts are always ugly.' We laughed. We were walking over the heath that first summer, the gorse flowers fading to a paper-yellow, the smell of coconut disappearing on the wind that blew in from the sea. Jonathan said you needed to keep your room separate from the house and the people who visited. It was a place for serious writing and thinking.

Once, when I was newly pregnant with Nan, I woke in the night without you beside me. I went outside and looked through the window in the door of your room and saw you resting your head on top of your typewriter. I tapped on the pane but you didn't move. I wasn't sure if you were asleep. In the morning you were back beside me and you pulled me to you and made me promise that if you were ever missing from our bed I mustn't come to find you. I laughed and you said, 'I'm deadly serious, Ingrid. Everyone needs a place to escape to, even if it's

177

only inside their head.'

'I'll promise,' I said, 'if you promise me the same.'

We were lying face-to-face, separated only by the paisley curl of our baby inside me. Awkwardly you held out your right hand and we shook on it. Do you remember?

And there was the time, years later, in the middle of the argument where the teapot got smashed, when you shouted that I wasn't allowed in your room because I was too fucking nosy and asked too many fucking questions. 'How's it going? How many words today? Thought of a title yet?' And you accused me of reading your pages when you were out, of snooping and checking up on you, of dripping my wet hair on to your words when they were still spooling out from your typewriter. It was fucking inhibiting, you said, and the reason you stayed in your writing room was no longer to write, but because you needed to fucking protect your intellectual property.

But the reason I wasn't allowed in there wasn't any of these, was it, Gil?

4th August 1977: The first time since Nan had been born that I'd gone further than Spanish Green's village shop. I'd saved the money for the bus and the train fare a few pence at a time from the housekeeping you gave me, hiding it away in an empty custard-powder box. I took Nan (three months and four days old) in the Silver Cross pram, and I was more proud of that baby carriage than I was of the baby. I'd bought it, mail order, with the little bit of money my aunt had left me. It was a shiny black boat on high white wheels. There was a satisfying pop when I pressed the cover in place, a firm click when the arm mechanism of the hood was locked, and a small bounce from the suspension when I walked. I put lipstick and mascara on for the first time in five months, my back was straight and my head up. I wore my platform sandals, a pair of flared patterned trousers with a comfortable elasticated waist, and a 1940s blouse with a floppy bow at the neck which I'd found at the village-hall jumble sale. I was ready for London. I pushed the pram down the road to the bus stop and let Mrs Allen coo over the baby, tell me how glamorous I looked, and ask whether I was off somewhere exciting.

'To see my best friend, Louise,' I said.

The bus driver helped me on with the pram and the other passengers smiled and didn't mind that we were blocking the aisle. At the train station I stood on the platform as the 9.37 came in, and realized, with the same feeling as if I'd turned up a day late for a school exam, that the pram wouldn't fit through the carriage door. I contemplated leaving it and Nan on the platform and stepping on to the train without her, but Nan and I, and the Silver Cross, spent the two-hour journey bumping around in the guard's van amongst the bicycles, guitar cases and oversized boxes. As the train pulled out of the station, Nan began to cry. I jogged the pram, pushed it to and fro, and picked her up. She cried harder, her eyes crimped shut, face red and

179

mouth open. She was normally a good baby, contented. Through Winchester and Basingstoke I paced up and down the dirty swaying van, moving her from one shoulder to the other, patting and stroking. She didn't stop wailing. At Woking I changed her nappy and at Clapham Junction, in front of a group of Boy Scouts with bikes, I undid my blouse and hefted one of my enormous breasts out from my bra. I saw it anew — a huge white udder, larger than Nan's head. She was having none of it, she carried on crying, her little body tensed and her head thrown back. The boys stared at me as I cried with her, wiping under my eyes, my fingers black with smudged mascara. When the train pulled into Waterloo we were both sobbing.

Louise met me on the platform. Her hair had been set and she wore a camel-coloured suit, buttons up the front of the jacket, high heels. Her eyebrows had been plucked and her bosoms were tiny.

'My God, Ingrid,' she said, looking me up and down, hair bouncing. 'What the bloody hell happened?'

'I've had a baby, that's what!' I shouted at her, rocking the pram and making Nan bawl louder.

'I can see that.' She glanced inside and with a sharp 'Come on, then' strode off. I followed on behind, looking sadly at her neat bottom in her fitted skirt.

She'd kept the flat on after I left, and when we'd negotiated the Underground, the narrow street door, and the stairs up to the third floor, Nan was still crying. The smell, the light and the furniture were the same, and a wave of nostalgia washed over me for the other life I could have had. I didn't let it show. Louise had thrown a patterned cloth over the sofa, a new rug was hiding the ripped lino, and she'd put a vase of flowers in the centre of the table. She lit a cigarette.

'I thought we could go out for lunch,' she said over the noise of Nan mewling. 'I reserved a table at Chez Alain.'

I took my hand from inside my blouse and stared at her.

'Don't worry,' she said, smiling. 'My treat.'

'With the baby?'

'I've got a job, research assistant at the House of Commons. I started last month. It's amazing.' She took a lipstick out of her handbag and applied it, looking in the mirror over the gas fire.

'But I thought you were going travelling.' I lifted my breast out of my bra and latched Nan's whimpering mouth on to my leaking nipple, and finally her noise changed to wet sucking.

'This opportunity came up and it was too good to miss.' Louise's voice distorted as she stretched her lips. There was a tightness in my chest at the memory of the rebuke she'd given me when I'd gone back on our plans. 'I bet you haven't been to a restaurant in weeks,' she said. 'It'll do you good.' Her reflection in the mirror held the lipstick out to me. I shook my head.

'I don't know. It depends if Nan falls asleep,' I said.

Louise smacked her lips together. 'If she doesn't, we can stick her in the bedroom, she won't disturb the neighbours there.' She sat at the little square table where we used to eat our bean and potato stews, and tapped her cigarette against an ashtray.

'I can't leave her here on her own.'

She paused and said, 'No, silly me, of course not. We'll take her with us. Come on.'

With Nan asleep, we renegotiated the stairs and walked to Chez Alain, bumping the Silver Cross up the steps.

'Madam,' the French maitre d' said before we were even inside, 'we don't allow children in the restaurant.'

'But I've reserved a table,' Louise said.

'I'm sorry.' He didn't look apologetic. 'It will disturb our diners.'

'That's ridiculous. I have a reservation and I would like some lunch.'

Nan was grizzling. I shook the pram and she began to cry. I could feel the sweet sting of my let-down reflex and the milk beginning to flow. The man shrugged, already turning away.

Louise and I sat on the bench in St George's Gardens where I'd read your books only fourteen months previously. (How could so much have changed?) She tore into the pork pie we'd bought from Levitt's. I shifted away, embarrassed to be feeding Nan in public, bending forward, trying to release my breast at the same time as fitting Nan's head under my blouse.

'For God's sake, Ingrid,' Louise said, her mouth crammed with pastry and pork. 'Just get it out. What does it matter if anyone sees? You

182

never used to be such a prude.'

I could feel those old tears stinging my eyes. It took two hands to get Nan latched on. 'Tell me about your job,' I said.

She told me how she'd seen Barbara Castle's back as the MP walked along a corridor in the House of Commons, and how when Parliament reconvened after the summer she was going to find the courage to introduce herself. Louise was excited, full of life and London. She held the pork pie up to my mouth so I could eat and keep Nan in place. I lunged and took a bite, fatty pastry spilling over my lips. Louise poked a piece back into my mouth with her finger and we smiled, and I was dismayed to feel my eyes watering again.

'So, motherhood isn't all you thought it'd be?' she said, finishing the pie, sucking the grease from her fingers.

'I'm loving it. It's wonderful.' I swiped my cheek against my shoulder. She wanted to say I told you so and I wasn't going to let her.

'And your husband? He's wonderful too, I suppose?'

'Yes, of course. He adores Nan. He's writing every day, his next novel will be finished soon.'

'And life in the sticks?' She snorted.

'You have no idea what my life is like, Louise, so how can you judge it?' I raised my voice and Nan twitched. She had come off my nipple and fallen asleep but I didn't want to risk waking her again.

'I can imagine.' Louise crossed her legs — in tan tights although it was summer — and folded her arms. 'You're unhappy, you regret what you've done, but now you're stuck. You didn't get your degree and you're financially dependent on a man. You have a baby, but no money and nowhere to go. You live in the back of beyond and you have nothing to fill your time or your mind except nappies and breastfeeding.'

I shook my head, starting to interrupt, but Louise hadn't finished: 'Your husband spends his time working on some fiction you don't believe will sell. When the baby pops off the boob you cry yourself to sleep and then get up the next day and do the whole thing again.'

'How dare you!' I stood up and hefted Nan to my shoulder, feeling a trickle of milk run down my stomach under my blouse. 'You know nothing about what it's like to be a wife and mother. Nothing.'

'And I don't want to,' Louise said, and then more calmly, 'I can help you.' She put her hand on my arm. 'If you want to leave him, I could help now, with the money.'

I pulled away from her. 'I don't think so.' I put Nan in the pram, not bothering to tuck her in. She'd had enough food and was floppy with sleep.

'Just think about it.' Louise stood up too.

'I have to go.' I released the pram's brake. 'Thank you for . . . ' I was unsure. 'The pork pie,' I said, and wheeled Nan out of the park.

I spent half an hour in the ladies' toilet at the railway station, sitting in a cubicle to compose myself before the train came. I had to keep the door ajar to make sure no one walked off with

184

that damned pram. The station was crowded with youths with spiky hair and rings in their noses, and girls in jeans so tight the fabric might have been sprayed on. No one in London was wearing patterned flares or platform shoes. The punks lounged over the public benches, smoking, pushing each other and laughing. When I walked past one of the girls, her eyes rimmed in black and her face pasty, she opened her mouth and stuck out her thick pink tongue, curling it over her bottom lip to touch her chin. I realized she was about twenty-one, the same age as me.

I tried to call you from a phone box outside the station, parking the pram up against the grimy windows so I could see the baby, but terrified of the trouble I'd be in if someone were to run off with her. London was too crowded, too noisy, too dirty; it scared me.

It was dark when I got off the bus beside the village shop. Nan had slept all the way in the guard's van, on the ferry, and on the bus while I dozed. The smell of the sea, the pitch-blackness, the beautiful silence after the bus had pulled away, made me determined to prove Louise wrong. I would try harder to be happy. I was home. Nan and I took a detour through the car park to the edge of the beach so I could hear the sea shushing against the sand, and further away a hollow gulping as the water bumped against rock. I would have liked to walk along the beach and up the chine, but not even a Silver Cross could have coped with sand.

Your car was on the drive and there was a light on in the house when I arrived home. I pulled the pram backwards up the three steps and parked it, with Nan still inside, at the end of the veranda. The front door was unlocked and, when I opened it, music was coming from the sitting room, where a light shone.

'Hello!' I called out. 'We're home!' The music finished, and there was the fuzz and click from the end of an album. I pushed the door open — the room was empty. I lifted the needle and stopped the turntable. The lights were off in the bedroom, but when I put my head in the door I saw that the bedcovers were still untidy from where I'd left them unmade that morning. I went up the hall. I don't know why I felt the need to check everywhere, but I looked in the spare room too, now the nursery. Nothing had changed. I stood in the kitchen doorway. No one was there either, but the air smelled of hot oil and old food. The silence in the house was thick and it felt like there was somewhere else I hadn't looked.

When I'd first arrived at the Swimming Pavilion, you and everyone else in the village didn't lock their doors. But when the holiday park was built, with its prefabricated chalets and offer of cheap holidays by the coast, the permanent residents of Spanish Green began to use their keys at night. I knew you wouldn't have left our front door open without good reason.

I'd walked into the hall and was facing the bathroom, also empty, when I heard the noise: similar but lower in tone to the cry of a young

186

seagull; the sound of an animal, made every minute or so, repetitive, insistent. I listened. It was coming from outside the house. I returned to the veranda, where the sound was louder. I checked on the sleeping Nan and stepped into the garden. There was a light on in your writing room, and I followed the cry along the path of bent grass. I thought a bird must have flown in and become trapped. I took two steps up to look through the window. The paraffin lamp was burning, casting a yellow light across your writing table and a small patch of floor, leaving the rest of the space in shadow. I pressed my nose to the glass.

It took me a while to make sense of the shapes: at the end of the room I saw you, kneeling on the floor in front of the bed, your spine curving away from me so I could see your highlighted vertebrae, throwing triangular shadows as if you were a lizard or dinosaur. At first I thought you were bending forward to pray. I could see the crack of your bottom and the soles of your feet, one crossed over the other. Under your knees, for comfort I supposed, was a pillow from the bed. The birdlike cry came again and you bobbed your head. I tried to understand what I was seeing even while I was thinking, Gil can't be praying, he doesn't believe in anything.

Do you know that drawing? Look at it one way and you see an old crone with a hooked nose; look again and you see a beautiful girl in a fur coat with a feather in her hair. Finally, I saw the woman, spread-eagled on the velvet cover of the bed, your hands pushing her thighs open, her

187

calves and feet either side of your body. As I watched, she reached forward to put a hand on your head, guiding you, pulling your face into her. She lifted her own head, with light brown, short hair, and opened her eyes. Like Nan's when she was born, this woman's eyes were glassy, and although she looked straight at the window, she was lost in the moment and didn't see me. She opened her mouth to make the cry again, her body convulsing in rhythm to the sound she made.

Ingrid

[Placed in *We Are the People Our Parents Warned Us Against* by Nicholas von Hoffman, 1968]

25

At about five o'clock in the morning Flora gave up trying to get back to sleep. Nan was breathing steadily and deeply as Flora crept out of their bedroom. She took a towel from the bathroom, put her mother's dress over her head and went to the beach. The morning was fresh, mist lying low in the hollows, and the rising sun was obscured by a haze which forecast a beautiful day to come. The beach was empty when she swam to the buoy, the water as cold as ever, until it was time to come out and it became miraculously warmer than the air. As she strode on to the beach, a dog walker, a man she didn't recognize, stopped to stare.

'The nudist beach is that way,' he said, pointing along the coast.

Flora glared, picked up the dress and her towel, and slipped her feet into her flip-flops. Only when she was at the top of the chine did she put the dress back on.

She'd expected everyone to still be asleep, but when she went into the house Flora heard voices in the front bedroom. The bed was empty and Nan was crouching beside one of the carved legs, while Richard was lying on his back with his head under the frame, like a mechanic under the chassis of an old car.

'Shall I get a torch?' Nan said.

'Where's Daddy?' Flora said.

'He's in your bed, sleeping,' she replied without looking up, and to Richard, 'It might be screwed together.'

'What's going on?' Flora said.

'Richard's taking the bed apart.'

'Well, trying to.' His voice was muffled.

'You can't do that,' Flora said. 'Why would you want to do that?' She gripped one of the posts. Her fingers remembered the pathway of every vine as they spiralled up towards the pineapple finials, every curled leaf and closed bud. The oak was an oily black in the middle sections where centuries of fingers had grabbed, stroked and clung on. Hidden in the foliage on each post was a tiny animal: mouse, minnow, viper and wren. Flora liked to speculate about how the minnow, out of water, could have survived all this time. The tiny fish's mouth gaped, tilted upwards as if gulping for air, and when, as a child, she had dared to put her little finger in between the minnow's lips, the cavity was deeper than its full length. On the 2nd of July 1993 — a year after her mother was lost — Flora had marked the anniversary alone by dropping one of Annie's teeth into the yawning hole.

Nan took a deep breath. 'If the bed came in, we must be able to get it out.'

'You can't do this,' Flora said to Richard's legs and the back of Nan's head.

'I don't think it's that simple.' Richard moved further under the bed. 'A carpenter must have put it together in the room. There aren't any screws, it's proper dovetail joints.' He came out

190

from underneath, coughing. 'There's a lot of stuff under there — suitcases, more books.'

'Oh Lord,' Nan said. 'I'd forgotten about all of that.'

'Wait!' Flora shouted now to get their attention. 'This is Daddy's bed. You can't just take it apart. I'm going to talk to him.' She went to leave.

Nan caught hold of her sister's arm. 'Flora,' she said. 'There's a new bed coming, an adjustable hospital one.'

'Why would he need one of those? Have you asked him if that's what he wants?'

'Let him sleep.' Nan's grip tightened.

'Not if you're going to pull his belongings apart as soon as he's out of the room.' She yanked her arm free, wheeling it above her head. 'I'm sure he'll have something to say about this.'

Nan tried again to catch Flora's arm, as if that alone would pin her down, keep her silent. Flora turned sideways.

'Be quiet,' Nan hissed. 'You'll wake him.'

'What are you going to take next?' Flora yelled. 'The sofas? Or how about the paintings? Would you like one of the paintings too?' She marched to the windows which overlooked the sea. 'I'm sure they're here somewhere.' She pushed at the top half of a pile of books stacked against the wall, hardbacks and paperbacks scattering. Behind them was a small seascape in a deep frame. 'Here you are.' She yanked at the painting, but it was attached to the wall with mirror plates and didn't move. 'Sorry, Nan, it seems you can't have a painting unless Richard

191

wants to take it off with his fucking trusty screwdriver.'

'Flora,' Nan said, and came across the room. 'Stop this. Please.'

'Stop what? Stop what?' Flora was screaming.

'I've been trying to tell you for days. This isn't just about a sprained wrist and a black eye,' Nan shouted over her. Flora saw Richard's face, his mouth a thin straight line. 'You do realize that, don't you?'

'I have no idea what you're talking about.'

'He's dying.' Nan held her hands out as if ready to catch her sister. There was something inside Flora that refused to budge, a boulder that wouldn't roll.

'Who is?'

'For God's sake. Why must you make every conversation so difficult?' Nan had her palm across her forehead, and Richard had stepped away until he was backed up against one of the bedposts. A thread of cobweb clung to his hair above his left ear. And for a second Flora thought that Nan was talking about him.

'Because you never say what you mean!' Flora moved towards Nan, her head thrust forward, a bull about to charge.

'Our father is dying. He has pancreatic cancer!' Nan shouted, and gripped Flora by the shoulders. And in a reaction that was instinctive, animal, Flora lifted her hand, which had formed into a fist without her knowing it, and punched her sister in the chest. Nan cried out, buckled and fell back, at the same time as Richard leaped forward. 'Flora, Flora,' he said, trying to contain her, but she flailed her arms and hands, slapping and hitting until he ducked and moved away, out of her reach.

'No,' she said, sitting down. Through strands of hair stuck to her face by tears and snot she saw Richard with one hand over his mouth. On all fours Flora crawled over the books, their covers torn where they had been trodden on, her feet catching on the skirt of the dress, to Nan, who opened her arms and held her like a baby. And then she was aware of Richard, crouching beside them. He smelled of fabric conditioner and deodorant, colours too light to pin down.

'Please can the bed stay?' she said into Nan's chest. Nan didn't answer, but against her ear Flora heard and felt her sister's speeding heart slow and grow steady.

26

The Swimming Pavilion,
14th June 1992, 4.10 a.m.

Dear Gil,

On Friday, Flora's teacher phoned. She asked if I would 'come in for a quick chat on Monday'.

'What's it about?' I said, but thinking, What now? (Why is it I never imagine it will be good news?)

'I'd rather you and your husband came into school. It won't take long.'

I wanted to tell her that you won't be coming with me because you're not here and I don't know where you are, although I can imagine. But instead I said in my cheeriest voice, 'Of course, I'll catch the school bus with Flora on Monday.'

I'm no good at motherhood.

After I saw it wasn't writing you were doing at the end of the garden, after the crying and the packing, and the begging, you wrote me another letter. I didn't keep this one, but it was short and I remember it.

Ingrid,

I know I've blown it. I know that nothing will undo what I have done. I am a stupid fucker. A stupid fucker who loves you.

Please don't leave me.

Gil

194

You left it, the letter, on top of a large flat cardboard box which you'd placed on the bed. Inside the box was a dress: layers of long pink chiffon below a sleeveless bodice sewn with silver beads and sequins, antique, expensive. Without thinking I took it out and held it up to me, running my fingers against the fabric, and then, suddenly remembering, shoved it back in the box. I've never worn the dress, but I did hang it in the wardrobe because I couldn't ever quite bear to throw it away.

Despite the letter and the dress I wouldn't let you sleep in the house. Every evening you said goodnight to Nan and you looked at me with your sad eyes, and I made you leave for your writing room. I wanted you to lie in the bed where (literally) you ate the cake you wanted. At night the house belonged to me and our daughter. At night it would go like this (it still goes like this): I try to stay up as late as possible but by 10.15 p.m. my eyes are aching in their sockets and it's impossible to resist laying my head on the kitchen table or falling asleep where I sit, so I get ready for bed. I stretch out under the bedcover and sink into sleep. At 2.35 a.m. by the numbers on the digital alarm clock, I am awake. There isn't a period of waking; I am just awake. I hope that if I lie motionless with my eyes shut, sleep will find me again. At 2.56 a.m. my eyes are dry and scratchy and my butterfly mind is flitting from one monstrous problem to the next, unable to settle or resolve anything. At 3.12 a.m. I am angry with myself, with sleep, with the girls, with you. I kick the mattress and push my fingers into my closed eyes until they might burst. I sit up, drop my chin forward on to my chest and stay like that until 3.21 a.m. when I pull the cover from the bed and stand at the window to look at your writing room. There is never a light on, of course. If it's very cold I pace from the sitting room to the kitchen, or more recently I wrap myself up and sit at the veranda table and write to you.

At 4.33 a.m. the fear that there won't be any more sleep until the evening kicks in. I feel sick at the thought that soon the day will start and I will have to get Nan and Flora up, make them breakfast and packed lunches, search for stray plimsolls and money for a school trip, and for the whole day I'll have to stay awake to stand the smallest chance of sleeping through the night. At 5 a.m. I give up and go for a swim.

There were months of me moving about the house like a nervous horse ready to bolt, and you being too nice, falsely bright, like a stable-hand with a bridle and bit held ready behind your back. Our conversations were inconsequential, about what to have for dinner and when you could drive me into Hadleigh to buy food if I missed the bus. We didn't touch each other, we didn't kiss, I wouldn't let you. I thought about leaving, often. Once or twice I got as far as dialling Louise's number but put the phone down before she answered. Another time, I packed that blue suitcase but couldn't work out how to carry it together with all the things Nan needed, as well as push the Silver Cross. So I unpacked it and put the clothes away.

And I thought about leaving without her.

Several times that summer, people turned up uninvited (even by Jonathan) for the sunshine and the beach, to camp in the grass like the year before. You avoided them, but I was grateful for their company, and if I'm honest I was grateful because those girls in long skirts and bare feet loved Nan. One day, I came across a girl — a woman (she must have been ten years older than me) breastfeeding her. The woman was topless, sitting on a mat with her friends, smiling down as our daughter fastened to her nipple. At the time I couldn't work out how she was able to do it, how she had the milk, but later I understood. When she saw me the woman's face and chest flushed, she slipped a finger into the side of Nan's mouth, unlatched her and held the bawling baby out to me, but I shook my head and sat beside her. She smiled again and guided Nan's gummy mouth back to her nipple.

★　★　★

And then Jonathan came to stay.

He'd been down for a day or two after Nan was born, but now he arrived with a toy bear that growled when it was upturned, two bottles of Kilbeggan, and a round of Gubbeen for me.

We were both so thankful for his arrival that we moved from our defensive positions, and on his first evening the three of us stayed up late, passing the baby in the opposite direction to the whiskey and the cheese.

197

'Smells like the bog,' you said when I unwrapped it.

'I camped on the farm where they make it and helped with the milking,' Jonathan said.

'Jonathan — the world's best lay-abed — got up to milk the cows?' I said, my mouth full of soft yellow cheese and cracker.

'Needs must when you're a travel writer.' He laughed and then stopped. 'A terrible thing happened while I was there.' We watched his face. His eyes shifted away from ours and momentarily he pressed his hand against his mouth. 'A child fell in the bog and was lost.'

'Oh God,' I said.

'Lost?' you said, holding Nan tighter. 'How the hell do you lose a child in a bog?'

'Her brother dared her to cross it. She sank and he couldn't pull her out.'

'Oh God,' you said. 'How old was she?'

'Six. Her brother ran to the dairy and a group of us ran back with him, but he couldn't remember the exact place where she went in, and we found nothing. Nothing. The whole village came out to search.'

'And you didn't find her?' I said.

'She was gone,' Jonathan said.

'Not even a body to bury? I can't imagine anything worse.'

We were silent until you said, 'Of course that isn't the worst thing. Finding the body is surely more terrible, more absolute. With a body there is no possibility of hope.'

'I'm telling you,' Jonathan said, 'the child was gone.'

198

'Maybe she was,' you said, 'or perhaps one day she'll come walking back into Bally-whatever saying she bumped her head, forgot who she was and wandered off. Without the body her parents are free to imagine, to hope for anything.'

'But maybe they'll be hoping for ever,' Jonathan said. 'What kind of life would that be? You can't exist like that, with not knowing.'

'It's about believing two opposing ideas in your head at the same time: hope and grief. Human beings do it all the time with religion — the flesh and the spirit — you know that. Imagination and reality.'

'That old Catholic upbringing rears its head again,' Jonathan said. 'Pass the whiskey, I need cheering up.'

The two of you carried on drinking and talking until Nan fell asleep, and I lay on the sofa with my head resting in Jonathan's lap and shut my eyes to listen as I drifted in and out.

'I bumped into Louise when I was in London,' Jonathan said.

'Ingrid's Louise?' you said. 'I haven't seen her since the wedding.'

I heard more whiskey glugging, the chink of glass on glass.

'I took her out to dinner.'

'Really?'

'Well, OK, she took me out to dinner.'

'She's still into women's lib?' Your voice was less distinct; you must have got up, turned away from us.

'I suppose. She did pay.'

'And you paid her back in kind, did you?'

199

'The kind where you only leave a deposit? No, I'm not her type.'

There was a click as you switched on the record player and a shuffle while you put an album on the turntable. The music started, the needle finding the beginning of a track. Wedged on the opposite sofa, Nan gave a single squawk and you turned it down.

'If there was an offer on the table I'd be very happy to carry out a thorough audit of her fixed assets,' you said quietly.

'I'm sure you'd depreciate them.'

'Let's say there would be a definite upward movement of goods and services.' You both sniggered like schoolboys and Jonathan's leg muscles twitched under my head.

'So, how's family life?' Jonathan said.

'Good, fine.' You were unconvincing.

'Because I have to say there's been a bit of an atmosphere.'

'Has there?' You sounded defensive.

'You're missing being the bachelor about town, is it?'

'I've finished with all that,' you said more loudly, and I wondered if you'd guessed I was listening.

'Really? I didn't think you took your marriage vows so seriously. You know, I never imagined you would settle to life in the country. Wasn't this place meant to be somewhere for writing and parties? I thought you'd escaped for good when your father died.'

'What do you mean? What's Ingrid been saying?'

'I haven't spoken to Ingrid,' Jonathan said. There was a pause. Perhaps you both looked at me, trying to decide if I really was asleep. 'Don't be cruel to her, Gil. She deserves better. If you're going to fuck around, let her go.' You were both silent, drinking, until Jonathan said, 'I didn't think being barefoot and pregnant would be Ingrid's thing either. I thought she wanted something more.'

'I saved her,' you said without a trace of irony.

'What the hell from?'

'A sad and lonely life.'

'Bloody hell, Gil. I think you really believe that.' If you replied I didn't hear. 'Well,' he continued, 'you'd better write faster. Get the next book written before she pushes out another sprog.'

'That's the plan,' you said, and yawned. 'I've got to go to bed. I can't keep up with your late-night drinking now I'm a family man.' I heard you go down the hall towards the bathroom.

Over my head Jonathan swilled the whiskey in his glass and knocked it back. I smelled the fumes on his breath as he bent over me. Moments passed and then he whispered, 'Ingrid.' His fingers moved the strands of hair from my face and stroked my cheek.

I opened my eyes and looked up at him. 'In Norway,' I said, 'when a person drowns you're meant to go out in a rowing boat with a cockerel.'

'Oh yes?'

'When the boat is over the body, the cockerel

201

is supposed to crow. And then you can retrieve it so they can be properly buried.'

I don't know what Jonathan would have said — would he have preferred to know or to live with hope? — because we heard you pad back along the hallway from the bathroom and I sat up.

'Come on, sleepy head, time for bed,' you said to me. You came forward and took my hand as if the past few months had never happened; it was the first time we'd touched in weeks. You didn't look at Jonathan as you pulled me off his lap and led me into the bedroom.

Although I was still breastfeeding Nan, and Jonathan received the occasional cheque from his travel writing, with three of us to feed and keep in whiskey, money was always an issue. We lived off vegetables and lentils, and sometimes I bought the remains of a fisherman's catch, going cheap. I thought it was this that made me sick one morning, but when I threw up a second time, I knew. You'd always insisted on using the withdrawal method for our contraception (some Catholic thing, I supposed). I should have been firmer, I should've insisted on taking the pill, should've taken it without you knowing. I'd already been dreaming of when Nan was older, of the places I could go, the things I could see, even if you didn't come with me. The walls of the Swimming Pavilion were closing in. And when you caught me kneeling beside the toilet I didn't need to explain.

'The second of six, remember?' you said when we were all in the kitchen. You hugged me and slapped Jonathan on the back.

'We can't afford it,' I said.

'Of course we can.'

'I can't scrimp and save any more.'

'I'll get a job. It'll be fine.'

Jonathan laughed, stopping when he saw your face.

'What?' you said. 'You think I can't?'

'What kind of job?' Jonathan said.

'I don't know.' You dismissed the question with a wave of your hand; nothing was going to spoil this news. 'Something in Hadleigh — fisherman, baker, candlestick maker, behind the bar with Martin.'

Jonathan rolled his eyes. He thought it was funny.

'Talking of Martin,' you said. 'A celebration is called for, I think.' You rubbed your hands together. 'A lunchtime drink?'

'You finished the whiskey last night,' I said.

'How about that fine public house up the road? The one Martin opened up about' — you looked at your watch — 'an hour ago?'

'I don't think that's a good idea,' I said.

'Oh, come on. What the hell is wrong with both of you?'

'We don't have enough money to go to the pub!' I was shouting. 'We need more milk, more washing powder, more food.'

'Don't be such a spoilsport, Ingrid. I promise you it'll be fine.' You swept me up in your arms and waltzed me around the kitchen, bent me

203

over backwards and kissed me with Jonathan watching.

We walked up the road to the Royal Oak, you carrying Nan, and Jonathan and I trailing behind.

There were several people in the pub: that farmer and his wife (the ones whose barn burned down in the lightning storm); Joe Warren, who'd now lost all that weight; Mrs Passerini, with her yellow fingers, perched on her usual stool at the end of the bar; a couple of cattle-feed reps in their suits having a lunch-time pint; and of course Martin serving the drinks.

'Gil,' he said, smiling and holding his hand out. 'Long time no see.'

Mrs Passerini got down shakily from her stool, put her cigarette in her mouth and lifted Nan out of your arms. She didn't cry, just kicked her fat legs in her little white tights, and gurgled.

'I've got an announcement, Martin,' you said. 'Pass me a piece of cutlery.' You stood at the bar and took the long-handled spoon out from the pickled-egg jar and chinked it against the glass. The pub quietened.

'Ladies and gentlemen,' you said, 'we're here to celebrate that the Colemans are bringing the average age of this village down to sixty. My beautiful wife, Ingrid' — you waved me over and pulled me in to your side — 'is having another baby!'

I was passed around like Nan — hugged by beery neighbours, my stomach stroked by their wives — and you didn't have to buy a single

204

drink. At two thirty in the afternoon I left with Nan, and Martin locked the door behind us. You hadn't asked him about a job.

It was cold that January, and while I waited for you and Jonathan to return I got into bed with Nan to keep warm. When the evening arrived and neither of you had come home, I put the oven on, keeping the door open to warm the room, and cooked and mashed some carrots. After Nan fell asleep I ate the last of the bread, sitting alone at the kitchen table. I went to bed and heard the front door open and someone go into Nan's room, the spare bed creaking up against the adjoining wall. I rapped my knuckles on it, and Jonathan returned the knock. I lay in the dark and stared at the nearest bedpost rising up and disappearing into the shadowy ceiling, my fingers threaded together across my stomach. I was numb. I heard you and a crowd of people come back long after closing time. Your celebrations continued in the kitchen.

I must have slept because when I woke in pain in the dawn you were snoring beside me and I hadn't noticed you come to bed. The sheet under me and my legs were red and sticky with blood. In the kitchen I leaned over the back of a chair, breathing in through my nose, out through my mouth. When the cramp passed the only sensations I felt (facts and truth, remember) were relief and guilt.

I went to the toilet, and as I flushed our second baby away I listed all the untelling I would have to do that day, starting with you, Gil,

205

and afterwards Jonathan, and then our neighbours. And I worried, considering the number of
empty bottles in the kitchen, none of which
you'd have paid for, whether they would believe
I'd ever been pregnant.

Ingrid

[Placed in *Money* by Martin Amis, 1984]

27

In the afternoon, Flora sat opposite her father on the veranda. It was still warm and the bees droned in the honeysuckle that her mother had planted and now ran wild over the side of the house. She and Nan had excavated one of the high-backed armchairs from the sitting room, placed it in a strip of sunshine and tucked Gil into it with a blanket. The last time she was home he had just been her father, a reclusive eccentric who was always there in the Swimming Pavilion or his writing room, even when she wasn't thinking about him. Now, he was an old man who was dying. She hadn't been able to discuss her new knowledge with him, she wasn't even sure it was new — perhaps she had known as soon as she'd seen him struggling out of the car two days ago.

After the punch, Flora had apologized over and over to Nan. The sisters sat side by side on Gil's bedroom floor, and Flora learned that their father's early symptoms of indigestion and sickness had been ignored, firstly by himself, and then by his GP, until it was too late. There had been some treatment offered which Gil had refused, saying it would only delay the inevitable, and insisting on coming home as soon as he was able.

From the veranda they watched the sparrows pecking at the crumbs of toast Nan had thrown out, taking turns with a dust bath in a dip they had made in front of the gorse bushes, and then Flora watched Gil sleeping, his eyeballs moving under his closed lids like a dreaming dog's. She took her sketchpad from under her chair and got out a charcoal pencil, putty rubber and a small piece of rag that she kept wedged in between the sheets. The smell of drawing was cream, a clotted and buttery yellow.

She moved into the shade to stop the glare coming off the blank page and drew her father, his head tipped against the wing of the chair, his right hand resting in his lap, the other in the sling, his good cheekbone polished to a knuckle by the clear light reflected off the sea. With the rag she moved the charcoal across the page, lifting it with the rubber, smudging it with the tip of a wet finger.

'Have you had an argument with your young man?'

Flora looked up. She'd thought he was still sleeping.

'Not really.' The angle of his head had changed and she redrew the line that ran from his temple past the hollow of his cheek to under his chin.

'It's not worth it,' Gil said.

'What isn't?'

'Upsetting someone you love.'

Flora glanced up. 'Who said I loved him?'

'You never know when you'll see them for the last time.'

Flora stared at her drawing, tore it out of the pad and screwed it up.

She began again, a series of dashes, shadows

and lines, the bones in Gil's head no different from the chair's structure. She liked to see how much could be left out of a drawing while keeping it recognizably human. People's brains always wanted to fill in the gaps — imagine a nose where there was only a hint of a nostril, or the fully formed whorl of an ear where she drew a short coil. Everyone saw a different picture. Flora's fingers were grimed with black and there was dirt under her nails. The man on the paper didn't look like her father: he was healthy and young, and he would live for ever. She ripped this page out too and tore it in half.

'Aren't you going to show me?' Gil said.

'They're rubbish. I can't do it any more.' She leaned forward in her chair, picking at the rinds under her nails. 'Daddy?' she started, but when her father looked up she didn't know which question she wanted to ask — whether he was certain he had seen Ingrid in Hadleigh, what it felt like to know he was dying, or why he really wanted all the books burned. Instead she said, 'Did I tell you that it rained fish the other day, when I was driving here in Richard's car? They were bouncing off the roof and the bonnet.'

'I don't know why you think you can't draw any more, Flo. It seems to me you did a bloody good drawing in *Queer Fish*.' Her father winked.

She looked through her sketchbook: Nan hanging out the washing, Martin in his slippers reading the paper, Richard sleeping, his glasses skewed on his face.

After a few minutes Gil said, 'There's something I wanted to ask you.'

'What?' Flora said.

'Bring your chair closer.'

Without standing, she shuffled her chair towards his.

'Closer,' he said. She moved until the arms of their chairs were touching. Behind him some optical illusion made the sea appear higher than the land, as if it were being sucked away in the presentiment of something momentous. 'It's always been you and me, Flo, hasn't it? I should have let your sister in more, and your mother of course. But that's done now. There's something I want you to do for me.'

'What is it? I'll do anything you want, Daddy.' She sought his hand from under the blanket.

'I want you to get me a baby's boot. One of those knitted ones.'

Flora pulled her hand away. 'A what?' she said.

'And it must be blue. Blue wool. I don't need a pair, just one will do. I wondered if Nan might have them at the hospital. I can't ask her myself, she'll think I've gone mad.'

'Christ, Daddy.' Flora laughed. 'I thought you were going to ask for something important. You nearly made my heart flip.'

'It is important. It's very important. I need it, Flora.' Gil's face didn't change.

'Come off it, Daddy. You can let me in on the joke now. What do you need it for? A one-legged baby?'

He didn't answer.

'You're serious, aren't you?' Flora stopped smiling.

'Completely.'

210

'God, Daddy. What is all this?'

'I'm going to bury it.'

'What?' Flora said again. 'Why?'

'It's just something your mother . . . ' He stopped mid-sentence as if checking his words. 'So you won't ask Nan?'

'I don't understand.'

'Forget I ever asked. Forget it.' Gil tucked his hand back beneath the blanket, rested his head against the wing of his chair and said something under his breath.

'What?' Flora said. He didn't repeat it, but it may have been, 'Baby shoes, never worn.'

★   ★   ★

Later, when Gil had gone inside, Flora picked up her torn drawings and walked to the end of the garden with a box of matches and burned each page, letting the black flakes float into the nettles.

28

The Swimming Pavilion,
16th June 1992, 4.35 a.m.

Dear Gil,

Yesterday, before the morning bell, Flora's teacher met me in her classroom. She showed me a letter and asked me whether I'd written it:

Dear Mrs Layland,
It is with my deepest regrets that I write to tell you Flora was unable to come into school yesterday. Her father came home to spend some time with his daughter and that is the reason she didn't come in. I also write to let you know that he is still home and so Flo might not be in in the future.
Yours sincerely,
Ingrid Coleman

I cried in front of Flora's teacher, not because the letter was so clearly written by a desperate child, and not because Flora is missing school or lying, although that's what Mrs Layland thought, but because she doesn't need me.

On the 9th of February 1978 you drove me to the check-up appointment you'd made with my doctor. I didn't want to go: what was there to learn? I'd been pregnant and now I wasn't. You'd barely spoken after I'd woken you that morning.

212

I thought I heard you crying in the bathroom, but the noise stopped when I rattled the door handle and called your name, and when you came out you sat in the kitchen, brooding over a cup of coffee.

Jonathan stayed a week longer, but in the end I don't think he could stand the melancholic atmosphere that settled over the house. I was sad to see him go, although not having him around was one less thing to think about.

At the surgery you remained in the waiting room until the examination was over and Dr Burnett called you in.

'I'm pleased to say everything is where it should be.' The doctor addressed you. You didn't laugh and he continued: 'Miscarriage this early is much more common than you'd think. And Mrs Coleman is only . . . ' He looked at the envelope that contained everything he knew about me.

'Twenty-one,' I said.

He peered over his half-moon spectacles as if surprised I'd spoken. 'Twenty-one, yes,' he said. 'Still almost a child herself.'

'But what's wrong?' you asked.

Dr Burnett removed his glasses. 'Mr Coleman, there is nothing wrong with your wife. Go home and carry on doing the things you've been doing and I can assure you she'll be pregnant again in no time.' He put his glasses on again and wrote something about me in a spiky hand at the bottom of a piece of card and slipped it into the envelope with the others. 'Plenty of good food and rest.' He clicked the end of his pen. The appointment was over. I half rose, but you stayed in your seat.

'You'd advise then,' you said, 'that she shouldn't go swimming?' The question was unexpected.

'Swimming?' the doctor said.

'In the sea,' you said. 'In the middle of the night, in the morning, in the evening — any chance she can get.'

Dr Burnett glanced at his watch. 'Dear me, no. Rest is what's called for here. She should avoid all physical exercise.'

We argued in the car on the way home, your knuckles white around the steering wheel.

'Looking after Nan isn't restful either,' I said. 'But are you going to get up in the middle of the night when she's teething, when she's got a temperature? Are you going to clean up when she's been sick, change her nappies? Are you going to stop writing so that you can push the pram up to the shop because there isn't any food in the house?'

'It's fucking swimming, Ingrid,' you said.

'Swimming isn't strenuous, Gil. I happen to find it restful.'

'This isn't about you, for God's sake.' The hedgerows rushed past us.

'I know what it's about. You don't need to tell me.'

'This is our baby, and you're happy to take a risk with its life because you'd rather go for a fucking swim.'

'Gil!' I shouted. 'There isn't a baby. I lost it, remember, while you were getting drunk.'

You became patronizingly calm, but your teeth

214

were clenched. 'I meant next time, Ingrid, of course.'

I stared out of the passenger window at the sea. In my head I was saying, If there is a next time. Neither of us spoke for the rest of the journey.

Four months later you sold a short story and when the money came through, in true Gil style you spent it on a holiday to Florence. An early birthday present or our second honeymoon, you said. I arranged for Megan, from the village, to take care of Nan while we were away. Megan was a year younger than me, happy to have some time off from the dairy, I thought. She picked Nan up with a confidence I still didn't have, held our daughter on her hip in a way that made me feel like I'd been faking motherhood for thirteen months.

She stood with Nan on the veranda as we got into the car, and she looked at me with pity, and naively I thought she must have heard about the miscarriage. She held Nan's tiny wrist so that our daughter waved us goodbye as you reversed the car out of the drive. By the time we reached the main road, my eyes had filled with tears. You put your hand on my knee.

'It'll be fine. Megan will look after her. What's the worst . . . '

' . . . that could happen,' I finished for you, smiling feebly. But I didn't admit, not even to myself, that the reason I was crying wasn't because I was already missing Nan, but at the relief of getting away from her.

215

Florence, 15th to the 19th of June 1978. You had it all planned out. In the mornings we'd go for thick strong coffees at one of the little cafes on the Piazza della Repubblica and you'd order us two cornetto semplice. We'd stroll in the Boboli Gardens, and in the Accademia we'd stare up at Michelangelo's *David*. After a long lunch we'd go back to bed for the afternoon. Later, you'd take me to La Specola and show me the three supine wax women that you fell in love with when you were fifteen, no matter that their insides are on display for everyone to see. You'd tell me how you visited them every day to escape the claustrophobia of your bullied mother and the wheezing pump of your father's portable oxygen machine as the three of you did a latter-day version of the grand tour. We'd eat dinner at ten, finishing with chestnut ice cream and more coffee.

The sun was warm and Florence was beautiful, the hotel and the room perfect. We sat on the stone window seat and you kissed me with the sounds of the street coming in: car horns, raised Italian voices, and the click of women's shoes on paving. You started to undress me, one button at a time, but I had to prise myself away and run to the bathroom so I could vomit into the toilet bowl. A queasy feeling had come over me as soon as we'd stepped on to the train at Pisa, but I'd ignored it.

'Can I do anything?' you said from outside the bathroom as I retched. You couldn't hide the excitement in your voice.

I laid my forehead against the cold tiled wall

216

and called out, 'It must have been something I ate on the plane. I'm sure I'll be fine in a moment.'

You didn't come in. I heard you opening the suitcase clasps, then the drawers and the wardrobe, putting your notebooks and pens on your side of the bed, whistling through your teeth. The nausea rose again, my eyes watered, my forehead turned clammy and I retched once more. I remembered to be thankful for the decent hotel, the clean bathroom with a toilet unsoiled by anyone other than me, even if we couldn't afford these things and I'd be paying for them in reduced housekeeping money long after we returned to England.

After a while, when you heard me flush and run the tap, you came to crouch beside me where I sat on the floor. The tiles were embossed with a map of Italy, the sea around it an unreal blue, capped with white waves from which fish-like sea creatures jumped. 'Do you think . . . ' you said, a stupid smile across your face. 'Is it possible, already?'

I flapped you out of the bathroom and was sick again.

'I'm sorry,' I said when I made it to the bed. 'I've ruined our holiday.' You lay beside me, your head propped up on an arm, and stroked my hair.

'Poor Ingrid. There's nothing to be sorry about. We can be happy again now.'

I was pleased for you. But I didn't feel the same.

'Promise me you won't tell anyone yet,' I said.

'I promise.' You kissed my forehead.

'There's no point in both of us staying in. Not on our first evening. Let me sleep and in the morning we'll go out together.'

You had the decency to be silent for a moment or two.

'Go,' I repeated.

'If you're sure?'

'I'm sure. Find a nice restaurant and have some dinner.' I sat up against the pillows, drew in my legs and wrapped my arms around my calves. A merman's tail had been imprinted into the skin of my ankle where I'd kneeled on the bathroom floor.

'Can I get you anything?' you asked before you left.

In the way that sickness will pass quickly, when I'd rested for ten minutes I felt full of energy and not at all tired. I got up and sat again in the open window, my feet pressing against the frame, watching the mopeds in the street below bounce along the cobbles.

I washed my face, brushed my teeth and chose a dress (the one with the sailor collar), and strode out into the city. I walked without any sense of direction, taking in the Italians promenading through the squares. I was excited to be alive.

I stopped in a crowd to watch a man playing 'Für Elise' by running his wet fingers around the rims of water glasses set out on a table. It was then, when the crowd was clapping and he was bowing and I was feeling maybe even happy with the thought of something new starting, that I saw you sitting alone at a table outside a restaurant, the yellow light from the windows spilling over your shoulders. I stayed within the crowd and spied on you, watching with a stranger's eyes and playing with the fantasy of going up to your table and introducing myself. You were so handsome, so self-assured, watching the people walking past, and I was prepared to forgive everything.

You called the waiter over, for the bill I supposed, but the conversation was whispered and although the man brought a piece of paper and took some money, you continued to sit and wait. The crowd around me applauded the water-glass musician again, threw coins into the suitcase he had open in front of his table, and moved on, another group of tourists replacing them. I must have listened to that music five or six times before the waiter came to your table again, this time with a woman. She was about my age, but taller, or tall in her high heels and miniskirt. Even from a distance I could see her eyes were ringed in kohl, and her lips garish. She sat at your table and crossed her legs. You shook hands with the waiter and the woman leaned in towards you and when you said something she laughed, so that a couple walking past the restaurant turned to look. When you stood, the woman held on to your arm — proprietorially, I thought with a stab. You walked towards the Medici Chapel and I followed. What else would you expect me to do?

She took you to an apartment building behind the empty market stalls on the Via del Canto dei

Nelli. I don't know why I'm telling you — you must remember. Please let me believe that you remember, because if you've forgotten it means this prostitute who you bought on a Thursday night in Florence was only one in a long list of women on trips to London and wherever else you went. I never expected to be the kind of jealous woman who lets her imagination run away with itself.

I sat on the steps of San Lorenzo, hugging my knees, and saw a light come on in an attic window. Of course it might not have been yours (hers), but I imagined it was. I thought about you ducking your head in a room where the walls sloped, where the wooden floorboards were flecked with paint from slapdash decorating, and where there was one low window which overlooked the red-tiled roofs of Florence.

'Do you live here?' you might have asked in English, just to say something. Her skin was the colour of caramel, her black hair poorly cut, and although she'd laughed at your joke at the restaurant table she didn't understand what you said and might have been from any number of countries. She didn't answer, or maybe she shrugged and you were relieved you didn't have to make conversation. It was a transaction. You were buying and she had something to sell; it was no different from the dinner you'd eaten. She was another digestif you allowed yourself because you had something to celebrate.

In the attic room (small but clean), maybe the woman undressed and you took off your own clothes, looking around for somewhere to place them that wasn't the bed or the floor. There, I have made a chair appear for you to save getting your trousers or white shirt dirty. She took a condom from a bedside drawer, and although you shook your head and offered her more money, you relented when she insisted. (I have convinced myself that she insisted.) Your erection didn't flag when you protected the three of us; I don't think it's the loss of sensation you worry about, it's the missed opportunity of insemination.

You had sex with her first on the bed, vigorously. You were only forty-one. Then, through gestures and manoeuvring, you had her lean forward on the windowsill, so you could come while looking out over the floodlit Duomo.

I was back in the hotel bed, pretending to be asleep, long before you returned. The next day you described in detail the antipasto (salami, grilled asparagus, tiny peppers stuffed with soft cheese), the pasta e fagioli, the sublime agnello dell'imperatore with its wreath of bay and rosemary, and how afterwards you'd strolled across Ponte Vecchio for a grappa in a bar in Piazza della Passera. I never challenged your story.

But when we got home, I did tell Jonathan everything. He's a good listener, he didn't interrupt me, he let me relate all of it while we sat with our backs against the Agglestone, watching Nan with her legs splayed out in front of her, playing with the sandy soil.

'I'm going to leave him,' I said.

221

'Really?' Jonathan said quickly. 'You've decided?'

'Probably.'

He sank back into himself.

'I just haven't worked out how I'd live. What job could I do? No education worth talking about, no experience, and a baby to look after. There's not enough money for any alimony.'

'There are ways,' Jonathan said without looking at me. With a fingertip he drew a spiral in between Nan's chubby legs. She leaned forward, patting the ground and laughing, raising red dust. He drew it again.

'There are always ways.' I sighed, and gave a half-hearted laugh. 'Perhaps I could turn to prostitution. Get Gil to pick me up. That'd give him a surprise.'

'You don't know that's what he was doing.'

'Why is it you always defend him?' I said. Nan rocked herself forward and grabbed on to the rock, levering herself upwards until she was standing. 'Maybe you're right, maybe it was all in my imagination. I saw him going into a house with a woman. I don't know what he did in there, not really.'

Nan looked over her shoulder at us, smiling, pleased with herself. She let go of the rock with one hand.

'You're right,' he said. 'Perhaps she was his therapist.'

'Some kind of therapist!'

'I was joking,' Jonathan said. 'Look, I just want you to be sure. I don't want to be the one to persuade you.'

'You don't think I should leave him, do you?'

'I didn't say that.'

'Oh, Jonathan, you're so old-fashioned. So Catholic.'

'Take a lover of your own then,' he snapped.

Nan let go of the rock and, shocked to find she was standing unaided, toppled backwards on to her bottom and after a pause began to cry. Jonathan picked her up and swung her on to his shoulders. We walked home in silence.

The next day I said I'd buy one of the new home pregnancy tests, but you insisted I take a bottle of urine to Dr Burnett.

'More accurate,' you said.

'Cheaper,' I thought.

It was positive.

I finished this letter an hour ago. I'm sorry about the places where the ink's run, but I've decided I can't write any more. What's the point? These letters and my stupid idea of putting down the truth only causes me pain, and most likely you'll never read them. So this is the last.

    Addio,
    Ingrid

[Placed in *Italian* (*Teach Yourself*) by Lydia Vellaccio and Maurice Elston, 1985]

29

In the kitchen a few days later, Nan said, 'I telephoned Jonathan this morning.' She was standing with her back to Richard and Flora. Her words dropped into the washing-up bowl in front of her, as if telephoning Jonathan were an everyday occurrence and she was hoping they would sink and no one would notice she had spoken.

But Flora said, 'Our Jonathan?' They didn't know any other Jonathan. The thought of his coming was one of relief; that there would be someone other than Nan and Richard to tell her what she should be doing. Three or four times a year Jonathan and Flora met in London. He took her to an exhibition, the aquarium or an art gallery, then out to dinner; somewhere expensive with white linen tablecloths and heavy silver cutlery. And he would ask about her art, and she would tell him what she was working on, both of them knowing they were making conversation until they could get round to the subject of the Swimming Pavilion, Gil, and finally, over glasses of cognac, Ingrid. Jonathan wanted to know how Flora's father was, what he had been doing, and she would try to make their visits to charity shops or walks along the beach sound interesting. In return Flora wanted old stories about her parents and Jonathan — hippies camping in the garden, playing cricket in the hallway, telling ghost stories and getting drunk on Irish whiskey. Like a child at bedtime she never tired of listening and would mine each story for every tiny detail. Although he never said it, Flora was sure that Jonathan searched for Ingrid in crowds like she did. He looked for her on the tube at Lancaster Gate, in the throng of tourists watching the seahorses being fed, or in the tour group standing in front of Monet's *Bathers at La Grenouillère*.

In the kitchen, Nan turned. 'Dad asked me to invite him.'

'What?' Flora said. 'To the house?'

'Who's Jonathan?' Richard said. Flora ignored him. She was irritated that he was still there, four days after her fight with Nan, eating their food, hanging around, talking to Gil with the bedroom door closed. She wondered what Richard had told the bookshop about why he needed the time off; whether he'd said it was because he'd been asked to be at the deathbed of a famous author, or if he'd admitted he was there to burn a houseful of books.

'Dad wants him to bring Louise and . . . ' Nan began.

'Louise?' Flora jumped in.

'I was as surprised as you are.'

'Is Jonathan his brother?' Richard said. Flora wondered if during the night he bashed out all the information he had gathered during the day on Gil's old typewriter.

'He's Dad's best friend,' Nan said.

'Was,' Flora corrected.

'I'll have to get some more food in. Cook

225

something nice. A salmon, perhaps.'

'And Louise — who's she?' Richard asked.

Flora looked up at Nan, who was drying her already dry hands on a tea towel. Nan stared back, her mouth set, her eyes pitiless, and Flora realized she was probably wearing the same expression, a mirror of her sister's. Richard looked between the two of them.

'Oh,' he said. 'That Louise.'

30

Gil,

I wasn't going to write again. I mustn't write, it hurts and doesn't solve anything, but I have to put this down on paper. I need to get it out of my head and right now there's no one else to tell.

I went down to the sea again this morning for a swim. (Early.) I shouldn't have gone. Oh God, I shouldn't have gone. It was still dark and cold so I wore your greatcoat, the one you got from a young man in Moscow in exchange for a borrowed pair of suede shoes. ('Tell me the Moscow story, Daddy,' I can hear Flora saying, swamped by the coat, her little head poking out the top.) I was naked underneath it; I've always liked how the heavy wool scratches and tickles. It smells like a musty version of you.

The beach was empty. The tide was going out, leaving a wide ribbon of seaweed creased on the sand and swaying in the shallows. I walked around the Point to Middle Beach, where the sea is always clear. I unbuttoned your coat and, I don't know why, but I checked the pockets first before I took it off. Flora must have been wearing it again, because I found the queen of hearts from the pack of cards which has those ladies on the back, two sheets of Green Shield

227

Stamps and my purse! Still with ten pounds and a few pence inside. I put everything back, folded the coat, left my flip-flops on top and ran into the sea just down from the beach huts.

The water was steady and black. An inch below the surface my body disappeared as if it didn't exist. I swam straight out towards the rising sun, which was under-lighting the clouds with a dramatic orange as if I were swimming into a Renaissance landscape. It shone a path over the water's surface, saying 'This way, straight on', but I tired and turned back towards the shore. I swam a lazy breaststroke, keeping my head above the water, and in the distance I saw a light: a campfire in the dunes.

Do you remember when we used to go to the sea together in the middle of the night to cool down, that first summer? We'd strip off, grabbing on to each other, yelping and laughing, and run across the sand and into the sea through the night air, as warm as noontime.

When I reached the beach the flip-flops and the coat had gone. My first thought, and I feel guilty writing it, was that Flora must have followed me, but she wasn't there. I searched the length of Middle Beach and in front of the last hut I found a discarded and crumpled queen of hearts. There was no sign of my purse or the other things. I could have gone home. I should have gone home, but I was so angry. I needed that money, Flora loves that coat! Then I remembered the campfire I'd seen from the water and, without stopping to think, went in search of it.

I crouched in the dawn, watching two men drinking and laughing. The flickering orange from their fire set their skin alight and I recognized your coat, slung around one of the men's shoulders. The other appeared to have square tattoos on his cheeks and forehead, and it took me a moment to see that these were the Green Shield Stamps. Behind a tuft of marram grass, I growled, long and low.

'Did you hear that?' greatcoat-man said, looking up.

'What?' the other said, drunk, I think, and slow to react.

I rustled the grass and greatcoat-man stood. 'There's something out there.'

'It's the weed giving you the heebie-jeebies. Here.' The man held out his hand to the other, the lit tip of a cigarette glowing.

I jumped forward into the ring of firelight like a wild woman or a tiger. I made a grab at the coat; even if my purse was no longer in the pocket, I was bloody going to get it back. But the man was on top of me before I could stop him, still wearing the coat, his weight pinning me, a hand across my jaw, pushing the side of my face into the sand away from the fire, and giving me a mouthful of grit. I don't know what happened to Green Shield Stamp-man, I didn't see him. I think the one with the coat had expected me to be male; his arm was tensed, flexed, and his hand a fist. But he must have realized what, or who, was beneath him and his grip changed, as if it wasn't a fight he was after. With one hand constricting my throat he pushed his thighs

229

between mine. I don't think I shouted. I tried to shake my head, tried to say no, please no, tried to get out from under him, but his hand pressed harder. And I stopped struggling. Struggling, I decided (have decided), would (will) make it worse. As the man was unzipping his trousers, my left arm became free and I moved it out across the sand, my hand scuttling sideways until it came across a cylindrical object, smooth and light. An empty beer can. My hand dropped it and moved on towards the flames. While the man on top of me grunted with the effort of keeping me down and releasing himself, my hand closed around a thick stick lying at the edge of the fire. I lifted it up, the end glowing white with heat and ash, and I lowered it over the man's back, pressing it against the olive wool of your coat. There was the smell of burning fabric, and I forced the stick down harder. He didn't notice until his T-shirt began to burn, and for some moments more, while he was screaming, I clamped that man to my body with my arm and the stick, until he managed to roll off me, swearing and yelling. He flung the greatcoat away and I grabbed it, dropped the stick and ran.

I didn't slow until I reached our beach at the bottom of the chine, and it was only there that I felt my own pain. The sun had fully risen, a yellow light streaming through tattered clouds, and I saw the white scalded skin across my palm and fingers. I stared down the beach while I squatted in the waves with my hand under the surface, and I began to laugh. The bottom of your coat was sodden with seawater.

When I got home, goose-pimpled and muddy, I went into the girls' room. I'd been gone less than an hour. I bent over them, the ends of my hair dripping on to the cheeks of our sleeping children. They hadn't woken; nothing bad had happened to them while I'd been gone.

I bandaged my hand, and when Nan asked about it I said I'd burned it while boiling eggs for breakfast. She wanted to see, wanted me to go to the doctor, but I told her not to fuss. And an hour ago, when the girls left to catch the school bus, I stuffed the coat into a bin liner and, with the pole that props up the washing line, pushed it as far under the house as it would go.

Ingrid

[Placed in *Warne's Adventure Book for Girls*, 1931]

31

On her way out of the house in the afternoon, Flora pressed her ear up against Gil's door to listen to the conversation he was having with Richard, but their voices were too low for the words to make sense. She considered knocking, but Nan shooed her away. On the beach Flora kicked through the foam that fanned like a bridal train across the sand. She walked from Dead End Point to the cliff, staring at the ground, trying not to think about her father, and not looking at the people on the beach, controlling her habit of searching for women with fair skin and straight hair. She thought about going for a swim, but even that seemed pointless. She flapped out her towel, lay down and closed her eyes.

She tried to imagine what Louise would look like now. Just before Ingrid had disappeared Louise had been elected to the House of Commons, and Flora had seen her picture in the paper, wearing a fitted jacket, a pearl necklace and matching earrings — not someone she could imagine her mother being friends with. The newspaper had been spread out on the kitchen table and Flora had seen that Ingrid had doodled in red pen on the photograph: devil's horns rising out of the coiffed hair.

Flora might have dropped off to sleep, she wasn't sure, but she was aware of a shadow across her face. She opened her eyes, shielding the glare with her hand. Richard was looking down at her.

'What?' she said.

'I wasn't sure if you were sleeping. It's not good to lie too long in the sun.'

'I wasn't asleep.'

'Someone with your colouring — it's very easy to burn.' Richard had a long-sleeved T-shirt on, shorts and walking boots.

'I've lived by the sea for my whole life, Richard,' she said.

'Anyway, Nan wants to go shopping and I said I'd go with her. Your father shouldn't be left on his own.'

'Oh God, is he worse?' Flora jumped up.

'He's sleeping. He's the same.'

Gil breathed — a slow, rasping exhalation, and a too-long gap in which Flora waited, holding her own breath. She rested back in the chair beside his bed and closed her eyes, then was jolted awake by her father saying, 'I haven't seen you do any drawing today.'

'Do you want me to do one now?'

He closed his eyes again and she took that as a yes.

When she returned with her sketchpad, the charcoal, the rubber and her rag, he said, 'Sit me up.'

She lifted him under his armpits, the folds of skin nearly empty of muscle. She drew what she saw: his head and shoulders propped up by the pillows; his prominent cheekbones, the hollows below them, his eyes smudged by black, and all the creases and lines in his sallow face. The swelling had gone down now, but some discolouration remained. She looked harder this time, recording how his eyes receded inside the cavities of his skull, his thin, downturned lips, the sag of skin under his chin.

'Do you remember when I found that whale's head on the beach?' Flora said.

Gil opened his eyes. 'A real whale's head?'

'No, plastic or fibreglass I think.'

'A toy?'

'It was life-sized. I wanted you to hang it on the wall.'

Gil shook his head.

'But you must remember.'

'No. I don't.' His eyes moved to Flora's sketchpad. 'Let me see.' When she showed him he said, 'It's good. I look like my father just before he died, as if parts of me don't work like they used to and other bits have fallen off.' He smiled and pushed the bedcovers away with his good hand. 'I need the toilet,' he said.

'Can I bring you the bedpan? Doesn't Nan usually bring you the bedpan?' Flora was nervous of looking after Gil on her own.

'And I always refuse it. She'll have me in nappies next.'

Flora didn't tell him she'd seen a packet of adult-sized incontinence pants in the airing cupboard. She offered her arm and together they shuffled down the hall, negotiating the books. She waited in the kitchen, staring at the washing Nan had hung on the line. She put the kettle on,

234

searched in the tin for biscuits, yawned, and stared out of the window again. After five minutes Flora pressed her ear up against the bathroom door and heard her father whispering.

'Daddy?' She tapped on the wood. 'Are you OK in there?'

'I'm fine,' Gil called. 'Go to bed, Flo. We'll see you in the morning.'

'Daddy, it's the afternoon.' She crouched at the keyhole but it was blocked by hardened toilet paper stuffed there by a seventeen-year-old Nan when she had tired of her little sister peeping in. Flora stood and knocked harder.

'It's just your mother,' Gil said.

'Daddy.' Flora rattled the handle. She glanced down the hall, worried Nan would return soon, worried she wouldn't. 'Please unlock the door.' She heard the bath curtain being pulled and a couple of seconds later the door bolt was drawn back. Gil had his toothbrush in his hand, a swirl of striped paste on the bristles.

He moved to the bath. 'Look,' he said, one hand on the edge of the water-marked towelling curtain, the bath hidden. The toilet and the sink spun around Flora; the altitude in the room was too high, the air too thin. Her father drew back the curtain with a flourish, like a conjurer delivering his most celebrated trick. The bath was empty. But the magician didn't notice his mistake, didn't realize that the trapdoor hadn't opened, that the coloured handkerchief was showing from his sleeve, that the rabbit had hopped from the stage.

'Do you see her?' Gil said, looking in the

235

mirror over the bath. 'Do you see her? There, beside the sink.'

Flora saw herself and an old man, half his face yellow, grey bristles sprouting from a sagging neck, his eyebrows wild. There was no one else in the room.

'Yes,' Flora said. 'I see her.'

32

Gil,

We had another power cut last night. The three of us were in the sitting room when the lights flickered twice and then died. While Nan went out to the road I waited with Flora, holding her hand. She still doesn't like being inside the house in the dark.

'The whole village is out,' Nan said when she returned. 'I'll get the candles.'

'Shh.' Flora gripped me. 'Listen,' she said, with such urgency that Nan and I didn't move, waiting for something. 'There's a noise,' Flora said, 'in the kitchen.' And there was a slow creak, the sound of a footstep. 'It's the loose floorboard.'

'Which loose floorboard?' Nan said.

'The one in front of the cooker.'

I could hear the terror in her voice.

'Don't be ridiculous,' Nan said, and marched up the hallway to find the candles, and of course there was no one in the kitchen.

I need to teach Flora that there is nothing to be scared of, that she can do anything she wants, be anyone she wants to be.

After I finished my previous letter I thought about what had happened on the beach. At first I was angry that you weren't there to help me. You brought me to this place, gave me children and left; everything that's ever happened to me in my adult life is because of you, and now you expect me to be able to manage on my own, like a fledgling deserted before being taught how to fly. And then it occurred to me that I survived that incident on the beach by myself, I didn't need you or anyone else to rescue me. I did it on my own.

After my conversation with Jonathan in front of the Agglestone, I decided I would stay. No, perhaps it was more that I made no decision. Leaving was too momentous, too frightening, something I only thought about in the abstract. And while I stored our time in Italy away and tried to forget it, my third pregnancy was something I was surprised to find I welcomed. It wasn't only that I stopped being sick earlier and felt healthy, but that it made me strong, invincible. I began to join in with your enthusiasm and the list of names you taped to the fridge door (Herman, Leo, Ford, Günter). I, too, was certain it was a boy.

Jonathan called me after you'd told him.

'You're still there then?' he said.

'I feel fantastic.'

'Do you want me to come down?'

'It would be good to see you, but you don't have to come on my account.'

'Is Gil listening?'

'No, I mean it. There's something about this baby, a connection. He's not something alien like the others. He's part of me, I'm part of him.

238

Perhaps I was meant to do this mother thing after all, it's just taken me a bit longer than everyone else.'

'If anything changes . . . ' Jonathan said.

'It won't.'

' . . . I'm just at the end of the phone.'

One morning in July I asked Martin if I could borrow his lawnmower. We leaned on the gate to the Swimming Pavilion and looked at the grass — coarse and knee-high — and instead he loaned me his scythe, sharpening it with a whetstone, and in the gap between the pub's lunchtime closing and the evening's opening, he showed me how to use it. I swept the blade before me, only managing two or three jagged arcs before the muscles in my shoulders complained. (Different ones, it seemed, from those I used for swimming.) I cut the grass while Nan was sleeping, and it took me a week to shave it short enough to be able to mow it. After that I dug a flowerbed below the veranda, a laborious job through the compacted earth. Milkwood Stables heard about my plans and dropped off a pile of manure. Every day I worked in my wide straw hat, long trousers and one of your old shirts. Sometimes Martin would lean on the gate to watch and shake his head, telling me what I needed was a rowan and sea buckthorn windbreak and how the flowers Mrs Allen's sister had sent would never survive in our salty air. As the baby grew inside me, so did the garden.

When I think back on those months of swelling and happiness, my recollection is that I was alone in the Swimming Pavilion, or, at least, it was just me, Nan and the garden. But you were there writing, because that summer you submitted your third novel. And it was rejected.

We were living off the tiny trickle of twice-yearly royalties from your first two books and the money your mother had left in trust for you; it wasn't enough. Margarine sandwiches for supper, tea leaves reused pot after pot, and hiding from the milkman when he came knocking. Martin gave you a job behind the bar but asked you not to return for a third shift after you drank more than you poured for the customers. You worked for a few weeks at the stables but the horses scared you. You lasted six months or so at the dairy, but getting up early was never going to work for long. (Funny, after that conversation we'd had with Jonathan about milking cows in Ireland.)

The garden and the swimming were my release from the worries about money and from the relentless grind of motherhood. The water was good for what was happening inside me. Without you knowing, I crept out of the house and down to the sea in the dark, my feet finding their way around the rocks at the top of the beach. I hid the damp towel from you, washed the sand from my hair and the salt from my lips before you kissed me. I was gentle with the baby, I didn't swim hard or far, we were never in danger. There was something magical about those mornings, imagining the child suspended in its fluid, while I was suspended in mine, both of us in our natural states.

I swam until the cold weather came, when instead of going in the water, I went down to stare at the sea — flat and grey, or brilliant as the sun rose, or, best of all, with the wind raging and the water throwing itself at the rocks.

In the village shop one afternoon, Mrs Bankes found me hiding behind the shelves, counting the money in my purse, trying to decide if I could afford a packet of butter. Nan was sitting up in the pram, pointing at everything and saying 'jam' no matter whether it was window cleaner or gravy browning.

'She's such a good girl, isn't she? Never struggles or wants to get down,' Mrs Bankes said to me. 'You're such a good girl,' she said to Nan in a sing-song voice.

'Jam,' Nan said.

'Let's hope the next one will be as easy,' Mrs Bankes said. I looked at my daughter and then, because it seemed to be expected of me, I reached out to stroke down a stray curl of her hair. 'I expect you're hoping for a boy. It's always nice to have one of each.'

'George,' I said, my hand on my belly, the name coming out of nowhere.

'Lovely. After George the Fifth, I suppose. Such a nice man.'

'No,' I said. 'Bernard Shaw, or maybe Orwell.'

Mrs Bankes carried on as if she hadn't heard me. 'They say we're in for a cold winter, even down here. I hope you've got plenty of warm clothes ready for that new baby'

'I've kept Nan's — in the loft, I think.'

The shopkeeper leaned towards Nan. 'Your

241

little brother is going to be wearing pink? That won't do. That won't do at all.' And one of Mrs Bankes's hands flew down from over her head, and her finger pressed the end of Nan's nose. Another child would have cried, but Nan smiled, a kind of adult smile — tolerant, patronizing. Mrs Bankes stood up straight again. 'You're going to have to get knitting. I think we have some blue wool in the back here, and I'm sure I'll have some needles you can borrow.'

'I can't knit,' I said. 'I don't know how.'

She tutted. 'Come up tomorrow lunchtime and I'll show you.' She bustled me out of the shop. At home I found a packet of butter and a pot of strawberry jam tucked under Nan's blanket.

For the next month I spent every lunchtime in the shop, Nan stirring buttons in a saucepan, and Mrs Bankes and I side by side in front of the meat counter, as I learned to knit. The wool was baby-blue and soft. I finished one little boot, lopsided and too large for a newborn, but still I kept it under my pillow so I could hold it at night.

On the 23rd of November, in the evening, I was sitting in the kitchen casting on like Mrs Bankes had taught me, starting the next blue boot, wondering whether you were enjoying your birthday in London and trying not to worry about where you were exactly, when there was a familiar pop and my waters broke, two months prematurely. I put my hand between my legs as if I could stop the flow of liquid, but it ran off the chair and pooled on the lino. I must have cried out, because I heard Nan calling 'Mum mum mum mum' from her bedroom. I dropped a tea towel into the puddle.

I rarely used the telephone, too concerned about the bill, but that night I stood over it, thinking about what number to call. We still had that pop-up address book then, and for several minutes I slid the pointer up and down the alphabet, trying to recall the name of your agent, but as I dialled the last digit of his number I realized how late it was, and when the phone rang in an empty London office I felt the first contraction, a mild, low ache, like the others. Jonathan was in London that weekend and I remembered the name of the hotel he was staying in. The operator gave me the number, but when I phoned they said he'd gone out. I knew he'd be drinking with you, putting the tab on expenses. I left an urgent message with the receptionist. The only other person I knew in London was Louise. I hadn't seen her for more than a year; we exchanged Christmas and birthday cards with letters, mine becoming a round robin with bad news smoothed over like the wash of a tide across dry sand. Louise answered on the fifth ring.

'Fitzrovia 386?'

'Louise? It's Ingrid,' I said.

'Ingrid.' She said my name without any intonation. There were voices in the background, the chink of cutlery on china. 'Ingrid,' she repeated, this time her voice starting high and dropping lower. 'How are you?'

'I'm very well,' I said. And then another pain

caught me and I clenched my teeth together and breathed through it. 'I'm having a baby.'

She paused, and said, 'Another? Congratulations.'

'No. Right now.'

'Shouldn't you telephone a doctor or a midwife or someone?'

'I will. But I'm trying to find Gil. He's in London.'

'In London,' she said.

'Yes, at a meeting with his agent, or out with Jonathan. I didn't know who else to call.'

She covered the mouthpiece and spoke, and I heard more people talking and a burst of laughter.

'And you're having a baby?'

'It's coming, but it's too soon.' I didn't want to cry.

'Ingrid, listen.' She sounded more pragmatic than she'd ever been before. 'I'll find Gil for you. When you put the phone down, call the hospital, tell them you're having a baby, get them to send an ambulance. Right away. And Ingrid, don't worry.'

Two days later when I was in my own bed again, one of those thick sanitary towels between my legs, and staring at the empty cot beside me, you went alone to the Royal Oak. I can't write it, I can't put down the words that describe what happened, and anyway, you were there. The hospital scene still replays in my head, and sometimes it's easier to let it. They whisked our boy away before I had a chance to say goodbye, and never gave him back to us even in an urn or a coffin. I'd taken the knitted boot to the hospital, grabbing it at the last minute from under my pillow, and although there was only one, I'd been excited to see it on him. It disappeared in that hospital room, and I never found out where it went. In good moments I like to think the midwife put it on one of his tiny feet. I never told you, but I longed for it; just that one thing that had belonged to our son. What would I have done with one blue bootee? I don't know; kept it under my pillow, or buried it perhaps and said Annie's prayer over it.

I heard you bought your own drinks in the pub that time; you bought the bottle. I don't blame you, sitting at the bar in the far corner, on Mrs Passerini's seat, while Martin and his regulars whispered, casting worried glances at you.

'Let the children come to me, do not hinder them,' you said into your glass, according to Martin.

And that idiot George Ward, at the other end of the bar, almost under his breath, said, 'Must have got the priest in there pretty damn quick if that baby made it to heaven.' He didn't say it quietly enough, because you got off your stool, staggered up to him, and when he turned, you punched him in the face. Martin told me he heard George's nose crack under your knuckles as he staggered backwards, blood running from his nostrils (so much blood). You swayed, took another swing and then Martin was around the front of the bar, holding you off, saying, 'Gil, it's all right, Gil, Gil.' As if soothing a baby.

Sometimes I think about George Ward in the accident and emergency department, lying on a bed behind a curtain, holding a blood-soaked bar towel to his face while his nose was reset, and at the same time, somewhere in the same hospital, there was our own George, cold and alone. A little fish, swimming too early from his private sea.

Ingrid

[Placed in *Joe Strong, the Boy Fish* by Vance Barnham, date unknown]

33

Richard and Flora sat opposite each other on the sofas, books crowding around them. Gil and Nan had gone to bed. Flora tried to ease a paperback out from one of the towers behind her, *Joe Strong, the Boy Fish*, written on the spine. Above her, the tower shifted.

'Careful,' Richard said. Flora pushed the book back in and took another from higher up. A hardback called *Pruning Fruit Trees and Shrubs*. She flicked through it, and heart-shaped pieces of sugar paper fluttered out over her lap.

'*A heart-felt invitation*,' she read from the typed text. '*Please come to Michael and Clementina's engagement party on 14th February 1957.*' The paper was soft, fragile, purple faded to pink.

'Perhaps they fell out of love before Valentine's Day,' Richard said.

She chose another. *Moby-Dick*. A giant flat-nosed whale reared up from the sea, dwarfing a wooden boat of sailors. Inside the front cover someone had glued in a bookplate. '*This book belongs to*,' Flora read out, '*Sarah Sims*.' The writing was laboured, the pen scoring the paper, and she imagined a young girl, hard-working, her tongue sticking out in concentration. Under her name, Sarah had added, *But I don't want it.* Flora laughed and held the page up for Richard to see. 'Your go,' she said.

He reached behind him and extricated a book, patting the stack so that it dropped with a jolt but didn't topple. '*Red Sky at Midnight*,' he said, reading the title. He flicked through the pages, but nothing fell out. He turned them more slowly and stopped when he reached the middle. He smiled.

'Marginalia.' He lowered his voice, lengthening his vowels, making his consonants more pronounced, a good impersonation of Gil: 'It's a female vulva, drawn by a fucking male of the species.'

Richard handed her the open book.

'Nicely drawn,' she said. 'Good technique.'

She picked another, *Thrilling Stories for Girls*. On the flyleaf someone had sketched a small barren island surrounded by water. In the style of a textbook diagram the cross-section of the island had been labelled with an 'escape shoot' running down through the middle, hidden by a hinged hatch disguised as the island's peak. Under the water, a 'secret submersible' waited for passengers.

'After Mum went I was embarrassed about how we lived,' Flora said, closing the cover. 'The garden like a jungle, the number of books in the house, that I had a sister who behaved like a mother, a father old enough to be my grandfather, who locked himself away with his typewriter, but never wrote a word.'

Richard pushed his glasses up his nose and waited.

'I never invited anyone home.' Flora put her heels up on the edge of the sofa, wrapped her arms around her knees. 'I didn't have many friends, but there was one girl, Kathy. I made friends with her so I could go to her house after school rather than come back here.' Flora picked at a scab on her knee. 'The first time, when we stood on Kathy's doorstep, she shuffled her feet and said, 'There's something I need to tell you about my mum.' I remember thinking, Shit, she's going to say her mother's disappeared. But she said, 'My mum's really fat.'

'She was right, her mum was enormous. She overflowed the sides of her armchair and wore flowery dresses which rode up when she sat down, and showed her meaty legs. If someone had pricked them with a fork they would have spat grease. Kathy was apologetic, but I loved her mum. That term I went home with Kathy after school at least twice a week and ate dinner on my lap with her family in front of the telly. I liked to pretend that her car-mechanic brother was my brother too, that her father, who commuted to a normal job in an office, was my father, that her semi-detached estate house was my house. I'm sure now that her mum felt sorry for me, for what had happened, but I didn't know it at the time. She would give me a hug before I left, and it was like I was sinking into her flesh, as if she could take me into her body and I could become her child. I would lie in bed on the nights I had been to Kathy's and remember the smell of her mother's bosom, the whiff of cooked food coming off her clothes and the sweat rising up from her cleavage. Mixed together I thought they made the smell of a mother: carmine pink.'

'Pink?' Richard said, but Flora carried on talking.

'It was Kathy that I first read *A Man of Pleasure* with, under the bedcovers, shining a torch on the rude bits. I think one of her uncles owned a copy. Most of it went over our heads, of course. It was later I realized the significance of those words at the beginning, and even then I didn't fully understand.'

Richard began to say something, but Flora interrupted. 'Wait. I have to tell you all of it now I've started.

'After a few months Kathy hinted that she wanted an invitation to my house in return. She'd say stuff like 'Your dad's famous. I've never met anyone famous before' or 'Is it true you live in some swimming changing rooms?' And I considered what I'd have to tell her on the doorstep about *my* mum, but I didn't know how to say it — *There's something I need to tell you: my dad's a writer who doesn't write but collects other people's books, and this is my sister-mother, and by the way my mum's disappeared, but don't you dare say she's dead.* She would have known about that though. Everybody did.

'The last time I visited Kathy's house one of their neighbours was round. Her mum and this woman were sitting in the kitchen, having a cup of tea. Kathy and I were playing at being spies or something; we were listening outside the door, pretending we were riveted by knitting patterns or recipes. Then their conversation changed.

''I see Flora's round again,' the neighbour

said. 'That poor girl.'

' "She comes round nearly every day after school,' Kathy's mum said. 'Can you imagine? It doesn't bear thinking about. And her father, hiding away in that shack of his, or gadding about goodness knows where.'

' "I worry about the older sister,' we heard the neighbour say. 'Having to be a mother to a ten-year-old at, what? Fifteen?'

' "Oh, but what about that poor little Flora? Losing her mother when she's still so young." '

Flora paused in her story, looked across at Richard. His face was blank, still waiting. 'Losing her mother,' Flora repeated. 'They thought *I* lost her.'

'It's just a turn of phrase. They didn't really think you were responsible . . . ' Richard started, but Flora shook her head.

'I stared at Kathy and I was sure she thought that too: my mother disappeared when I should have been watching. And I *was* watching — I was hiding in the gorse, outside the house.' Flora nodded towards the window. 'Nan had made sure I caught the school bus that morning, but I got off at the next stop and walked home. I couldn't wait for Mum to leave the house so I could sneak indoors to get my costume and go for a swim. I watched her go and I didn't stop her.'

'But if you had gone to school you wouldn't have been there to stop her.'

'I ran out of Kathy's house,' Flora said, talking over Richard. 'She called for me to come back, but no one came looking. Perhaps Kathy told

251

them I'd gone home.'

'Oh, Flora,' Richard said, and leaned forward to touch her ankle.

'I know, what a terrible childhood.' Flora barked out a laugh. 'There's more. The following day in class the girl I sat next to passed me a note. I recognized Kathy's handwriting. I opened it under the desk. It said, 'I know what you done.''

'What?' Richard said.

'I told you, she thought *I* had lost my mum. And I believed it as well. Maybe I still do.' Flora didn't tell Richard the rest of the story: that she'd taken the note home and when she was sitting at the kitchen table she read it again. Nan was out, but Gil was there, cooking a fry-up. She wanted him to see it, to read it and tell her that she wasn't responsible for losing Ingrid.

Her father set a plate in front of her, the egg sliding over the sausage, its yolk heart broken and leaking into the beans. She wasn't sure she could eat it. Gil looked over Flora's shoulder and read what Kathy had written.

He tutted. 'It should be 'I know what you *did*,'' he said. 'Not '*done*'.' Flora slipped the note under her plate and later put it in the bin with the food her father didn't make her eat, hadn't noticed she didn't eat.

Flora got up from the sofa and stepping between the books went to the French windows and stared out at the sky, where dark clouds raced across the moon. 'I think we've had the last of the good weather.'

'Flora?' Richard said.

'I'm fine. It was a long time ago.' With her back to Richard, she saw her mother closing the door of the Swimming Pavilion, the book in her hand. Flora strained to see the title — a question, perhaps. She remembered crouching in the space she had made in the middle of the gorse, a thorned fortress. She remembered willing her mother to hurry up, to leave. And when Ingrid had turned, stepped into the sunlight wearing the long pink dress, walked around the corner on to the lane and disappeared into Spanish Green, Flora hadn't thought about her again.

To Richard she said, 'Let's go to bed.'

34

Gil,

Today I had a phone call from Flora's headmistress. I could hear our ten-year-old daughter complaining in the background while I was told what she'd done wrong. She'd been found standing on the main road outside the school gates with her thumb out. She told me later she was hitchhiking to London to go and live with you. I asked her how she'd find you in London when she doesn't know where you're living. She said she'd go to a bookshop and find the name of your publisher and then go to their offices. (Clever, independent girl, our youngest daughter. Maybe I should have let her go.)

I find myself thinking about you less as I write these letters. I mean today's Gil, where you are, what you're doing. Meanwhile, the Gil of the past fills my head. I work in the garden when the girls are at school; there's always something that needs doing. The view from the house to the sea needs clearing, there's a cordyline which has grown too big, and I should have pruned the tamarisk in March. I sometimes think about what the garden would become if I weren't here to look after it. (The nettles at the top of the bank reclaiming their old territory, the grass going to seed after a few weeks, the flowerbeds

254

full of interlopers.) Is imposing our will on nature wrong? All that work to keep the garden as I want it — the weeding, the pruning and the mowing. Perhaps it would be more honest, more truthful, to let the land slip back to how it wants to be.

★   ★   ★

Do you remember the time Flora ran away when she was seven? Another of those things we never talked about. You were in London at an event, due to return the next morning. The weather drew me down the chine after the children had gone to bed. I liked to lie on the sea's rocking surface and let the waves sluice me and the rain pock my skin. When Flora climbed out of her bedroom window I wasn't there to stop her. But you came home early on the last ferry of the evening, or you hadn't gone at all, and must have found Nan crying, the girls' window open and our youngest child flown.

I came up the chine in my bare feet. The path was muddy and I was watching my step when I heard the voices of your search party calling out for Flora, and when I glanced up, torch lights were bobbing through the copse. I knew I should have been looking after the children and so I ran through the woods, my towel dropped somewhere behind me, but by then you'd already found her, and when I pushed through the small group of people crowding around you, Flora was in your arms. In front of our friends and neighbours you slapped me and the crack echoed across the Downs like a gunshot.

I don't deserve to be looking after our children.

Ingrid

[Placed in *The Last Gamble* by Harold Q. Masur, 1958]

35

'Keep still,' Flora said, straddling Richard's hips. 'Or your bones will be wonky.' He lay on the bed built into the far end of the writing room. The morning light coming through the window and the open door warmed the colour of his skin, and she concentrated on drawing his elbow joint, trying to visualize how the knuckle-like end of the humerus slotted around the bones of his forearm.

'It rained fish,' Flora said, still drawing, 'the night I borrowed your car.'

'Fish?' Richard said.

'Yes.' She began on his other elbow. 'They fell all over the road — tiny mackerel.'

'I've read about that,' he said. 'Water spouts or miniature tornadoes form over the sea or sometimes ponds and suck up small aquatic animals — fish or frogs — and drop them somewhere else.'

Flora sighed and shifted her knees on the bed-cover. 'I wasn't after the scientific explanation.'

'What then?'

'Don't you think it's significant?' Flora lifted her pen from Richard's skin, considered her drawing. 'That it happened just as I was coming home? Some kind of omen?' She looked up at his face but saw no connection in his expression to what she was saying. 'Forget it.' She went back to her work.

After a while, Richard said, 'I can't believe I'm in the room where Gil Coleman wrote *A Man of Pleasure*.' He turned his head towards the door. Flora looked too. It still felt illicit to be there with Richard, in her father's space. The side window, which was propped open, gave a view over the nettles and a glimpse of the sea. A fold-down flap below the sill created a narrow table which could be used for writing or eating, and a wooden folding chair was hanging high up on the wall until it was needed. At the door end, an old oven glove, two chipped mugs and a paraffin lamp dangled from hooks above the stove. Under Richard, the puce-coloured cover, bald in patches and water-stained, was rucked and pushed to the side, revealing grey, musty-smelling sheets and pillows. A colour like the undersides of mushrooms came and went.

'How much of it do you think happened here?' Richard said.

'What?' Flora said. 'You don't think it was autobiographical, do you?' She laughed and the lines she was drawing on Richard rippled. 'For fuck's sake.'

'That's what everyone said.'

'I didn't think you would listen to literary gossip.'

'OK, at least it was here he wrote it, at that table, looking out at that view.'

'I suppose so. We weren't allowed in.' She stuck the tip of her tongue out from between her lips. She'd got as far as Richard's wrist and the carpal bones were complicated.

'Why not?'

'It was the rule.'

There had been one time she'd gone into the room on her own. For a reason Flora could no longer remember she had climbed out of her bedroom window one night. Nan was in the kitchen; she wasn't sure where her mother was. It was raining, a thick, warm rain that soaked through her pyjamas as soon as she jumped down on to the flowerbed. She ran along the gravel paths in between the lawns, thinking her father might be writing, but although the light was on and the door unlocked, his room was empty. Flora stood on the threshold for a minute, and even though she understood it wasn't allowed she stepped inside. The place smelled of her father, musky, rich, otter brown, like the man. The bedcovers were thrown back, as if her father had just got up. She would have liked to crawl under them but was distracted by his typewriter and a curl of paper that rolled out from the top. 'I ran my hand over the downy curves of her buttocks,' she read. Flora wasn't sure what 'buttocks' meant, and she leaned in closer to read the next line. Her wet hair dripped on to the ink, the letters spreading one into the other.

She hurried from the room, across the garden, running out to the lane, and took the uphill footpath through the small beech wood, the trees stained by streaks of copper where the rain dripped in slippery runnels. She slapped their trunks with the palm of her hand as she passed, as if she were whacking the meaty rumps of giant horses. By the time she emerged from the trees she was warm and panting and the rain had stopped. The path came out on the rising slope of Barrow Down, where the grass was cropped short by rabbits, and the land rolled in undulating waves. In a burst of energy Flora ran up to the highest point. The footpath continued rightwards along the coast to Hadleigh; to her left the shorn grass fell away to the cliff at the end of the beach, while in front of her the ground was level, facing out to sea. She spread her arms wide and ran into the wind and across the grassy slope towards the cliff top. The edge here had been eroded into a narrow spit two feet wide and twelve feet long that pointed accusingly out to sea at Old Smoker, the column of chalk to which hundreds of years ago the land must have been attached. The forty-foot-high sea stack rose straight up out of the water like the funnel from an oversized and sunken ocean liner, and once upon a time Old Smoker's Wife, a smaller rock, had hunkered low beside him. Along the middle of the finger of land a track had been worn through the grass by daredevil teenagers and reckless adults. Flora and Nan, and all the children they knew, had been forbidden to walk out along this peninsula, had been forbidden, Flora suddenly remembered, from walking on the Downs unaccompanied. She took one step on to the track, the width of a shoe, and then another — one foot in front of the other, heel to toe, until she could no longer see the land hulking behind her. Below on either side was the pitchy shifting mass of the sea, which Flora couldn't look at for fear of tipping, so she stared straight ahead at the clouds scudding across the moon and at the immensity of Old Smoker rising like a beacon-less lighthouse from the water. Flora held her arms out and the wind lifted her hair. She took another step forward, sweat breaking out on her fingertips, and another step until she was at the very end of the spit. If she were to take one more there would be nothing under her foot, only empty air and a long fall, tumbling through space to the water and the rocks below. A gust came, strong from behind her, willing her to step out, the force of it pushing her forward. She dropped to her knees, clutching on to the tufts of muddy grass at the edge, and when she was calmer, shuffled backwards up the path, using the grass either side to pull herself to safety.

Flora met the search party as she was going down through the trees: torch lights moving amongst the branches and people calling her name: her father, Martin and some other neighbours. Gil picked her up and hugged her and the small crowd gathered around. She was never sure if the next part was true memory or nightmarish imagination, because Flora recalled a white wraith flowing out from under the tree shadow, its skin luminous in the moonlight, and her father stepping forward to strike it so that the creature turned and fled, before her father carried her home.

The autumn after her mother had disappeared, Flora went again to the narrow track leading out to sea, and, lying on her stomach with her head over the edge of the cliff, she let fall one of Annie's teeth. The small white nugget was in her fingers and the next moment it was gone, too tiny, too insignificant to be seen; she imagined it spinning downwards and passing through the surface of the water without a disturbance, then carried along by the tide, deeper and deeper and further out to sea, until it settled amongst the weed and the rocks.

'You can't draw on my hand,' Richard said, snatching it away and leaving a snaking black line down to his middle finger. Flora looked up, surprised her model had moved. 'I will have to return to work soon.'

Flora had forgotten Richard had a job, that there were places of business where people took money and sold things from nine to five thirty on the other side of the ferry crossing. The sea, the land, the Swimming Pavilion often did that to her; made her forget that the rest of the world existed. 'Well, if the bookshop is more important to you than having your limbs and appendages in full working order, and staying in bed with me . . . ' she said, and went to jump off him, but he caught her by the arm and pulled her back to bed.

Later, with Richard asleep behind her, she looked at the sky and the clouds passing by the window on their way from the sea to the village, feeling the dry warmth of the stove mixing with the fresh air. After a time she whispered, 'Richard, are you awake?' and his breathing changed as he returned to consciousness. 'Are you really going to burn Daddy's books?'

'Of course not.' He kissed the nape of her neck

and the bristles on his chin raised goose pimples along the length of her body. She pushed against him so he would wrap his arms more tightly around her.

'Have you told him that you won't do it?'

'Not yet. He's so insistent, I'm not sure how to tell him. How to deny Gil Coleman his dying wish? But I won't burn them. Not books.'

She got up and put the kettle on the stove. 'I can't wait until Jonathan gets here. He'll know what to do.' She crouched to pull open the air vent at the bottom of the stove.

'I'll tell Gil I won't do it,' Richard said, putting on his glasses. 'Later today, I promise.'

36

Gil,

For nearly four years the dry sticks of George's dismantled cot lay in the loft, weighing on my head wherever I was in the house, the smell from the box of Nan's old baby clothes under the bed changed from fresh laundry to dust, and the space under my jaw and against my shoulder where a baby's head should rest remained empty. The world had become harder, more abrasive; sheets scratched, clothes irritated and people grated. It was when I was underwater or in the garden that I felt relief. But precise moments of grief, like the pangs of childbirth, are hard to recall after the most intense pain has passed: nature's trick to ensure we survive and continue to reproduce.

We must have carried on with normal life, I suppose; I gardened, making the rocky zigzag path down the bank to the beach, and planting it with sea kale, horned poppies and fennel. Our neighbours would leave cuttings wrapped in damp newspaper on our doorstep, or pots of lady's bedstraw, kidney vetch and sea lavender. I planted, watered and cared for them, and I looked after Nan. And you started another novel (all pretence of trying to find a job which paid long given up). I could tell it wasn't going well.

264

We stayed at home and counted the pennies. When you sold a story we celebrated with Jonathan, who was often with us, typing up his travel notes, helping with the heavy work in the garden while you were in your writing room. He no longer brought crowds of people with him, only sometimes a woman (remember that American who came for Christmas in 1980?). I tried to like them, tried to make them welcome, but most of them were ridiculous. The American insisted Jonathan buy the ingredients for a gingerbread house, even though none of us liked gingerbread, not even her. It gathered sticky dust in a corner of the kitchen until March, when its roof fell in.

Every night you didn't sleep in the house I went swimming. Once, after it rained for two weeks and the streams burst their banks, I walked inland as the sun came up, to the field at the rear of Milkwood Stables where the land dips down to the brook. I hung my clothes over a fence and stepped into the grey water. The thought of the submerged paths and hedges and barbed-wire fencing lying just beneath the surface was exhilarating.

And I often swam in Little Sea Pond before it became popular, with its official signposts and designated paths. The water was briny and the mud cool. I laboured out between the reeds and turned to face the bank, lowering myself backwards, letting the water support me until I lay supine, my head reclined, my hair trailing. If I remained motionless I could open my eyes and watch the colour of the sky change from deep purple to orange as the sun rose. Returning to the land was never so elegant, but despite the sulphuric smell of the disturbed mud, swimming there made me feel alive.

There was a morning in 1980 — October, I think — when I swam beyond my usual marker (the buoy) and struck out for Old Smoker. The rock is a long way, but I was a strong swimmer (I still am) and it was good weather, overcast but calm. I was nearly there when, without warning, the sea around me flowed with a strength I would never have believed possible. Like an invisible monster it took me and swam with me, out to sea. I fought, tried to kick and push towards the beach, but the thing was powerful, determined. I yelled, but after only minutes I was too far out to be heard, too tiny to be seen by anyone. The creature wrenched me under, turned me over, filled my mouth with water. Once, twice, I rose to the surface, spluttering, coughing and shouting, and then I was under again, spinning until I was adrift, lost. Under the surface, the water boiled as if storm clouds were massing and dispersing at great speed, and I spiralled through them, a leaf in a whirlwind. My chest burned and beams of light shone all about, illuminating the air bubbles attached to the swaying eelgrass which was sometimes above me and sometimes below. I remember thinking how beautiful it was under the water, and that I must tell everyone about it, but then realizing quite calmly that I wouldn't be able to because I was drowning and I would never see anyone again. But perhaps the sea just required me to submit, because once I'd given up struggling, my head popped out of the water like a cork and my legs pedalled in the undertow and I went with it. The sea current took me to Old Smoker and shoved me against its side, lacerating my knees and my cheek, but I clung on, embracing the flinty chalk. When I'd caught my breath I edged around to the south side of the pillar, out of the tearing flow. I took a moment in the slapping water on the leeward side to look up. Old Smoker rose vertiginously into a clearing sky, and when the sun appeared, the chalk on the southern side was blinding. Have you ever pressed your face against the wall of a skyscraper and stared up? The building will appear to overhang, to loom and force the dizzy visitor backwards. In a few hundred years Old Smoker will disappear, eroded and vanished into the sea like his late wife.

From the chalk stack I swam south, past the shingle bays that have no access to the land, until I reached Hope Cove, and there I dragged myself out of the water on to the tumble of seaweed-coated rocks that have fallen from the cliffs. I clambered, naked, on all fours, over the boulders, my knees bleeding, my hair hanging in clumps — a mermaid with a severed tail. A family had set up camp on top of a flat rock, with buckets and nets for catching shrimp. A mother uncapping a Thermos flask, a father untangling a crabbing line, and a child of about seven sitting on a hard picnic box, all watched me crawl towards them, their mouths open. I was lucky.

I remember now the intoxication that I felt after the incident on the beach, drunk on survival. I laughed every time I looked out to sea; I'd fought the water and won. All things were miraculous. I found joy not only in the garden, but in washing clothes, in counting out coins in the village shop in front of the patient Mrs Bankes, in being woken at five by Nan when I'd just fallen asleep.

Did you notice the change in me? You didn't say so if you did, but you spent more time at home, and we made the kind of love that we had when we'd first met, and you began again to ask me what I wanted you to do, what we could do together. I made up stories about making love in the sea, in the sand dunes, on the back seat of your car, but none of them was enough. 'Tell me what you'd like us to do with Jonathan,' you said. The story hadn't been in my head until you planted the idea, but I enjoyed letting it grow, develop, blossom. And I told it to you each night, inventing and describing it line by line, the three characters, the plot, the twist, the denouement. Dictating you a novel, so that in the morning you would hurry to your writing room and all day the tap, tap, tap of your typewriter keys would sound across the flower-beds and lawn.

'You know that the things you've been describing are just imaginary?' you said one evening when we were alone at the kitchen table. You were flicking the corners of a book, looking at the drawings a previous owner had sketched on each corner. A cat stood up on its hind legs and danced a modern dance with a fish. I knew what you meant without your having to explain, but you went on: 'I don't want us to do those things with Jonathan in real life.'

'OK,' I said.

'You know what I mean?' The cat raised its front paws and bent over backwards, the fish balancing on the cat's nose. 'Promise me you won't really sleep with Jonathan.' You stopped flicking and looked up at me.

'OK,' I said again.

The cat flipped the fish into a somersault and opened its mouth, and as the mackerel came down, the tabby snapped its jaws closed.

And then once more, I was pregnant. We didn't tell anyone, you just wrapped your arms around me as we sat on the bench at the top of the zigzag path. The feeling I'd had with George didn't return. In the night my mind filled with plans for escape which by morning seemed ridiculous and untenable. Flora arrived two weeks late, screwing up her eyes and crying, kicking her legs at the world, her tiny hands clenched into fists. You fell in love with her (your Flo), I could see it in your eyes, and in the way you held her.

'Number two,' you said. 'Four more to go.'

But your counting was off. By my reckoning we were at number four already. I did my best to hide my disappointment when Flora slid out of me, a slippery eel caught by a midwife in the hospital. But here, in this place of truths, I can say it. Flora wasn't George. Flora wasn't even a

269

boy, and I grieved again for the child I'd lost.
  Ingrid

[Placed in *Twelfth Night* by William Shakespeare, 1968 edition]

37

Flora was sitting on the top step of the writing-room stairs when Richard came out of the house.

'I told him.'

'What did you say?'

'That it wasn't in me to burn his books. That it was a bit too much like *Fahrenheit 451*.' He sat beside her, nudging her along. 'But he was OK about it. He didn't seem surprised.'

'Didn't he say anything at all?'

'He quoted some German at me, and when I asked what it meant he said it was from a Heinrich Heine play.'

'Who?'

'A German Romantic poet. 'Where they burn the books, so too, in the end, will they burn the people.' He asked me to do something else though. He wants me to help him down to the sea. This afternoon.'

'That's impossible — he wouldn't be able to get there. How would he make it to the beach?'

'I said I would carry him.' Richard stretched his legs out into the sunshine.

'What's going on with you and Daddy? How is it you suddenly know what's best for him?'

'It's not that I know what's best,' Richard said, without rising to the anger in her voice. 'Perhaps it's just that I'm not family — you know, not so close.'

Flora turned her head away, dared herself to look straight at the sun.

Richard put his arm around her. 'Hey, I'm only talking to him about facing reality.'

'Did you know he asked me to get him a baby's boot? One of those knitted ones.'

'A what?' Richard said.

'And he only wanted one. He was very specific.' She turned and stared at Richard's face. He seemed genuinely surprised. 'I thought maybe you'd put him up to it.'

'Why would I suggest something like that?'

She shrugged.

'It'll be all right. It's one last trip to the water. What harm can it do?'

Without talking about it, neither Flora nor Richard told Nan what they were planning. After lunch, Nan said she was going into Hadleigh again, that there were some things she had forgotten. She came out to the veranda wearing a pencil skirt and a black top with a sequinned butterfly sewn across the chest.

'He's resting, but I've got my phone.' Nan reached inside the top and adjusted her bra strap. 'I'll keep it switched on, so call me if you need to.'

'Look at you!' Flora said. 'You're not just going to the supermarket.'

Nan stared down at herself and smoothed her hands over the top, the sequins moving and catching the sunlight, tiny flashes dancing across the front of the house. 'If anything changes, anything at all, promise you'll call me.'

'I promise. Turn around,' Flora said, motioning with her hand.

'I can come home straight away.' Nan peered over a shoulder, trying to see her bottom packed into the skirt. 'Is it OK, do you think? Not too much?'

Richard gave a long low whistle and Nan smiled coyly. 'I thought I'd better go and ask Viv about Dad's book.'

'You look great,' Flora said. 'Amazing.'

'I have my phone,' Nan repeated. 'You know the number.'

'Don't worry,' Flora said. 'Everything will be fine. Have a lovely time.'

Flora walked in front, down the chine, carrying a blanket, a pillow and a folding chair which Gil said he didn't need, but she had insisted on. Richard carried Gil.

He wore a large straw hat, one of those which lived on the pegs in the hallway and were no longer owned by anyone, and a pair of women's sunglasses Flora had found in the kitchen-table drawer. He was thinner than a few days ago, but he could open his left eye now and the purple on the lid had changed to a lurid yellowy-green. He reclined in Richard's arms without embarrassment, examining and commenting on the sky and trees as he passed beneath them, as if it would be his last opportunity.

When Flora stepped on to the sand she saw Martin standing by the edge of the water. The wind was light and the sea lolled, only bothering to break into lazy wavelets when it touched the beach.

'Daddy,' Flora said, 'what's going on? Why is Martin here?'

'You can put me down now. Thank you, Richard,' Gil said, and he made his way towards the sea. 'Martin,' he called.

'How are you doing?' Martin didn't come forward, and Flora saw that he held a rope in one hand and behind him a boat was lodged in the sand.

'Who's Martin?' Richard said to Flora.

'Shit,' Flora said under her breath. 'I knew it wouldn't be a simple trip to the beach.' She went forward to help her father. Gil and Martin shook hands.

'Your shiner's coming along well,' Martin said. 'Nice to see you on the beach. Not too choppy, good day to go out on the water.'

'You got the boat, then, and the bird?' Gil peered behind his friend.

'Couldn't get a rubber dinghy or a motor, but I thought a nice little rowing boat would be fine. This young man looks like he's got some muscle on him.' Martin raised and bent his own arm, clenched his fist, laughed. His bicep didn't get any bigger. 'We could have managed it ourselves once upon a time, eh?' Martin said, slapping Gil on the shoulder.

'But you got the bird?' Gil asked again, staring at Martin over the top of his sunglasses. 'There's no point in having the boat without the bird.'

Martin stood back to reveal a small skiff, a knocked-about blue with two benches inside and a rill of dirty water slopping about in the bottom. It would have been big enough for three if it weren't for a small wire cage jammed in the bow. Inside, a cockerel jerked its head, staring at them with one beady eye and then the other, its wattle swaying.

'Daddy,' Flora said, 'what *is* this? I thought we were bringing you to look at the sea.'

'I'm going out on the water,' Gil said. 'I'm not sure Martin's up for the rowing, so it'll have to be one of you two.'

'But the chicken?' Richard said.

'Cockerel,' Martin said.

'It's a little trick Flora's mother told me about,' Gil said. 'A long time ago . . . well, not so long ago.' He stepped forward into the water beside the boat, his trouser bottoms turning a darker grey. 'Hold it steady, Martin.' Gil lifted one shaky leg and the cockerel croaked in the back of its throat.

'Wait, Daddy, wait,' Flora said. She dropped the folding chair, flung the blanket and cushion into the skiff and moved to her father. 'Richard,' she said, 'come and help.'

'I don't think this is a good idea,' he said, but he stood beside the old man, put an arm around his chest and lowered a shoulder for Gil to lean on. Flora and Richard manoeuvred his limbs like those of a stiff-jointed doll until they got him sitting on the bench in the stern, opposite the cockerel. Gil clung on to the side with his good arm, catching his breath, his sun hat knocked off and hanging down his back. The others stood on the beach, undecided, while the bird watched.

'What is going on, Martin?' Flora said in a low voice.

'Don't ask me. You know what Gil's like. He wanted me to meet him here this afternoon with a boat and a cockerel. It took some getting, I can tell you. I had to pay twenty pounds just to borrow the bird for the afternoon from a farmer over near Sydenham. He'd better not come home with a single feather ruffled or I'll be done for.'

'So one of us has to row him? But where to?' Flora looked at the sea. A couple of yachts were moored far out, and the silhouette of a container ship sat low and motionless on the horizon.

'He always liked a bit of an adventure,' Martin said. 'God, we used to get up to some stuff around the village, you wouldn't believe.' He seemed about to go on to give an example and then changed his mind. 'Look, the man is dying.' His voice was quiet, and the three of them glanced at Gil, who sat with his head pushed forward on his scrawny neck, staring at the cockerel, which was eyeing him back. 'Take him out on a little row around the bay and home again. That's all he wants. So what if he's taking a cockerel with him. People have asked for stranger things.' He didn't give an example of these either.

'You go,' Richard said to Flora. 'It would be good for you to spend some more time alone with him.'

'There's enough room for us both.' Although she wasn't sure there was, with the cockerel's cage.

'I'll wait with Martin.'

They turned the boat and pushed it out, and when it began to float, Flora jumped in, settling in the middle and holding the oars. She rowed with her back to the cockerel, facing her father. Flora liked the action of rowing: there was something satisfying about pressing her feet against the sides of the boat and feeling her shoulder muscles work, the closest she had come to swimming without being in the water. The skiff gave a blip as it rose and dipped in the swell; Gil took off his sunglasses and closed his eyes, wedging himself into the corner formed by the stern and one side. His arm was stretched out and his hand gripped the side of the boat.

When they were about a hundred metres out, Flora turned the skiff and rowed hard against the current which flowed towards Old Smoker. She got into a rhythm, pulling the oars through the water, lifting and rotating the blades. Behind her the cockerel's croak had changed to a *puk, puk, puk.*

'I read about this trick that you can do with cockerels,' Gil said, opening his eyes.

'I thought you said Mum told you,' Flora said when the blades were out of the water.

'Well, yes. Whichever,' Gil said. 'They have a sort of sixth sense.'

'I have to rest for a bit.' Flora pulled in the oars and bent forward, panting. They had gone past Dead End Point and were opposite the beach huts where a few owners sat out on wooden decks. Without the forward motion the boat wallowed in the waves, which were bigger

277

now they were out from the lee of the cliff, and Flora felt the wind chilling the sweat that had formed down her back. 'Are you cold, Daddy?' Gil was hunched, his free hand tucked between his legs. Flora picked up the cushion and the blanket from the bottom of the boat, but they were both sodden and she dropped them back. A bigger wave caught them broadside and spat at all three of them. The cockerel's noise changed to an open-beaked bray, starting high and plummeting to a throaty cough. It wasn't a crow but more melancholic, a lament. As soon as it finished the bird began the sound again. Flora twisted around to look behind her and the boat rocked. 'I think it's seasick,' she said.

'If you row over the spot where a person drowned the cock will crow,' Gil said.

'What?' Flora turned back to him.

'Or maybe it's where their body is, under the water. I've forgotten exactly.' Gil's eyes were closed as if he was concentrating, and his hand again gripped the side of the skiff, his knuckles white.

'Is that what this is all about? You think Mum drowned? But you saw her in Hadleigh.'

'I saw something. Who knows what it was. Something my imagination served up for me.'

The cockerel was louder now, and Flora saw people on the beach stop to stare out at them.

'Do you think it's all right?' Gil craned his neck to look around her. 'Maybe it's seasick.'

Flora rolled her eyes. 'Your imagination?' she asked.

Gil ignored her. 'Perhaps we should let it out

278

and then it might crow.' The cockerel's noise was hideous, and it tried to flap its wings but the cage was too small.

'I can't row all over this patch of sea,' Flora said, picking up the oars. 'We're not even up as far as the nudist beach. I think we should go.' When she looked at the land, they were drifting back the way they had come, around Dead End Point.

'Open the cage just for a moment,' Gil said. 'Then at least it might be less distressed.'

Flora shifted to manoeuvre her legs over her seat. The boat listed and cold seawater slopped over the edge. The bird's cage tilted and the terrified creature grew even louder. Contorting her body, Flora reached to unhook the catch. The bird jumped, battering itself against the top.

'Careful,' Gil said.

'I am being careful!' Flora shouted over her shoulder, but he didn't mean the cockerel. When she turned with the wailing, flapping bird in her hands, one of the oars was overboard and bobbing beside the boat.

'I can get it,' Gil said, leaning awkwardly.

'No, Daddy!' Flora shouted above the cockerel's shrieks. It jabbed its head forward, aiming for her face, and she let it go. The bird perched on the side of the boat and glared at them and the strange wet land they had brought it to.

'There,' Gil said, pointing at the oar which Flora could plainly see. 'Get it.'

Using the remaining oar as a paddle, she tried to move the skiff forward as the floating oar travelled ahead of them in the current. The boat jerked and bumped, and there was a scraping as they hit the underwater rocks at the Point.

'Push us off! Push us off!' Gil said, and Flora jabbed at the rocks with the oar so that the skiff bumped again and Gil held on tighter. With each bump the bird bounced and then resettled on the edge, until Flora pushed with all her strength and with an ungainly flapping flight the bird took off, landing a couple of metres away on a seaweedy rock which poked up out of the waves. And then they were clear of Dead End Point, being returned to the beach, Flora paddling to keep them angled towards the sand, the waves washing them back in.

Richard and Martin were waiting and beside them was a furious-looking Nan. Flora twisted to get a glimpse of the cockerel, and Gil watched it too as it puffed out its chest, tipped up its head and crowed. Gil wheezed out a laugh and Flora began to laugh too. Richard waded out a little way and took the rope tied to the bow to pull them in.

'Bloody hell, Gil,' Martin said. 'How am I going to catch that effing bird now?'

Nan's face was white with anger.

They made a bedraggled procession as they walked up the chine, Richard carrying a wet Gil in his arms.

'He could have drowned,' Nan hissed at Flora. And Flora wondered, for a moment, if that was what he had wanted after all.

38

The Swimming Pavilion,
28th June 1992, 4.45 a.m.

Gil,

Yesterday the three of us caught the bus into Hadleigh. I thought it'd be fun, we would have fish and chips on the beach, and I'd buy us some clothes, even though you're late again with the money. We went to the shop that calls itself a department store because it sells everything in one room, and Nan and I combed through the racks of clothes. Flora sulked. She didn't want to be there, wasn't going to wear anything from that 'shitty place', she was going to catch a 'bloody bus to London or anywhere else but here'. I cajoled and reasoned, ignored and bribed, but after five minutes Flora walked out, and Nan and I ran after her, just in time to see her turning the corner on to the promenade and disappearing into the amusement arcade. We gave her ten minutes and then I sent Nan in after her.

'She won't come,' Nan said when she returned.

I went into that jangling, eye-jarring place, which was murky with smoke. Tiny aluminium ashtrays overloaded with cigarette butts shuddered on top of every machine.

I found her at the back of the room. 'Flora, we need to go now.'

'Five more minutes,' she said.

'Now.' She walked off, scanning the bottom trays for stray coins. I followed her. 'Nan's waiting. We need to go now.'

'I'm not ready,' she said.

'We're going, whether you like it or not.'

'OK.' She moved to another machine.

'And you have to come too.'

'Why?' Flora didn't look at me.

'Because I say so.' My voice was raised.

Our youngest daughter bumped her hip against the glass of Rio Carnival, girls with coconut-shell bras cavorting alongside the sliding plates of two-pence pieces. A cascade of coins dropped into the crevice at the side and disappeared.

'Bugger,' Flora said.

I could see the woman behind the change counter watching us, eyes squinting. 'Now, Flora.'

'What if I don't want to?'

'I don't care what you want. We're going.'

Then Nan was there. 'Mum,' she complained. 'I'm hungry.'

'OK, Nan,' I said, surprising myself at the volume, and she backed away from me.

I grabbed Flora's wrist and yanked her. She became limp and silent under my hand, and I dragged her along, avoiding the blaring machines.

'Mum! Let her go.' Nan was crying, tugging on my arm. The lonely men with their plastic pots of 50p's, and the women with their blonde hair and cigarettes, stared. Bad mother, they were thinking. Bad mother. Nan, pleading with me to let her sister go, was thinking, Bad mother.

When we got outside, Flora ran to the steps down to the beach and huddled against the promenade wall as if I'd beaten her. It took Nan half an hour to talk her round so we could catch the bus home, without doing any more shopping or having fish and chips. The girls sat together and I sat alone near the front. And it was while I pressed my forehead up against the bus window, and with the warm smell of dusty upholstery in my nose, that I wondered if my children might be better off without me.

* * *

In September 1990 you delivered *A Man of Pleasure* to your editor and the advance was larger than we could ever have imagined. Previously he'd taken a month to return your phone calls, but now you were in demand for London lunches, deals and meetings. You phoned to speak to the girls every night you were gone, but I was left explaining to Flora why her father wasn't here to put her to bed, and to Nan why she no longer had to worry about switching off the lights so I wouldn't cry when the electricity bill arrived. It took me weeks to get used to the idea that I didn't need to tally the prices in my head as I walked around the supermarket, and that I could take a taxi home from Hadleigh rather than the bus.

You gave me the manuscript of *A Man of Pleasure* only after I'd repeatedly asked for it. You handed it over in a brown envelope and

283

warned me to read it when the children were in bed and to hide it afterwards. And when your novel was printed you wouldn't allow a copy of the book in the house. I wasn't shocked or disgusted at the story; I knew it already from when I'd whispered the whole book to you in bed at night. But the final draft you gave me to read that autumn was missing one crucial element, wasn't it, Gil? The one line that was more terrible than all the lurid scenes of debauchery I'd invented and you'd copied down in such arousing detail.

The book was as controversial as your publisher and agent had hoped, but the reviewers who looked beyond the subject matter said your third novel was 'lean and understated', 'measured and poetic', 'from a writer at the top of his form'. Jonathan didn't see it like that, of course, especially since you hadn't even bothered to change his name. I agreed with all the things he shouted when he came down that final time, and I'd have liked to tell him the truth of who the real author was but I was too afraid of what he'd think of me, too afraid I'd never see him again. Neither of us ever told anyone whose head the real story of *A Man of Pleasure* had come from.

You were keen to point out to interviewers that it was your fourth book, and I've always thought how I'd like to have been that brave. What did I reply when a hairdresser or a new neighbour asked how many children I had? I curled my fingers into fists, pushed my nails into the palm of my hands and answered, 'Two.' I

284

always answered 'Two', and hated myself for it.

You were delighted with the book's success, and the money rolled in. You gave interviews on radio and television where you were jokingly coy about your private life. You were handsome and charming. Isn't it ironic that the publicity focused so much on the book's author? No one, not even you, was interested in its readers.

I was usually too busy with the girls to go with you to many of your literary events. 'You won't like them,' you told me. 'They're full of boring, bookish people standing around talking about themselves for too long.' But I went up for one of your television appearances: ten minutes in an armchair on an arts chat show with a tumbler of whiskey in front of you.

In the television studio I stood in the margins amongst the cables and the cameras to watch you in the spotlight. You mesmerized us — studio crew, audience, interviewer (and me); we were alternately laughing and hushed, listening to everything you had to say. I was so proud. They loved you, your book, your stories, and your looks. I loved you too.

I loved you and nodded when the production assistant, standing beside me, whispered, 'Isn't he great?' And I smiled when she said, 'He's a bit of a rogue though.' I still loved you when she continued, 'Apparently he's got a wife and children in the country. Keeps them there out of harm's way, I suppose.' I said nothing. 'He took my friend out for drinks a few weeks ago,' the girl whispered. 'And then he asked her to stay the night in his hotel room. 'Aren't you married?' she said to him, and he said, 'What the eye doesn't see and the mind doesn't know, doesn't exist.''

I didn't look at the girl as she spoke, I watched you on your black swivel chair, legs crossed in the grey slacks I'd ironed, wearing the socks I'd washed and hung as a pair on the line outside the kitchen. Even the interviewer was laughing, unable to get his questions out coherently. I remembered our first summer, lying in the long grass outside the Swimming Pavilion, your head on my lap as I read to you, holding the book high to block out the glare of the sun.

'Did she take him up on his offer?' I said. 'Your friend?'

'I can't blame her,' the production assistant said. 'He's pretty old, but God, I would. Wouldn't you?'

I waited until we'd driven off the ferry, paid the toll and were on the dark straight road, heading home.

'I met a girl tonight,' I said, 'who told me you'd fucked her friend.' I said 'friend' in the way that people write to agony aunts about their friends who have slept with their boyfriend's brother and want some advice.

'What?' You gave a short laugh, like a yap.

'So you didn't?'

'What?' you said again.

'Fuck her?'

'Fuck a friend of a friend of a friend?' You said it like it was a joke.

I didn't answer, and when the silence became

uncomfortable you said, 'Come on, Ingrid. It's a silly girl gossiping. She probably knew who you were and was hoping for a reaction.'

'So you're denying that you fucked her?' I said.

'I thought it was her friend I was supposed to have fucked,' you said. 'And when exactly was this meant to have happened? I have been very busy, you might have noticed, earning us money.'

'Pull over.'

'We're nearly home. Let's talk about this later.'

'Pull over,' I repeated sharply.

You drew up on the sandy edge of the road. A couple of cars passed us, their headlights moving over our bodies like lighthouse beams sliding across rocks. 'I'm not going to do this all again,' I said.

'Do what?' You took your hands from the steering wheel and clasped them together in your lap.

'Be made a fool of!' I shouted. 'Be the last to know!'

'You're no fool, Ingrid.' You wouldn't look at me.

'And yet you treat me like one,' I spat out.

'This is about the book, isn't it? You think I went too far.' You turned towards me and put a hand on my arm. You didn't blink. 'You don't need to worry that Nan or Flora will read it. We won't keep a copy in the house.'

'For God's sake, not everything is about your work, Gil.' I pulled my arm out from under your hand.

'There's no need for you to be concerned.

You're the mother of my children — it'll always be you and the girls I come home to. I'd never desert any of you.'

'So you did take some stupid book groupie to your hotel and fuck her!' My fingers found my seat-belt button and the strap flew loose with force.

'It didn't mean anything, Ingrid. It just happened.'

Without thinking I reached out across the gap between us and struck your face with the flat of my hand. It wasn't hard, but you flinched and knocked the side of your head against the driver's window. You said nothing, still looking ahead, as if punishment was something you wanted, something you deserved.

'It means something to me!' I said, pushing your head with both hands and slamming it into the window. I grabbed at the handle beside me, yanked the door open and stumbled out of the car.

'Ingrid!' I heard you call. 'Ingrid, I'm sorry!'

But without looking back I ran into a gap in the gorse by the side of the road, slipping and tripping across roots and through sharp grass, sobbing as I ran. I kept running until my heart was pumping and my breath painful, and I had to slow to a trot. After a few minutes of walking I recognized the path and found my way over the dunes to the sea. Behind a bank of cloud the moon glowed and sprinkled its light across the moving water. The wind whipped my hair around my head. I considered wading in, thought about what would happen and whether

I'd be missed, and although I believed I knew the answer, I took off my shoes, tied the laces together, slung them around my neck and walked towards home on the firm sand that the retreating sea left behind. The car was on the drive when I got back, but you must have been in your writing room because you weren't in the house. I paid the babysitter, sent her home and went to bed.

In the morning I telephoned Louise, and she arranged everything for me. Two days later I went to a clinic and aborted our fifth child.

Ingrid

[Placed in *Brilliant Creatures* by Clive James, 1983]

39

Gil went to bed when they returned from the beach. Nan gave him some water and one of the tablets he kept beside his bed. Flora sat next to him on her mother's side, and Nan, still in her pencil skirt and top, in the chair.

'I'm sorry, Dad,' Nan said, 'but Viv doesn't have that book, the one you were holding when you fell. She asked what it was called, though, because she might be able to get you a copy, or she thought there could be another in the shop. Sometimes Viv has duplicates.'

'It doesn't matter,' Gil said. 'It was that particular one I wanted.' He coughed, his jaw clenched against the pain.

'Shall I get the doctor?' Nan stood up and plumped his pillows.

'No more doctors,' Gil said.

'Did the book have something in it, Daddy?' Flora asked.

'Just another note. Too late now.' He coughed several times, his head bending forward with the effort.

Nan held a glass with a straw up to his lips for him to suck on.

'You don't want to see this, you girls. An old sick man.'

Nan looked accusingly at Flora as she held the water.

'Better to be remembered like your mother

290

— still young, still beautiful.' His eyelids dropped slowly, and Flora wondered if he saw Ingrid wearing her wide-brimmed hat and pushing a garden fork into the sandy soil, or standing in the sunlight on the veranda.

They were silent for a while, Gil's mouth falling open, his bottom jaw slack. Flora thought he was sleeping, until, still with his eyes closed, he said, 'Ambiguous loss.'

'What?' Nan said.

He opened his eyes. 'I went to the library, and they looked it up for me on a computer.'

'What did they look up?' Flora said.

'It's when you don't know if someone is dead or not and you can't mourn. No closure.' He paused, as if gathering strength to continue. 'Apparently I once told your mother that it was better to live without knowing because then you could always live with hope.'

'You told me that too,' Flora said.

'Dad, it doesn't matter,' Nan said. 'You should sleep.' She tugged on the side of the bedcover, straightening a wrinkle which wasn't there.

'I was wrong,' Gil said. 'Reality is better than imagination. Your mother is dead. I know that now.'

'No,' Flora said. 'You saw her.'

'An apparition.'

Nan crossed her legs, said nothing.

'I don't believe you,' Flora said.

'I used to think I needed a body, some kind of proof; I didn't. It's all in here.' He lifted a hand halfway to his head and pointed. 'It's not possible to live in limbo. You need to accept it,

Flora. Bury her, say goodbye. All of us need to say goodbye.'

Two swimming costumes and a bikini hung limp over the bath-curtain rail. They were still damp, and sand was clumped in the gussets where Flora hadn't bothered to rinse them out. She opened the airing cupboard, crammed with old sheets, towels, blankets and stained and flattened pillows; coloured layers of cloth like the tinted sand in the tiny bottles sold by Hadleigh's tourist shops. Somewhere in the mass of fabric would be more swimming costumes and trunks like the ones she had found for Richard, left behind by long-gone summer visitors and stuffed amongst the linen. Only the top third of each shelf was ever used — washed, ironed, folded and returned by Nan. Flora wormed her arms into the dense bottom layers, her fingers searching for smooth, slippery material. When she was immersed up to the elbows she grabbed a piece of cloth from the rear of the cupboard and pulled it forward. A corner of a towel appeared. She hauled it out and recognized the faded sandstone colour, the bald patches where the nap had worn away, and the hole on one edge where the towel had been jammed over the peg on the back of the bathroom door. Flora held it up to her face, closed her eyes and inhaled; it smelled grey, the odour of fabric which has lain too long without being washed. Still, the image of her mother came, forever turning away in the pink dress, the scent of coconut from the gorse, the colour of golden honey, a book in her hand.

Flora went into the kitchen, where Richard was washing up the breakfast plates. Nan, standing beside him, was scooping a pot of sour cream into a glass mixing bowl. A large salmon was flopped in an oven dish, and salad ingredients and a bag of new potatoes were scattered on the counters.

'Do you remember this?' Flora said, holding out the towel.

Nan looked around. 'What do you mean, remember it?' She blinked. 'Flora, please put some clothes on. It's not right.' She dolloped another pot of sour cream on top of the first and added a handful of chopped parsley.

'Richard's seen it all before, haven't you, Richard?' Flora said.

He smirked over Nan's shoulder.

'It was Mum's towel,' Flora said to Nan.

Nan stared down at the bowl in the crook of her arm as if she couldn't bear to see her sister's body. 'I don't recall any of us having our own towels, although that would be preferable. It's always a free-for-all in this house, as far as I can see.'

'No, I mean the day she disappeared.'

'Put some clothes on, please.'

Flora wrapped the towel around her, tucking it in under her armpits. 'Well?' she said, and sat at the table.

Nan picked up a spoon and stirred the parsley into the white cream. 'It might be, I don't remember.'

Richard filled the kettle, lifted cups from the cupboard. 'Tea or coffee?' he said.

'If she took this towel to the beach that last time' — Flora tucked it more tightly around her chest — 'how did it get to be in the airing cupboard?'

'I don't know what you mean,' Nan snapped. 'Where else would it be?'

'How did it get here, and what happened to the other things Mum had on the beach?'

'The same way that the ridiculous dress which you insist on wearing got back,' Nan said. 'I put the things away, in the airing cupboard, in the wardrobe, on the bookshelves, wherever they were meant to go — which is a lot more than other people do.' She picked up half a lemon and crushed it in her fist so the juice flowed out from between her solid fingers into the bowl of sour cream.

'But how did they get home?'

'I don't know. Martin must have brought everything over the next day — Mum's clothes, the towel. Somebody picked it all up from the nudist beach and stuffed it in a bag. One of the search party, I suppose.'

'And her book?' Flora said. 'What happened to that?' She wasn't sure why it was so important to know how her mother's things had got home, where they were now. An answer to a question she couldn't quite pin down.

'Like I said, I put things away in their proper places.'

'Didn't the police want to see them?' Richard said.

Flora had almost forgotten he was in the room. 'The fucking police were only interested in whether Daddy had murdered her and buried her body under the house.' Flora stamped a foot. 'But as soon as their dense little heads had worked out that he hadn't, they weren't interested in anything,' she said. 'No suspicious circumstances. They were crap.'

'Flora,' Nan said, 'that's not fair. Mum was an adult.' To Richard, she said, 'She went for a swim; she left her clothes on the beach. The coastguard searched, of course, but . . . ' Nan trailed off.

'What about her passport?' Richard said. He opened a cupboard and found the teapot, brown and round with several zigzags running through it where it had been glued together. He held it up to the window, as if unsure it would hold water.

'It was never found,' Flora said, as if proving something.

'She hadn't used it for years — not since I was a baby. It would have expired anyway.' Nan stirred the sour cream with a spoon.

'You think she's dead too, don't you?' Flora said. 'I bet you've always thought that.'

Nan looked at her, sighed, and sat opposite, placing the glass bowl on the table between them. 'She wouldn't have left without writing a letter, a note, something. She wouldn't have done that to us. She went for a swim, got into difficulty and drowned. It's as simple as that.' Nan gave a small laugh, and when Flora didn't speak, she continued, 'Mothers don't leave their children.'

'Who says so?' Flora dipped a finger into the

295

sour cream. 'Fathers leave their kids all the time and there's barely a shrug, or maybe someone's a bit disappointed. Why should it be so shocking when a mother does it?' She put her finger in her mouth.

'Tea, I think,' Richard said.

'It's different for mothers,' Nan said.

'Why? Because mothers are meant to love their children more than fathers? Because it's supposed to come naturally?'

'I see it all the time at work,' Nan said. 'There's an instant bond between the mother and her child. The father might be in the room, might even be the first to hold them, will be delighted, but it's not the same.' She stood and picked up the bowl.

'It wasn't like that for this family though, was it?' Flora said. 'You just don't like to admit it. Our mother didn't have an instant bond with us. I'm not sure she had a bond with anyone. Probably all she had was duty, expectation and guilt. She could have left because it was all too much, and still be out there.'

Nan talked over the end of Flora's words. 'I don't know why you want her to come home if she was so terrible.'

'Being a mother didn't come easily to her. Not like being a father does for Daddy.'

'You have no idea, do you, little sister?' Nan shook her head. Richard waited with the tea caddy in his hands.

'I don't know what you mean,' Flora said. 'He's been a good father.' Nan took a deep breath and Flora waited. 'What?'

'The man's dying. It's not right to talk about this now.' Nan stirred the cream once more.

'When will it ever be right?'

'You really want to know? How about this? He was a womanizer. He slept with whoever he could get his hands on.'

Flora laughed. Richard swilled warm water around the tea-pot and counted three spoonfuls of leaves inside.

'When I was fourteen, fifteen,' Nan said, 'every time Dad went out, Mum and I used to worry where he'd gone, who he would bring home to that damn writing room.'

'That's ridiculous. Daddy wouldn't do that.' Flora's voice rose; she felt the rush of anger and expected Richard to intervene, to say something, but he was waiting for the kettle to boil.

'What did you think he was doing down there? Writing?' It was Nan's turn to laugh. 'For your whole life he only managed to produce one book. And what a book that was. I'm still not sure how much of it's true. I could never work it out.'

From the corner of her eye, Flora saw Richard look at her. 'Of course it's not true.'

'How blind have you been all these years?' Nan said. 'While you and I were in our beds, he was down the garden having sex with Megan or some other girl, and Mum would leave the house and go swimming.'

Richard took the milk out of the fridge and sniffed it.

'Megan?' Flora said. 'Megan who used to babysit? I don't believe you.'

'God, none of it matters now,' Nan said. 'Just forget it.'

'You can't drop a bombshell like that and then say forget it.'

'Look, he's been making things up his whole life. The big important writer that everybody loved, speaking to Mum on the phone, seeing her in Hadleigh. It's all been nonsense.'

The kettle rumbled.

'Not all of it,' Flora said, almost to herself, almost hopefully.

'Oh, Flora, there are so many things you conveniently remember wrong. Sometimes I wonder if you were living in the same house as Mum and me.' The metal spoon chinked against the glass of the bowl and some cream splashed on to Nan's chin.

'Nobody told me anything,' Flora shouted. 'I had to work it out by listening at doors, overhearing snatches of conversation and filling in the gaps. Don't blame me if I made it up.'

'Stop complaining,' Nan said. 'At least you had Dad. Who did I have watching out for me? Not even Mum when she was here. And you didn't have to suddenly become the adult at the age of fifteen because there was no one else to do the job of a mother.'

'No one ever asked you to do it.' Flora pushed her chair out from the table.

'Who else was going to make sure there was food in the house, that there were clean clothes, that you went to school? It wasn't going to be our father. Overnight I had to become a mother to a daughter I didn't want.'

Flora flinched as if Nan had struck her. The kitchen window clouded with steam.

'You have no idea how difficult it was finishing my training,' Nan continued, 'when I had to keep coming back here and worrying what you were doing — staying out all night, drinking, smoking, sleeping around. Don't think I didn't know. Like father, like daughter.'

Flora stood up, her chair tipping behind her and knocking over some books stacked against the wall. 'I was only out all the time because being at home was so fucking awful I couldn't bear to be here.'

'You can't blame me for that,' Nan said. 'That'll be because of the man lying in the bedroom who you think is so bloody amazing. The two things he was good for were providing the money and the house, and the first came from a sleazy book which makes me ashamed to be his daughter, and the second was inherited from his own terrible father.' As the kettle reached crisis point, Nan took hold of the bowl with both hands and hurled. Flora ducked as it flew over her head, shards of glass and sour cream spraying the kitchen wall, the table and floor. In the doorway Nan turned. 'Actually,' she spat, 'I wasn't telling the complete truth earlier. Yes, I think Mum drowned, but it could easily have been suicide, and if it was, it's your precious daddy who bears the responsibility.'

40

Gil,

I've been thinking about getting a job. (Although who'd have me — undereducated, inexperienced — with so many unemployed? Maybe I should learn to drive.)

In the suitcase under my bed there's a photograph Jonathan took of you and Flora sitting on the steps of your writing room: you're fifty and Flora's nearly five, in a month she'll start school. It's late afternoon, the shadows are long, the light is golden. For once she's wearing clothes — a bikini with a frill around the bottom. Her feet are crusted with sand, as if she's just come up from the beach. You sit beside her in jeans and a T-shirt, your arms folded on your knees, your head angled towards her. The sun highlights your cheekbones and the fair hair on your forearms. Flora is looking up at you, an intense, concentrated stare, and it is clear that you're deep in conversation. Studying the photograph brings back the childish sting of being left out. And the hardest thing to write is that Nan wasn't enough compensation for your connection with Flora. Nan has always been complete, self-sufficient; she hasn't needed anyone, least of all me. The one person in our family who I was meant to mother was my dead

300

boy, George. Maybe I should have gone a long time ago.

It was less than a year ago (last September in fact), when I saw the young man through the glass of the front door. I thought he was a junior reporter or an evangelist. He was holding a book with both hands as if it were ballast, a weight to keep him grounded on our doorstep, and if he were to let go he'd rise and bob in the rafters of the veranda roof. He tried to smile when he saw me approach, but it was strained.

'Who is it?' Flora called out from my bedroom, where she was lying on the four-poster, drawing. She was faking her headache, but that morning I hadn't had the fight in me to get her out of the house and to school. Perhaps it was the delay of my answer or my tone of voice that made her get up and mouth 'Who is it?' as I passed the open doorway.

'It's OK,' I whispered, although I wasn't sure it would be. A tabloid journalist had already stopped me outside the supermarket, asking if I wanted help carrying my bags, before he began to ask questions about the book's content and whether it was a true story, and grew aggressive when I wouldn't answer. No one had dared come to the house before.

I opened the door a crack. 'Can I help you?' I said.

He looked about Nan's age, maybe a little older, fifteen or sixteen. (Still a boy, not even yet a young man.) He had blond down on his chin, and a mouth and nose too big for his bony face.

301

He was familiar, but I couldn't place him. The boy paused, as if he'd forgotten his rehearsed lines or wasn't sure they were the right ones.

'Is Gil Coleman in?' he said.

I hesitated, but told the truth. 'No.'

He gripped the book tighter, and I looked down at it. Inverted, I saw the image of the unmade bed from above, pillows hollowed by the shape of three heads, the crumpled sheet suggestive of a woman's body. *A Man of Pleasure*, I read. I'd seen the cover — the jacket, you called it — even though, as you'd promised, we didn't keep the finished book in the house. You'd shown me the picture, proud of the fact that your name was larger than the book's title.

'Do you mind if I wait?' His voice was tremulous, still breaking.

'What do you want him for?'

'I just . . . ' He held the book up. An autograph hunter, I thought. 'Can I wait?' he repeated, nodding at the table. 'I won't get in your way.'

Normally I'd have said no, but something about him, how tired he looked, made me shrug and close the door.

When he moved towards the table I saw he had a guitar strapped to his back. The boy chose the chair facing the view over the lawns and the pebble path, lined with pots of geraniums, to the sea and your writing room. From inside the house I could hear him tuning the guitar, a repeated note curving upwards. When I walked past the bedroom, Flora was jumping up and down, hissing, 'Mum! Why did you let him stay?

302

Now I can't go out and sunbathe.'

'There won't be any sunbathing Flora. You're supposed to be ill,' I said. I went into the bedroom and, without looking out, whisked the curtains closed across the front window. 'Back to bed, Flora, or if you're feeling better you can get dressed and catch the bus into school.' She huffed and sat.

In the kitchen I continued preparing dinner, chopping and frying onions, browning beef, when I suddenly realized that Flora had been quiet for a long time — longer than she could normally manage. I hurried along the hall to the bedroom, drying my hands on my skirt. I could hear the guitar music, a tune being picked out.

Flora, still in her nightie, was peering through a gap in the curtains.

'Come away,' I whispered.

'Why? You let him sit there.'

'It's rude to stare.'

'He's staring too. He looks like a hungry dog, a sad hungry dog. Maybe we should give him some food.'

When we went outside, the boy was staring towards the sea, his guitar silent across his lap. I put the tea tray on the table. 'I guessed at one sugar,' I said, sitting. Flora leaned on the post beside the steps, watching.

'Thank you,' he said. He propped his guitar against the veranda railing, and when he picked up the cup his hand was shaking. I held out the plate of biscuits, he took one and he ate it in two bites.

'I don't know how long Gil will be,' I said. 'But I am expecting him home later today.' Of course I had no idea when you would get back.

'I don't mind waiting, if you don't mind me sitting here.' He stared at the plate of biscuits, and Flora nudged it towards him with one finger, withdrawing her hand as if she was worried he might snap at her. He took another and ate it.

'Have you come far?' I said.

'Oxford.' His mouth showed churned crumbs.

Flora took one step forward, all the time watching.

'That's a fair way for a signature,' I said. He'd put your book on the table, and I placed my hand flat on top of it, covering the picture of the exposed bedsheet. Now, of course, I know that under the paper cover is a blue board and, inside, an endpaper — the left-hand side pasted down. Your book's endpapers are pale — the colour of duck's eggs in the morning. Next is the right-hand endpaper — the flyleaf — blue again. Then there's the first white page with the title — *A Man of Pleasure*. Turn that over, and the name is repeated, and below it there's your publisher's logo. On the reverse side of that leaf is the copyright page. And opposite that? You know what's opposite that. If you don't, you should go and remind yourself.

'No, that's . . . ' the boy said, and then quickly, 'Yes. A fair way.'

'Aren't you a bit young for this sort of book?' I said, my fingers tapping the pillows on the cover.

'I'm fifteen,' he said, sounding aggrieved, but

304

his blush gave him away.

Flora, beside the table now, snatched the book from under my hand.

'Flora,' I said sharply. 'Give the young man his book, please.' She ignored me and flicked through the pages with her thumb, stopping where a corner had been folded down.

'It's OK. I know it's Daddy's book.'

'Flora.' A warning in my voice.

'He's been writing in the margins.' She looked at the boy. I held my hand out. 'All right, all right,' Flora said, and snapped the book shut. To the boy she said, 'Daddy would like that.' She put it down in front of him. 'He likes it when people write in books. That's his thing.'

He'd taken another biscuit.

'It's only some notes — my thoughts,' he said, 'as I read.'

'What's your name?' Flora said.

'Flora,' I warned again.

The boy smiled, and the change in the shape of his mouth made his features suddenly sit well together and he became handsome. 'Since I know your name, I don't mind if you know mine.' He held out his hand to her. 'Gabriel,' he said.

Flora took his hand and pumped it up and down. 'Pleased to meet you, Gabriel,' she said. 'This is my mum, Ingrid.'

'I could tell. She looks like you.' He winked and Flora laughed.

'Everyone says I look like Daddy. They say I've got his smile, but I want to have my own smile.' She sat in the chair between me and Gabriel.

'Are you ill too? Is that why you're not at school?'

'Sorry,' I said, but he didn't appear to mind the questions.

'Something like that,' he said.

'My sister had to go to school today. But I'm at home because my head ached when I woke up.' She took a biscuit and Gabriel picked up the last one.

'I'm sorry to hear that,' he said, smiling. 'It must be awful to feel ill on a day like this, when the sun is shining and the sea is just down there.'

Flora nodded vigorously.

'I was hoping you might be able to show me the beach,' he continued. 'I live such a long way from the sea. I can't remember the last time I saw a wave or some sand.'

I was saying 'I don't think so . . . ' at the same time as Flora was shouting 'Yes, yes, I can show you the beach. Can I, Mum? Can I?'

'Flora,' I said sternly. 'You're not at school because you said you were ill. You can't go to the beach.'

'Maybe we could all go?' Gabriel said, and smiled his charming smile. 'I'd love to see the beach, we could have a swim. If you like swimming.'

I hesitated for too long, and it was decided without me even agreeing. Flora charged into the house and packed a bag: towels, bucket, spade.

'You have to wear something,' I said to her in her bedroom. 'You can't swim naked.'

'OK,' she said, pulling off her nightie and dragging on her costume. In the hall she shouted

306

to Gabriel, 'Do you want to borrow some of Daddy's trunks?'

The daytime crowds were leaving the beach by the time we got there. I'd put my swimming costume on under my clothes, and Flora had tried to give Gabriel a pair of your trunks, but he said he'd be fine in his underpants. We spread out a rug on the sand and sat side by side while Flora jumped in the surf. Neither of us looked directly at the other, but I could see his body was lean, his skin tight, muscles beginning to form into a man's. I have become used to your body: the grey hairs on your chest, the cross-hatched skin on your neck when you recline, the beginnings of a paunch when you don't know I'm looking. I used to love them all, but in comparison Gabriel was like a newly hatched man.

'She loves it in the water,' I said. Flora was floating on her front, letting the small waves push her into the beach and using her hands on the sandy bottom to move out, away from us. 'We'll both do anything to come down here. She'll even tell lies to her mother.'

He laughed. 'Sometimes I don't see the point of school. I've got to go back in a week, but I'm going to leave next year.'

'What will you do?'

'Don't know. I've had enough of it though.'

'What do your parents think?' Immediately I asked the question I regretted it. I sounded old.

'They don't know yet.'

We sat watching Flora until I said, 'I do find it

hard to be cross with her, about wanting to come to the sea. It's the one thing we both love.'

'And do you tell lies too so you can go swimming?' He lay back on the rug with his legs out, propping himself up on his elbows.

'Sometimes.' I felt myself blushing, and raised my hand to my eyes, pretending to shade them from the sun.

'To your husband?' he said.

I didn't answer, instead shouting to Flora not to go too far out. She ran over, plonking herself between us. Gabriel yowled as her icy skin touched his. 'You're freezing! Get away,' he said, laughing. Flora shook her head over him so that drops of seawater flicked out from the ends of her hair. He scrabbled backwards and stood up. 'Don't you dare,' he said, and set off running with Flora chasing him in between the late picnickers, the metal-detecting man, the elderly couple in their folding chairs. When they returned they were both panting.

'Do you want to build a sandcastle?' Gabriel said to her. 'You should go for a swim,' he said to me.

Flora barely glanced up when I put my hand on her head and said, 'I won't be long.' When I was far out, I turned towards the beach, pedalling my legs. I scanned the sand for Gabriel and Flora but they weren't where I'd left them. It was then, when I couldn't see them, that I considered what I was doing: leaving my daughter with a stranger; he might be fifteen, but I had known him for two hours. I felt sick, kicked my legs, and started swimming back. And then I saw them where they were supposed to be; it was I who'd drifted in the current. At that moment they both happened to stand up, look towards me and wave: big arm waves, slow and synchronized with each other. I waved back and swam out to the buoy.

When I'd dressed, we walked up the chine rather than the zigzag path, Flora running ahead, still in her swimming costume, plucking the flower-heads out of the marsh thistles and leaving a trail of purple petals behind her.

'Are you going to have any more children?' he said.

I laughed. 'I thought that was one of those questions you weren't meant to ask, like how much are you paid, or whether you're happily married.'

'Are you?' he said.

We were both silent a fraction too long. And then I said, 'Gil always wanted six children.'

'And you ended up with two.'

I wanted to tell him about George and the others, but I didn't trust myself. Then Flora came running down to us.

'Can I have some chips? The van's at the top of the lane. Come on!' It was Gabriel's hand she grabbed, not mine, and he let her tug him around the corner.

He bought three bags of chips, drawing the money out of the back pocket of his jeans — a screwed-up five-pound note. I wondered if it was his last. I bought two more packets for you and Nan, and when we got home I put them in a low oven to keep warm. Despite the swimming and the afternoon, or perhaps because of it, it still didn't feel right to invite Gabriel indoors, so the three of us sat around the table on the veranda and ate chips straight from the newspaper, and I didn't care that our appetites would be spoiled for dinner, or, indeed, that I hadn't finished the cooking. Your book was on the table where we'd left it.

Gabriel picked up his guitar again when he'd finished eating. He wiped his fingers on his jeans and played the song he'd been playing earlier, singing about the moon and the rain and lovers, and teaching Flora the lyrics. I watched his fingers pluck the strings and his eyes close as he sang. Strange to think this was only ten months ago; it feels like years.

It was Flora who saw you first. She leaped from her chair and ran to you, shouting, 'Daddy! Daddy!' I don't know how long you'd been standing on the drive, listening.

Gabriel stopped playing, and I stood up guiltily, although there was no reason.

'What happened to the car?' I said, leaning over the veranda railing.

Flora was jumping up and down, pulling on your shirtsleeve. You'd taken off your jacket and had slung it over your shoulder. 'Daddy, I've got chips. Look, chips!' Flora took her last one out of the soggy paper and held it up to you. You bent and opened your mouth, and Flora put the chip inside, and you pretended to eat her fingers.

'I need some fish fingers to go with my chip,' you said, and Flora shrieked with pleasure. And to me, 'The bloody thing broke down. Luckily

Martin was passing and gave me a lift.' You started on Flora's other hand.

'We've got a visitor,' I said. Gabriel stood and moved towards the top of the steps, looking at you crouched on the path. He held his guitar by its neck. Slowly you took Flora's thumb out of your mouth and stood up.

'Hello,' Gabriel said, and your smile faded. Flora stopped laughing and turned to stare at our visitor.

'This is Gabriel,' I said. Convention, I suppose, made me introduce him.

'I know who he is, I just don't know why he's here,' you said. Flora slipped her hand into yours.

Gabriel took one step. He raised his hands to chest height, the guitar with them, a gesture of surrender, as if you were pointing a gun at him.

'Dad,' Gabriel said.

'Get out,' you said, and Flora buried her face in the cloth of your shirt.

The rest, of course, you know; you were there.

I woke at a quarter past three alone in the bed; in my nostrils, the acrid smell of burning. I traced it to the kitchen: in the oven the packets of chips which I had bought for you and Nan were still waiting to be unwrapped, the newsprint singed and smoking. I took them to the bin outside and sat on the veranda, tucking my feet beneath the blanket. The light in your room was out. I'd asked you to tell me Gabriel's birthday. You'd said you didn't know it, that you weren't even sure he was yours, but I

311

remembered his smile and knew where I'd seen it before. It was your smile; Flora's too. Later I learned from Jonathan that Gabriel had been born during the first summer we spent together and that his mother wrote to you, but you destroyed the letter (remember?), and denied the boy was yours because the woman refused to marry you. Would you have done the same to me and Nan if I'd said no? It should be funny how you reverse convention, Gil, but it isn't. Gabriel is only nine and a half months older than our first child.

But that evening, I had worse things to discover than your sixth child (an illegitimate son you wouldn't acknowledge). *A Man of Pleasure* lay on the table, left behind by Gabriel, and when I saw it, I wondered if he'd buy another copy so he could finish reading.

I unfolded his turned-down corner and opened the book at the very beginning — the endpapers, the flyleaf, the title page, the copyright information, and opposite it, the dedication you'd written. The one which had been printed in all the books on all the shelves in all the bookshops across the country: 'For Louise'.

Ingrid

[Placed in *Good-bye, Mr. Chips* by James Hilton, 1934]

41

Flora sat once more by her father's bed. His breathing had changed to a rumble like an approaching Underground train. She stared at his collapsed face, trying to re-imagine Gil into a womanizer, someone who had slept with 'whoever he could get his hands on'. A man who took women to his writing room while his wife and children slept a few yards away; the image didn't come. The knowledge, if that's what it was, also changed the way she thought about Ingrid, made her more concrete, a real person with thoughts and feelings, decisions to make and an understanding of their consequences. Flora would have liked to ask her parents why the words 'to father' have such a different meaning from the words 'to mother'.

When she wasn't sitting, she stood by the window, looking out at the concrete sky and the drive, hoping to hear the Morris Minor's throaty engine.

After Nan had thrown the bowl at the kitchen wall, she'd run out of the house without taking her car key; fled along the lane or to the beach. Flora and Richard didn't see which way she went.

'Let her go,' Richard said, holding Flora back. 'Give her some time.'

Flora wanted to chase after her, but she remembered Nan's warning about not leaving Gil alone, so she made Richard go down to the sea to look for her sister. When he returned he said he'd waded around Dead End Point and walked as far as the nudist beach sign and had seen dog walkers, kite fliers and birds, but no Nan. She sent him to the pub to bang on the door until they opened up; she wasn't there. Without clearing up the debris in the kitchen, Flora made jam sandwiches but picked at hers; she brewed a pot of tea which she poured but left to go cold, and when even Richard had tired of waiting, he agreed to go out in the car and drive through the lanes, and to the ferry to check whether anyone matching Nan's description had boarded.

Only after he was home again did Flora think of Viv, but when she telephoned the bookshop there was no reply, even though it should have been open. Flora sent Richard out again to Hadleigh. When he had left she wrote down Nan's numbers from the kitchen telephone and stretched the curled mustard cord of the sitting room phone tight across the hall and into the front bedroom, and when it wouldn't come any further she gave it a yank. It caught on a corner of one of the stacks of books, which toppled. Hardbacks about space and time, paperbacks about love affairs, tumbling together with poetry pamphlets and novellas, knocked the top off another stack and then another, like a line of dominos. She didn't pick them up. Sitting on the edge of the chair next to Gil, she dialled the bookshop and Nan's numbers, letting them ring until the answerphones cut in, and then trying again and again. She worried she had lost her sister too.

The noise of a car turning on to the drive made Flora jump up and run to the door. It was small and white, not the Morris Minor. A man unfolded himself from the passenger seat.

'Jonathan!' Flora said, and ran out of the house and down the veranda steps. He flung his arms wide and they hugged, then he held her away from him and stared at her face.

'Jesus, you look more like your mother every time I see you.'

'I'm so pleased you're here,' she said into the cloth of his jacket, breathing in the smell of him — cigarettes the colour of wet bark. She was aware of other doors opening, and when she stood back to look around him, she saw Louise, her fingers with polished nails clutching the top of the car door as if she needed the support.

'Hello, Flora,' she said. And before Flora could answer someone else stood up from the driver's seat; a man at once familiar and unknown. He raised a hand awkwardly.

'Do you remember Gabriel?' Jonathan said. 'He says he met you once, a long time ago.'

Flora was aware she was frowning and her mouth was open.

The man had stubble and long hair, but he could have been the same age as the teenager she remembered. 'Gabriel,' she said. 'I don't know whether Daddy . . . '

'It's OK,' Gabriel said. 'He asked me to come.'

'You are expecting us, aren't you?' Jonathan said. 'I spoke to Nan.'

'Yes,' Flora said. 'But I didn't know who . . . I

just wasn't expecting you all . . . now.'

'Is Nan here? I'm parched.'

'She went out,' Flora said, reversing, blocking the way into the house. 'I'm not sure when she'll be home.'

'But Gil's in?' Jonathan said.

'How is he?' Louise asked. She slammed the car door shut and came forward. Flora took two more steps away from them. Her ankles touched the bottom tread of the stairs.

'Tired,' Flora said. 'Very tired. I don't know if he's up to guests right now.'

'But we've come all this way,' Louise said, as if the length of her journey had some bearing.

'He's fucking dying,' Flora said, and she could see Louise wince.

'Flora, Flora.' Jonathan put his arm around her, turned her away from Louise. Gabriel closed his car door and leaned on the roof, watching. 'I know it's hard,' Jonathan continued. 'Harder than I can imagine.'

'Perhaps we should wait until Nan gets back,' Louise said from behind him. Gabriel came out from beside the car, his eyes passing over the house, the writing room, and down to the sea, to the view. She saw the garden with his eyes, the plants run wild, the grass high.

'Why don't you go in and tell him we're here.' Jonathan gave Flora another hug.

She tried to think what her sister would do. Invite them in and give them a cup of tea? Perhaps she should do something with the salmon that had been lying in its oven dish all morning. But instead what came out was, 'Did

316

Nan tell you that Daddy saw Mum in Hadleigh?'
The expressions on their faces made her want to
laugh: eyebrows raised, round open mouths. She
decided not to tell them about the other things
Gil had seen, like Ingrid in the mirror. Jonathan
grabbed her by the elbow, pulled her back to
look at him.

'Gil saw Ingrid?'

Flora put her hand in the pocket of her shorts
and found the toy soldier there. She rubbed its
head. 'Apparently, Mum was standing outside a
bookshop in the rain.'

'What did she say? What happened?' Jonathan
said.

'I only meant he thought he saw her; they
didn't speak.'

'Oh, Flora.' Jonathan sounded like he thought
she'd made it up.

'What?' Flora said. 'Why shouldn't she be in
Hadleigh? It's as sensible as anywhere.'

The four of them stood, none of them looking
at each other, until Louise said, 'Shall we go in?
I think it's starting to rain.'

'Jesus, what happened here?' Jonathan said,
looking into the house. Half-fallen book-stacks
lined the walls, but the earlier landslide had left
the narrow passageway rocky with splayed books
piled up and blocking the way to the kitchen.
The telephone wire was still stretched tight
across the gap — a tripwire set to catch unwary
visitors.

Flora led the way into the bedroom. Rain was
beating against the seaward windows and

thrashing the tin roof, and the air inside was stuffy and stale. Gil opened his eyes. She thumped her father's pillows like she had seen Nan do, efficient and nurse-like. A sickly smell of persimmon came off his pyjamas, and she worried that she was supposed to have washed him. He raised his eyelids slowly; even this, an effort. It was Gabriel he stared at first, taking him in, and Flora saw each cleft chin, the same square jaw; one man healthy and handsome, the other a decaying mirror-image. Gabriel and Jonathan stood at the end of the bed with Gil's emaciated body, his death's head on the frame of a stick-man reflected in their expressions. Only Louise was able to hide her shock.

'Would you like something to drink, Daddy?' Flora said. 'I could make you a cup of tea.'

Gil slid his eyes towards the beaker of orange juice on his bedside table, and she held it up to him so he could suck from the straw.

'Gil,' Louise said, stepping forward, putting her hand on his. 'It's so lovely to see you.'

He turned his head. 'Always a sight for sore eyes, Louise.' His tongue made sticking noises in his mouth. He moved his focus back to Gabriel.

'So,' Jonathan said, filling the silence. 'What's the story? How are you feeling?'

'Fucking awful,' Gil said, each word drawn out. 'Dying isn't all it's cracked up to be.' Only Gil smiled, thin lips and a mouth with too many teeth.

Jonathan took a packet of cigarettes out of his pocket and a box of matches. Louise caught his eye and shook her head. Reluctantly he put them both back. 'It's bloody hot in here,' he said, taking off his jacket and laying it across the bed. 'Do you mind if I open a window?' He didn't wait for a reply, but went to the one facing the veranda. He wiggled the catch until Flora followed.

'Don't you remember, there's a knack to it,' she said. 'The frames have warped. You've got to give it a tug before you can turn the handle.' The window opened. A torn and folded beer mat fell out: *Ridley's 1977*, and the brown smell of wet earth came into the room.

'Shh,' Gil said and cocked his head. They were all quiet. 'Can you hear it?'

There was the sound of the rain falling on the roof. 'The carpenter's plane,' he said. 'He's making the coffin outside the window.' Gil's shoulders shook and he made a *haw haw haw* noise, and it took Flora a moment to realize he was laughing. 'He shouldn't bother.'

Gil closed his eyes and they stood waiting, watching, and Flora listened for his breath's rattle again, or another car on the drive.

'Perhaps I should make some tea,' she said, but didn't move.

'I thought we could have a party,' Gil said, paused, breathed, looked up at them without moving his head. 'For old times' sake; for Ingrid. She always liked a party, didn't she, Jonathan?'

The visitors looked from one to the other.

'Did she?' Jonathan said, and as if realizing this was the wrong answer, continued, 'Of course she did.'

'Dancing, whiskey,' Gil said.

'Daddy,' Flora said. 'I'm not sure Nan would let — '

Gil lifted the fingers of his hand that lay on top of the cover, stopping her. 'She's not here . . . I decide.'

'Gil — ' Louise began.

'Whiskey,' he said to Flora. 'You know where.'

Flora hesitated, wondering still if she should put the kettle on instead. She hovered by the door. Gil paused, gathering strength, willpower. 'Think of it like a wake, one where the corpse is still sitting up and talking.'

'I, for one,' Jonathan said, 'could do with a whiskey.'

'And what's a party without music, Gabriel?' Gil said. Gabriel was gripping one of the bedposts with both hands, holding the fish with the open mouth.

'I didn't bring my guitar.'

'Shame,' Gil said, not taking his eyes from him. 'Fetch the turntable from the sitting room. You'll know what to put on. Jonathan, help him.' Gil closed his eyes, resting, but still none of them moved. 'Go,' he said, and crooked an index finger to call Louise to him.

Flora picked her way across the books in the hall, like the unstable floor in a fairground fun house. In the kitchen she took the bottle of whiskey from under the sink. She could only find three tumblers. She knew there were more, but with Nan gone only a few hours already things seemed to be missing or in the wrong place. She rinsed out a couple of teacups.

Louise stood in the kitchen doorway, her high-heeled shoes dangling from her hand; she must have taken them off to clamber over the fallen books. 'He wants your mother's dress,' she said.

'Don't come in.' Flora flapped her away.

'He said you'll know what he means.'

'Broken glass,' Flora said, nodding towards the floor.

'Where exactly *is* Nan?' Louise looked around the kitchen. Streaks of white were sprayed out across the wall with long drips running from them, ending in a globule of sour cream where they had slowed and congealed. The salmon, its one upturned eye now dull, was still flopped in its dish. A half-eaten sandwich lay on the counter without a plate, and dirty knives, and cups filled with grey tea, littered the surfaces.

'Why does he want the dress?' Flora said.

'He said something about acknowledging his responsibility. I didn't understand completely. Something else about how he should have said sorry properly, behaved better. Anyway, he made me promise to get it.'

Flora passed Louise the glasses, picked up the cups and the whiskey bottle, and went into her and Nan's room. The dress was on the floor where she had let it fall after she'd last worn it.

In the sitting room, Jonathan had shifted the record player out from against the wall and was clearing a space so it could be carried into the bedroom. Gabriel was holding the album with the picture of the man sitting at the kitchen table — Townes Van Zandt.

Gil lay as Flora had left him in the bedroom — propped up on the pillows, his eyes shut. Louise crept forward, Flora behind her. 'Don't worry, I'm still alive,' Gil said. 'Have you got the dress? We can't have a party without a dress.'

'I think he believes Ingrid is here,' Louise whispered to Flora, and louder, 'Is the dress for Ingrid, Gil?'

'Of course it's not for fucking Ingrid.' Gil's eyes were open now. 'It's for me. It was the last thing she wore.' He fumbled with the top button of his pyjamas.

'Oh, I don't know, Gil,' Louise said, looking at Flora, who thought that the old Nan, the pleasant, agreeable version, would have disagreed on principle with anything Louise thought.

'Of course,' Flora said, and went around to kneel up on the bed. Gil's hands dropped to the cover while Flora brought the loop of his arm sling over his head and undid his pyjama buttons.

'Couldn't we put it over the top of them?' Louise said.

'Do you wear your dresses over your pyjamas?' Flora said. 'No, I didn't think so.'

The skin on her father's chest followed the outline of his ribs, dipping in the cavities, stretching over bone. The beating pulse of his heart knocked against the thin membrane and Flora had to look away. She pulled his pyjama collar over his right shoulder and helped him bend his elbow to get his arm out of the sleeve.

Jonathan and Gabriel carried the speakers and

the record player into the bedroom and plugged it in. An acoustic guitar started, a man's voice.

'Louder,' Gil whispered.

'Turn it up,' Flora said. Gabriel increased the volume and this time she remembered the music, not from when she'd put it on after she came home, but from years ago: a boy of about Nan's age sitting on the veranda, teaching her the lyrics.

Gil's skin was mottled, the inside of his arm bruised. She pulled the pyjama top out from behind his shoulders and inched his other arm out from the sleeve, being careful with his still-bandaged wrist. His eyes were screwed shut, his jaw working.

Louise held out the dress that Flora had draped over the chair. When Flora looked up, Gabriel and Jonathan were watching. 'Why don't you pour the whiskey?' she said.

'More,' Gil said.

'More whiskey?' Flora whispered, looking into his eyes, and he raised his to hers.

'More music,' he said, as she pulled the pink dress over her father's head, smoothing it around him.

Gabriel turned the music up again so that it swamped them and the room, overwhelming the noise of the rain and Gil's laboured breathing, like the last gasps of the mackerel on the road. Jonathan passed around the glasses and the two cups. And Gil, with a tumbler gripped in his fist, held up his shaking arm and, one by one, Louise, Jonathan, Gabriel and lastly Flora chinked against it and drank.

42

The Swimming Pavilion,
1st July 1992, 5 a.m.

Gil,

Yesterday evening Jonathan and I were the last customers in the bar of the Alpine Hotel in London. At the bar Jonathan ordered a whiskey. The woman who served him was stuffed into what the management must have thought was traditional Swiss costume: an apron and dirndl, the tight-laced bodice forcing her breasts over the top like risen muffins. Her hair was plaited and coiled around her head, and I wondered if they only hired barmaids with long blonde hair and whether that was legal. I asked for a glass of white wine, but Jonathan bought a bottle. We sat opposite each other on uncomfortable wooden chairs, a punched-out heart in each backrest.

'Happy birthday, again,' Jonathan said, and we chinked glasses.

Over dinner we'd talked about how he was still single, how his writing was going, and how he had to get up at six the next morning to catch a flight to Addis Ababa. I told him about the death and burial of Annie, and we'd raised our glasses to her memory. There was only one subject left now.

'You need to decide,' he said. 'Take him back or get divorced and move out. That house has always felt like Gil's to me, stuffed with his mother's old furniture and all those books. I remember being surprised there was even room for you and the girls when they came along.'

'That's because your oversized body was always hanging off either end of the sofa.' We drank. A wash of nostalgia for those months when I was pregnant with Nan swept over me. 'Not to London, though,' I said, imagining you with Louise at that very moment, in the same city, in her bed, in her body. I banished the image. 'I don't think the children would be happy moving. Nan wants to go into nursing, and we couldn't leave yet anyway, not until after her exams, and God knows about Flora. I'd have to suggest the opposite and then she might do what I wanted. I had to pay Nan more than the going rate to get her to babysit her sister tonight.' I drank again.

'You could come and live with me.'

I choked on the wine I was swallowing. 'But you don't even have a house, Jonathan. You've been sleeping on people's sofas for the whole of your life.'

'I do, in Ireland.'

'What are you saying?'

'I don't know.' He let go of his glass and rubbed both his hands through his hair so it stood up from his head. 'Just that I want something better for you, that you deserve something better.'

'That's what you've always said, but none of this is your fault. Everything that's happened I've let happen. There's no one else to blame except myself.'

'That's not true and you know it. Gil had the affair,' Jonathan said. I glanced at him and then away. 'Affairs,' he corrected. 'And he chose to include that dedication, he wrote that book; Gil, always the risk taker.'

I stared at my glass, didn't dare look him in the eye. 'But I knew what he was like,' I said. 'You warned me that first night at his party, remember?'

'Did I?' Jonathan waved his empty whiskey glass at the woman behind the bar. She clasped the top of her bodice and pulled it upwards with both hands; it didn't move. She came over with another whiskey on a silver tray.

'If you can't blame Gil,' Jonathan said, 'then you should blame me.'

'What do you mean?'

'I reintroduced them, Gil and Louise. At a party he invited me to. I brought her along. They didn't like each other much before that, did they? God, remember your wedding? I never thought the two of them would turn into something serious. He's an idiot. I'm sorry.'

'I have to make myself stop thinking about them. What they're doing, where they are.' I rolled the stem of my glass between my fingers. 'It's torture even after all these months.'

'But, Ingrid,' he said, and he reached out his hand to still mine. 'He's not with her any more. I thought you'd heard.' I could see the shock on my face reflected in the surprise on his. 'I haven't seen him since we argued, but I spoke to Louise. She left him weeks ago. She told me she was going to phone you.'

326

What did I feel? Relief? And then futility, anger, Schadenfreude. I remembered the telephone call that Flora had refused to take. Louise and I haven't spoken since you left. I blame her as much as I blame you, of course; but her betrayal is different, worse perhaps. Louise has always been my voice of reason, or, if not that, a different opinion — someone who will question my choices, make me defend myself. Not only has Louise slept with you, had an affair, fallen in love (whatever its name), she's changed sides.

'So tell me about this house,' I said.

'I've been thinking of getting rid of the tenants from my mother's old house, and doing it up. Going back to Ireland to settle down. Maybe I can find a job teaching in a school or somewhere.'

'It's about time. How old are you? Fifty-three?'

'Fifty-two. Bloody hell, how can I be fifty-two? I'm tired of travelling. You'd love the house. Plenty of space for the kids.'

'They're fifteen and nine. It's not space they want any more. It's time away from their mother.' I laughed.

'Well, there you are then.' He topped up my glass. 'Bantry Bay is beautiful when it's not raining. The house just needs some patching up, a lick or two of paint.'

'You should find yourself a wife.' We smiled.

'There's nothing to keep you and the children in England. Just decide, and come with me. You could make a garden and I could write.'

It sounded frighteningly familiar.

'You once told me to stay with Gil when I was thinking about leaving.'

Jonathan looked unbearably sad. 'See, that's why you should never listen to my advice. What do I know about what happens inside a marriage?'

'I sometimes think you know more about it than Gil and me, or at least you're able to take a more objective view.' I leaned forward and cupped the side of his face with my hand. He closed his eyes, pressed his cheek against my palm, and the moment lengthened until he snapped his eyes open and pulled away from me.

'Fuck Gil,' he said, raising his glass. We chinked again.

'To Ireland,' I said. 'I'll pack up the house, pack up the girls and move out.' It was the drink talking, making plans without my brain being asked.

Jonathan waved his glass towards the bar again and poured me more wine.

'Thank you for the offer, Jonathan,' I said, concentrating on my words, which wanted to run together. 'I really appreciate it. Will you do something else for me, too?'

Jonathan shifted across the table and held my hands in his. 'Anything.'

'If something should happen — you know, to me — promise you'll keep an eye on Nan and Flora.'

'What do you mean? What's going to happen?'

I stared at him until he said, 'OK, I promise.'

When we got up to leave I staggered, catching myself against the table. The barmaid was sitting on a stool, waiting for us to leave. Two plaits of yellow hair lay coiled on the bar beside her.

'Are you drunk?' Jonathan said.

'Of course I'm bloody drunk,' I said. 'You made me drink a whole bottle of wine, plus what we had at dinner.'

'I think you need some coffee,' he said. 'Come on, upstairs.'

Jonathan took me to my room and sat me on a wooden chair in the corner against another heart-shaped hole and kneeled to take off my shoes. I bent forward, meaning to kiss his forehead, but he jumped up. 'Coffee,' he said, and picked up the kettle from the tray on the unit opposite the bed. He shook it and went into the bathroom. I got up, steadied myself and followed him. The tiny space had been tiled with pictures of edelweiss and hearts which swirled together. Jonathan jumped when I put my arms about his chest, and when I looked around his shoulder his eyes met mine in the bathroom mirror. 'I can't do this, Ingrid,' he said. It hadn't occurred to me that we were doing anything until he said it.

'Why? Don't you want to?'

He left the kettle in the sink, turned around and put his hands on the tops of my arms.

'It would be wrong.' He sounded sober.

'But downstairs you said we should live together, in Ireland.'

'Not like that though. You're still married.'

'So you don't want me either.' I went back to the bedroom.

From the bathroom's doorway Jonathan said,

'Come on, Ingrid. Don't get all maudlin on me. It's wine you've been drinking, not gin.' He laughed. 'Let me make you some coffee.'

He sat on the edge of the bed drinking a mini-bar whiskey. I sat in the chair holding a cup and saucer on my lap.

'Drink it up,' he said. 'I might even make you have another.'

'Oh, please don't. I'll be peeing all night. Look.' I turned the cup upside down over the saucer and shook it; a couple of drops came out. 'See, all gone.' I got off the chair on to my knees, put the cup and saucer down and inched the two feet across the carpet.

I know, Gil, you don't want to read this. But you have to, every word. No skipping or scan-reading; this, my love, is your punishment. All I ask is that afterwards you break that stupid rule of yours and you remove these letters from their books and get rid of them. (More things our children mustn't read.)

This is what happened, the facts, the reality. I've always found that reality is so much more conventional than imagination. And over the years I've imagined far too many things: your women, your places, your actions.

Jonathan's knees were together; I opened them and kneeled in the space between. I took his glass of whiskey and put it on the floor behind me, and then I kissed him. He tasted of alcohol and sweetness; of the first spoonful of Christmas pudding after the flame has gone out. I hadn't kissed another man for more than sixteen years.

He pulled away but I took his bottom lip in

330

between my teeth and bit gently. I lifted my dress over my head, undid my bra, stood up and took off my knickers. I waited in front of him naked, and he held my buttocks and pulled me to him, pressing his face between my legs and breathing me in, long deep breaths. It was me who had to break away then, had to reach out to pull his shirt from his trousers and unzip him. Everything we did, the kissing, the undressing, the touching, everything was done slowly, as if at any time we were allowed to change our minds. Neither of us did. And when he came inside me as I sat astride him, his hands on my breasts, I watched his old familiar face from the perfect angle, and not once did I think of you.

In the morning I was woken by the click of the hotel door closing. The empty space beside me was still warm. Jonathan had left a note on the pillow:

> I told you I couldn't do this. I'm going to see Gil to get him to meet you at the Swimming Pavilion. Go home to your husband.
> Jonathan x
> PS — Sorry about Ireland.

I am grateful that he felt you and me, our marriage, our family, was more important than his flight to Addis Ababa, more important than anything he and I could've had together, but I don't deserve it, any of it. I never meant for this to be my life.

331

Time, tomorrow, for one more letter.
Ingrid

[Placed in *The Swiss Family Robinson* by Johann David Wyss, 1812]

43

They left Gil sleeping, still wearing the pink dress, and with an empty glass beside him. Gabriel turned the music down and closed the window, and Jonathan took the bottle with a drop of whiskey remaining out to the veranda. The rain stopped and the eaves dripped on to the rail and splashed on the weeds below.

Jonathan lifted a fat hand-rolled cigarette from the top pocket of his shirt and held it out to Flora.

'I brought this for Gil, but perhaps the whiskey has done the same trick. You should have it.'

She took it from him, rolled it between her fingers, held it up to her nose: the faintest whiff of tobacco and marijuana, waves of dusky orange.

'Or smoke it now. Why don't you and Gabriel take it down to the beach?'

Flora looked at Gabriel, who shrugged. She stared at the window into the bedroom.

'Go on,' Jonathan said. 'He's sleeping. He's fine, and Nan will be home soon.'

Richard had phoned to say he had discovered a muddy and wet Nan on the promenade in Hadleigh. She'd got a lift in a passing van halfway there and walked the rest of the way across the fields. Nan had gone to find Viv, but a notice was pinned to the door saying the bookshop was closed due to staff illness, and Nan didn't know where Viv lived. Richard said he would take her for a warm drink and then he would drive her home.

Flora stood up, still hesitating. There was something she was meant to tell Jonathan, something that Nan would have said, but she couldn't remember what it was.

'Do you want to come to the beach again?' she said to Gabriel. 'Where we went last time?'

They sat on the rocks at the bottom of the chine and looked out at the sea, grey and choppy in the wind. A couple of boys were lobbing stones into the waves. It was chilly, the tide was in and only pebbles and a strip of seaweed showed along the edge of the water.

'I was sorry to hear about your mother,' Gabriel blurted out. 'Her disappearance, I mean.' He hugged himself and blushed. 'I still think of that afternoon I spent with the two of you. I should have got in touch, but I wasn't sure it would be welcome.'

They watched the boys flicking seaweed with sticks and bending to poke at whatever it was they had found underneath.

'What do you think about smoking this?' Flora said, holding the joint up.

'Yes, sure,' Gabriel said. 'Do you have any matches?'

'Shit,' Flora said. 'I don't suppose you do? What was the point of Jonathan giving it to us without matches? Do you think those boys might have a light?' One of them picked something up with two fingers, yelling with delight and disgust as he threw it at his friend.

'Here.' Gabriel took the cigarette and put it in his mouth. At the twisted end he formed his hand into a fist and flicked his thumb up. He inhaled and closed his eyes. He pushed his heels into the pebbles and took the joint out of his mouth. Still holding his breath, he said, 'Strong stuff.' Flora smiled, and he passed it to her. She put the unlit joint between her lips and breathed in.

'I used to tell Nan stories about you after we'd gone to bed,' she said, holding the joint in her fingers. She bent to pick up a pebble, dull and brown. 'What you looked like, what you were doing, stupid stuff, like maybe you were in a band and we had a pop-star brother. She was so jealous she never got to meet you.'

'I'm looking forward to meeting her now.' He took the joint, let it hang from his mouth.

'I would pretend that you had visited us again and played your guitar on the veranda.' Flora licked the pebble and ran her thumb across it. The matt surface sprang to life, a rich brown threaded through with veins of red. 'No one ever told us what happened,' she said, suddenly embarrassed. 'To make Daddy behave like he did.'

'It's a simple story,' Gabriel said, taking the cigarette out of his mouth. 'He and my mum went out with each other for a few weeks. She got pregnant. He was really into it for a while apparently, read all the books he could get hold of, but he wanted to get married and she didn't, she didn't buy into all that conventional settling-down stuff he wanted. And so he denied the baby — me — was his, said she must have slept with someone else, and then left.

'She hadn't, of course. But she wasn't bothered, we were happy, only the two of us. She wouldn't tell me who my father was for years, but I wheedled it out of her in the end. And when *A Man of Pleasure* came out she made me promise not to go and see him. I didn't listen. But once was enough.'

'I'm sorry,' Flora said. 'Here.' She took the joint from him.

'You don't have to apologize.'

They were silent while the boys ran past them and up the chine.

'A week or so ago it rained fish,' Flora said. 'When I was driving home from the ferry. There was a massive storm and loads of little mackerel fell on to the car and the road.'

'Fish?' Gabriel said, and was quiet for a moment. 'Maybe it was a sign that something was going to happen — or,' he touched her arm, 'maybe it was a sign that something had already happened — that your mother had come back.'

'I don't know about that any more,' she said. She nudged him with her shoulder and laughed. 'But I think I'm going to like having a brother.'

Gabriel laughed too, took the cigarette and said, 'I think this stuff is working.'

'It is,' Flora said. 'I can almost smell it. *And* I can hear music.' She sat still, listening. On the wind there was the beat of a distant song.

'I can hear it too,' Gabriel said.

It was then that Flora turned her head to glance up the steep bank beside the chine, where, if you knew what to look for, the outline of her mother's zigzag path remained. The house was too near the lane to be glimpsed from sea level and the writing room was out of sight too. Only the nettles at the top were visible, and beyond them, in the grey sky, plumes of a darker grey billowing upwards. Smoke.

44

Gil,

I'm sitting on the beach. I've been delaying writing my final letter, and thinking about all the others already written and hidden in your books.

Remember your first class, with the jam jar and the daffodil? You asked then for our darkest, most private truths. And so here, at last, in all these words, have been mine.

When you find this letter, when you find the rest of them, don't forget that you must destroy them all, tear them up, throw them away, burn them; don't leave them for the girls to read.

I know you're on your way home, Jonathan rang to tell me. I'm sorry, but this time I won't be there.

This morning Nan promised to make sure her sister got on the bus and went to school. Flora has her packed lunch (two slices of bread buttered up to the edges and a piece of Red Leicester, but the cheese mustn't be inside the bread or she won't eat it). You need to keep an eye on her, she's spirited, and that's a good thing. I think she'll be OK — Flora has you, and you have her. Nan too will be fine, I'm sure. Just don't let her become the carer, the do-er, the little mother, a role I know she could slip into so easily. Let her go off and be free.

Weed the garden for me now and again, mow the lawn. And don't forget your other children, Gabriel and George, and the two others, unnamed and unknown. Six. You were right, in a way.

So, one last swim out, level with the buoy, or maybe a little further.

I.

[Placed in *Who Was Changed and Who Was Dead* by Barbara Comyns, 1954]

45

Flora remembered being ahead of Gabriel running up the chine, but then she was behind him, watching his arms pump as he sprinted into the lane. When she ran on to the drive the music was so loud it was distorted, unrecognizable, but even through that there was the sound of water splattering on to tarmac and her first thought was that everything was all right because it was raining again, but it was the noise of flames eating wood.

Gabriel was already at the door of the Swimming Pavilion. The window of the front bedroom glowed orange and a lick of flame crept out from under the roof.

Flora stood on the bottom step. 'Daddy!' she shouted, and 'Jonathan!' The glasses and the cups were still on the table with the whiskey bottle, empty now. One of the chairs had tipped against the railing, and there were tiny drifts of sand under the table and she knew Nan would want her to sweep them up. With a high-pitched crack, the glass in the front door crazed and fell out. Gabriel ducked as flames belched through the hole. Flora heard the music even louder: Townes Van Zandt singing about rain and roses, and then it stopped. 'Daddy!' she screamed.

'Get back! Get back!' Gabriel ran off the veranda in a crouch. 'Call the fire brigade,' he shouted. Black smoke billowed from the door and through the tin panels on the roof where they were joined together, high into the air, blowing over Spanish Green, away from the sea. The windows in the sitting room shimmered. Flora patted her shorts pockets, searching for her phone, but only finding the soldier and the unlit joint.

'I haven't got my phone,' she shouted as she followed Gabriel, who was running around the side of the house. The bedroom windows popped and shattered when he passed them, as though a sniper were following him and firing.

'Get mine!' he yelled. 'In the car! It's in the car.' He put his arm up over his face and went closer to Flora's bedroom window. She ran to the car, pulled on the door. Locked. She stared at the house. The flames roared and crackled, pouring out of the burst windows like liquid, as if gravity or the whole world had turned upside down. Inside the house she heard an explosion and yellow fire surged up through the apex of the roof. Flora took two steps away from the heat, and then Gabriel came running back.

'The keys, Gabriel,' she shouted. 'Where are the keys?'

'Shit.' He pulled them out of his pocket, aimed the fob at the car and pressed, pressed again until the car beeped.

And then Jonathan was there with Louise.

'Oh, thank God,' Flora said. 'You're safe.' She clung to him. 'You're all safe. I thought Daddy was in the house.' She almost laughed.

'Fuck!' Jonathan shouted, shoving Flora towards Louise, and running forward, tripping, righting himself. 'Fuck!' The front of the house was a leaping, curling rush of fire, each strut and beam in the veranda backlit by dancing, crackling orange.

'Where's Daddy?' Flora said. 'You must have Daddy with you.' Louise put her phone back in her pocket. Flora grabbed her jacket. Yelled in her face, 'Where's Daddy?'

'I've called the fire brigade,' Louise said. 'They won't be long. I promise you, Flora, they won't be long.' She held Flora up under her arms. 'We were in the pub,' Louise said. 'Just for a quick sandwich. Ten minutes. Twenty at the most.'

Something gave way at the end of the veranda, the paint blistering and the wood turning black, the screech of the tin roof warping in the heat. Flora's knees gave way too. 'Daddy,' she called again. A crowd had gathered at the end of the drive, women standing in twos and threes, the men coming forward past Flora and Louise to see if there was anything they could do. The heat drove them back, and when the engines arrived they stood watching the firemen unrolling hoses and connecting things, rather than looking at the flames and the burning house.

A man in a beige jacket and yellow hat spoke to Jonathan, and two firefighters in breathing equipment went into the house, behind a jet of water. Louise tried to take Flora away, out to the lane where an ambulance had pulled up, but she shook her off and stood beside Gabriel further down the garden, watching.

With the sprays of water the black smoke turned to white billows and the ribs of the building stood out. And then the white billows gave way to wisps and smoulders. 'They could probably see it as far as the Isle of Wight,' Flora heard someone say, and their neighbour replied, 'Must have had something good in there to burn like that.' And she thought of the hundreds, thousands of books, their edges curling, all the words and things that people had left in them blackening and crumbling to ash. And then Richard, and behind him Nan, wearing his jumper, her hair straggly, were pushing through the people, Nan grabbing them and shouting to get her father out; Richard running forward and swearing like Flora had never heard before, and later telling anyone who would listen that Gil had seemed fine and happy when Richard had said he couldn't burn the books.

'I didn't know,' Richard said, again and again. 'I didn't know Gil would do it himself.'

★ ★ ★

Flora wrapped a blanket around herself and crossed the garden towards the sea. The grass was long and damp, and although the morning was cold, there was a charge in the air, an awareness of the heat to come. She sat on one of the garden chairs — part of the set which had been given to her by the woman who lived in the big house down the road; odd that the chairs and the table had stood on the patio once owned by her grandparents, perhaps had even been theirs. The blanket was one that someone had wrapped around her the night of the fire, and since she

343

didn't know who it belonged to, she wasn't able to return it.

'Couldn't sleep either, Daddy?' she said. 'It's going to be a hot day.' She laid her head sideways on the table. In front of her the rising sun was a white puffball growing on the sea's horizon.

When she woke, the wooden table had imprinted its ridges across the skin of her cheek. The chair beside her was empty, and Flora cried.

After the fire Richard had stayed with her for a week in the writing room. He had tried to persuade her to go back with him, but once he understood that there was no changing her mind, he arranged for a Portaloo to be delivered and got the outside tap working. The landlord of the Royal Oak — the man who had bought the pub from Martin, Flora couldn't remember his name — had found beds for Jonathan, Gabriel, Louise and Nan. One by one, over the following days, they had left Spanish Green, each taking Flora aside and trying to convince her to leave.

Two weeks later they had all returned to scatter Gil's ashes. There had been a moment of tension when Flora had laughed at Nan deciding that Gil's remains should be cremated. 'They're burning bits of books and letters and bedsheets,' she had said, but she stood beside Gabriel, Louise, Richard and Jonathan on a swaying fishing boat one morning as the sun came up, to watch Nan throw the ashes across the water. They had floated on the surface for a minute or two, light grey on grey-green, and then had sunk.

And a week after that, the coroner recorded an

open verdict. All Flora's questions again went unanswered.

After lunch she ducked under the police tape that encircled what was left of the Swimming Pavilion. Most of the contents and internal structure had gone, especially on the right-hand side where the fire had burned strongest. She stood inside the charred skeleton of a giant creature, within the ribcage of a whale or a dinosaur, rays of sunshine casting bands of light and shadow across the ground. The place still stank of burning, the only smell that was pure black. In what was once the front bedroom she nudged the debris with her feet and bent where she thought the bed would have been, picking up bits of unidentifiable things and examining them up close. She would have been happy to find a piece of the bed, one of the pineapple finials or the fish with the open mouth, but what she was hoping for most was something else: a fragment of tibia, a splinter of radius, a molar. She imagined sealing it in a glass dome with a label, handwritten in ink: *A relic of the writer.* She pushed her hair out of her face with her sooty wrist and shuffled forward through the mess.

'Flora!' It was Nan's voice, and when Flora stood up straight she saw her sister in front of the tape, the car behind her on the drive. 'What are you doing in the house? It isn't safe.'

'I didn't hear you arrive.' Flora stepped carefully over the fallen beams and blackened remains, walked through the gap where the front door would have been and crossed under the tape. 'I needed some charcoal,' she said. 'I thought I might start drawing again.'

'Drawing would do you good,' Nan said. 'But I have something else that might make you even happier.' She went to the boot of the car and Flora followed.

'What is it?'

'Here. Don't look.' Nan passed her a bag and lifted out a heavy box the size of a small suitcase.

'What have you brought?' Flora asked.

'Wait and see.' Nan was as excited as a child. She carried the box down through the grass and put it on the table. She undid the catches on the side and lifted the lid. 'It's a wind-up record player,' she said, pleased with herself, delighted with the look on Flora's face. 'I managed to get you an album I think you'll like. You have to turn your back.'

'Really?'

'Yes, turn around.'

Flora turned and she heard Nan take something out of the bag, heard her pressing buttons, winding the machine up, and the crackle as she placed a needle on the vinyl. The familiar opening chords of 'Rubylove' played out over the tangled plants of the garden. Flora spun, laughing, and Nan clicked her fingers up near her head. 'Greek, not Spanish,' Flora said, smiling.

'Who cares,' Nan said, and began to dance, giving her hips a little wiggle. She twirled where the grass had been flattened, Flora swaying with her. They found it impossible not to smile, dancing around the table with the sun shining on the sea below them, and singing along, making up the foreign words with anything that came to them, holding hands, laughing together, until the track finished and Nan flung herself, panting, on to the ground. Flora lay beside her sister, staring up at the blue sky, the grass prickling her legs.

'I should have told them,' Flora said.

'Who?' Nan said, still breathless.

'Jonathan and Louise.'

'Told them what?' Nan moved on to her side, propping her head up with her hand.

'What you were always telling me.' Flora put her hands over her eyes. 'That they shouldn't leave Daddy on his own.' Her blood pulsed in her ears, the whirr of an approaching helicopter. 'I'm sorry,' she managed.

'Oh, Flora. None of it's your fault.' Nan tucked some of her sister's hair behind her ear.

'You're wrong.' Flora closed her eyes, tried to stop herself from crying. 'It's all my fault.'

'What do you mean?'

'I saw Mum the day she disappeared.' Nan was silent, listening. 'I didn't go to school. I hid in the gorse and I watched her leave the house.' Once more, Flora saw Ingrid in her pink chiffon dress, turning into sunlight. 'And I didn't stop her.'

'But how could you have known? None of us knew she wouldn't come back. And besides, you were a child, it wasn't your job to stop her.'

Flora put a bent arm over her eyes, her chest heaving, and Nan pulled her in. They lay there, the two sisters, arms around each other, with the sun shining on them until the album finished.

In the afternoon, when Nan had left, Flora pulled out one of the drawers from under the writing-room bed, and took it together with a cup of tea to the table outside. The drawer was full of pieces of paper: snippets of typed stories, paragraphs describing landscape and birdsong, pages of sex. They had been scribbled over by her father, lines crossed out and annotations made in the margins: *Shit* and *Move here* and *Fucking rubbish*. They made her smile, and she found it difficult to understand that these words could exist when her father did not.

★ ★ ★

The next morning Flora walked to the village shop. She selected a loaf of sliced bread and stood in front of the upright chiller with the door ajar, the pain of the cold air welcome. The second Mrs Bankes, a younger, slimmer version of the previous one, coughed and Flora took out a packet of bacon. She picked up half a dozen eggs, and when she opened the box to check none of them was cracked something about their shape, their fragile brownness, made her grip on to the edge of the shelf for support. Tears plopped on to the box and spread into the cardboard. When she paid for the food, the second Mrs Bankes gave her too much change. Flora knew it was on purpose and she dropped the extra fifty pence into the collection box held by the plastic girl with the calipers outside the shop.

As she balanced the frying pan on the writing room's stove and tried to flip an egg, Flora heard the unmistakable rumble of the Morris Minor. She leaned on the bottom half of the stable door, eating bacon with her fingers, waiting for Richard.

'Hello,' she said.

He kissed her on the lips. 'How have you been?'

'Breakfast? I could fry you an egg.'

'Just a coffee. You should eat at the table, you know, sitting down,' Richard said.

She fetched another cup, poured him some coffee, and they went to the table. The drawer was still there, the pages weighted with a rock.

'Nan brought me a record player,' Flora said, but Richard was busy sifting through the papers.

'What are these?'

'Some bits Daddy wrote. Scraps really.'

He peered at the writing. 'Do you think there's anything publishable?'

She could tell he was excited. 'Richard.'

He looked up. 'Sorry. It was you I came to see. I brought a picnic. I thought we could go for a walk, to the sea. Or you could even go for a swim. What do you say?'

She felt the sting in the bridge of her nose and turned her head away.

'I'm sorry,' Richard said. 'It's too soon. We can go some other time. When you're ready.'

'No.' She smeared the tears across her cheeks, wiping her fingers on her shorts. 'No, it's fine. It's not that. I suddenly thought that I can't lend you any trunks and I haven't got a swimming costume. Stupid really. What does it matter? They're just things.'

They took the picnic, the blanket and a towel donated by the pub landlord, and walked to the nudist beach. They set the blanket in the lee of a sand dune and looked out at the water. A heat-haze blurred the horizon, while closer in four anchored yachts swung in the current, the *chink, chink, chink* of their halyards against the metal masts carrying over the water.

'Was this where your mother sat?' Richard said.

'Before she went for her final swim? I'm not sure. Maybe. It's a nice place.' Flora smiled. 'Shall we?' She plucked at the sleeve of his shirt.

Richard looked up and down the beach. The nearest people were fifty yards away, pink and brown bodies lying on towels. 'I'm not sure I've ever taken my clothes off in public before.' A group of hikers followed the line of the surf away from the village; they were so determined to look straight ahead, they might have been wearing blinkers.

'Nobody cares, no one's looking.' Still sitting, she kicked off her shoes and slipped her shirt over her head. She reached behind her and unclasped her bra. She put her arms up in the air. 'Freedom,' she said, and laughed. She took off her shorts and Richard unbuttoned his shirt, pulled it out from his work trousers. 'Come on, bottom half,' she said. He removed his shoes, tipped out the sand and placed them side by side. He tucked his socks into them and, lifting his bottom, took off his trousers and folded them on top of his shoes. His glasses went on top of his trousers. 'Ready?' she said. They both stood and slipped off their pants. Flora took Richard's hand. 'What's the worst that could happen?'

The water was like stepping into a shadow from hot noonday sun. They inched forward, rising on tiptoes as each wave lapped against them. When the water was up to the middle of his thighs, Richard said, 'There's something I need to tell you.' His tone was serious, and Flora felt nauseous, dreading already what he had to say. 'I don't know how to swim.' She stared at him. 'Really, I can't swim.'

She knew he was standing in the shallows watching as she moved off, but she didn't turn around. She swam hard and fast until she was level with the distant buoy and the muscles in her legs and arms complained. When she returned to the beach, Richard was sitting on the blanket. He had put his glasses and his trousers on. Flora stepped into her knickers, dragged on her shorts, and sat beside him.

Richard looked at her sadly and she stared back. She kissed him, and at the same time put her hand in her pocket and took out the toy soldier.

'Do you think this is going to work?' Richard said. 'You and me?'

Without him seeing, she pushed the soldier deep into the sand beside her: a burial her mother had never had and never would. In her head she said, 'May your bones be washed by the saltwater, your spirit return to the sand and the love we have for you be forever around us.' To Richard, she said, 'I hope so.'

Epilogue

A breeze sprang up over Hadleigh. Shoppers and walkers heading down the high street towards the beach angled themselves forward, their faces sculpted smooth by the wind. The tide was in and the waves crashed and seethed where they met the sand and the boulders, while further out the water rolled in the sun, topped by white spume. A teenager on the promenade threw a handful of chips into the air and the seagulls flapped around him like sheets of newspaper tossed into the squall.

The plastic bag that had been caught by the Tyrannosaurus rex six weeks ago filled with air, and the wind lifted it from the fibreglass claw. It sailed up and over the wire fence and came down in the car park, cavorting over the markings for the exit until it inflated and a gust carried it high like a thrown beach ball. The bag rose over the cars and the gardens and the terraced houses and the bookshop, up above the chimney pots, a small white balloon travelling north, until the houses petered out to fields and hedgerows.

It was caught by the spike of a barbed-wire fence, where it flapped and rustled, demanding release, until the bag puffed up again and was unfettered by the wind. It blew over the Downs, past Old Smoker, skimming the tops of the beech trees and the wooden roofs of Milkwood Stables. There, the offshore breeze buffeted the bag inland to the heath and flew it over the sandy paths, boggy patches and stunted trees. And where the land rose up to the Agglestone, the white bag was captured by the thorny stalks of a gorse bush, and when the wind yanked it again, it ripped and remained there, pinned in place. The breeze moved on, flowing around the rock, lifting gritty particles, scraping them over the limestone, flattening the boxer's nose even further, smoothing out the etched graffiti.

The woman came around the Agglestone and faced into the wind. It blew her straw-coloured hair about her face and she pushed it out of her eyes with the back of her wrist and then caught the strands in her fist, as if to get an uninterrupted view. Laid out before her was a woven cloth of purple heath and gorse, rolling down to the glittering sea, and in the distance the rooftops of Spanish Green.

Acknowledgements

There are many people I'd like to thank:

Adrienne Dines for helping with early direction. My first readers: Jo Barker-Scott, Louise Taylor, Henry Ayling, India Fuller Ayling and Tim Chapman. All those who have given such constructive feedback on this book in the St James Tavern, including Amanda Oosthuizen, Sarah Wells, Rebecca Lyon, Natasha Orme and Kate Patrick. All the Friday Fictioneers, past, present and future. The lovely people at Lutyens & Rubinstein, especially Juliet Mahony, and Jane Finigan for her support and enthusiasm. Everyone at Penguin and Fig Tree, including Anna Steadman and Poppy North, and in particular my fine and straight-talking editor, Juliet Annan. Caroline Pretty for catching my mistakes. Masie Cochran for her eagle-eyed advice, and all the rest of the wonderful team at Tin House, including Nanci McCloskey, Sabrina Wise, Erika Stevens and Allison Dubinsky. Diane Chonette for her amazing jacket design. Isabel Rogers for her cockerel-wrangling knowhow. Tommy Geddes for advice on 1970s university administration. Angela Lam for help with research on childbirth in the 1970s. Jill Kershaw for her patience with my medical questions. Matt Holt for Morris Minor information. Ursula Pitcher, Stephen Fuller and Heidi Fuller for their love and support. And Townes Van Zandt for my writing soundtrack.

Other titles published by Ulverscroft:

THE GIRL FROM BALLYMOR

Kathleen McGurl

Ballymor, Ireland, 1847: As famine grips the country, Kitty McCarthy is left widowed and alone. Fighting to keep her two remaining children alive against all odds, she must decide how far she will go to save her family . . . Present day: Arriving in Ballymor, Maria is researching her ancestor, Victorian artist Michael McCarthy, and his beloved mother, the mysterious Kitty who disappeared without a trace. Running from her future, it's not only answers about the past that Maria hopes to find in Ireland. As her search brings her closer to the truth about Kitty's fate, Maria must make the biggest decision of her life . . .

TO DIE IN SPRING

Ralf Rothmann

Walter Urban and Friedrich 'Fiete' Caroli are young hands on a dairy farm in northern Germany. By 1945, it seems that the war is entering its final stage. But when they are forced to 'volunteer' for the Waffen-SS, they find themselves embroiled in a desperate, bloody conflict. Walter is put to work as a driver for a supply unit, while Fiete is sent to the front. When the senseless bloodshed leads Fiete to desert, only to be captured and sentenced to death, the friends are reunited under catastrophic circumstances. In a few days the war will be over, millions of innocents will be dead, and the survivors must find a way to live with its legacy.